Turtl

crowded tables

ANNALEE THOMASSON

For Joann
Happy Summer! Make room.
♥ Joell

ANNALEE THOMASSON

BOOKS BY ANNALEE THOMASSON

THE WRIGHTSVILLE SERIES
In The Moonlight
Coming Home
The Estate
Wellington Shores
Leeward Lane

THE CROWDED TABLES SERIES
Crowded Tables

CROWDED TABLES

Paperback 978-1-7377904-5-7
eBook 978-1-7377904-# # #

Cover design by Annalee Thomasson
Author Photo by Jana Tyler, Magnolia Photography
Developmental Editing by Dune Press & Co.

DUNE PRESS & CO.
Wilmington, North Carolina
USA

For Deana.
Our tables have always been wonderfully crowded.
Thank you for reminding me.

ANNALEE THOMASSON

crowded tables

ANNALEE THOMASSON

ANNALEE THOMASSON

PROLOGUE
VAL

2013

"Raise a glass, ladies!" My friends circled in close as I lifted my third...or possibly fourth...rum punch above us. The crowd around us quieted, and the toast meant for my best girls was suddenly about to be broadcast to every island visitor.

Etta, Bailey, Addy, Jessie, and Maggie were my sister-friends, my ride-or-dies. We'd all come together in our first year at the University of North Carolina and had been glued to each other ever since. As much as we refused to acknowledge it, this weekend would be the last of our traditional once-a-semester getaway trips to Ocracoke Island. For two days and two nights each semester, we did our best to pretend life as we knew it on campus didn't exist. For just one weekend, we weren't drowning in our studies, racing the social clock, making a dollar, chasing men, or being chased by boys.

For this one weekend every few months, it was just us girls. And on the last night of our last trip, we all walked down the road for one final night at Howard's Pub.

A hush finally settled around us as we linked arms, sharing a familiar and understood smile and even a few tears. I began the toast we could all recite in our sleep. The girls answered line by line as we all choked back tears—of bittersweet joy and for whatever came next.

> To fair winds-
> and following seas.
> To kites high flying-
> in the breeze.
> To the dunes that shield us-
> from tides unseen,
> And the rise and fall-
> of each between.
> For the storms that come-
> to skill the sailor,
> And the catch we lost-
> to the woeful whaler.
> In the fisher of men-
> that we trust for the ride,
> And the guardian of the rest-
> to take the night.
> May we find our fins-
> on waves alike,
> And ride the tide
> of salty life!

Glasses clinked, and noise erupted as we all said a final goodbye to the years of our youth and weekends spent on the beaches of Ocracoke. From here on out, we'd be slaves to the job and the ways of the world.

At least the good old days were really, *really* good.

CHAPTER ONE
VAL

2022

Funerals are shit; this I know. I mean, it's not like I've been to a ton of them, but at this point, I think I've officially earned the right to an opinion—and that's mine: funerals are shit.

Obviously, it's the death part that actually sucks, but a funeral doesn't exactly help an already terrible situation. You can call it a "celebration of life" all you want, but at the end of the day, Golly is still six feet deep, rotting back into the clay of the earth. That's just not how I want to picture her. She was way too good for that.

If I had it my way, I would've had her cremated and then hopped on a private jet to spread her ashes in some magnificent place like the Grand Canyon, the peak of Mount Vesuvius, or in the lineup at Teahupo'o. Instead, I had to follow the legal directives she filed with Pop all those years ago before I was even a blip on the radar.

Golly and Pop were all I ever had—aside from the first six months of my life, anyway. My mother died an hour after I was born from some rare complication during childbirth, and my dad died in Iraq during Desert Storm—leaving me officially, legally, an orphan. According to the will my dad filed with the Marine Corps, his life possessions (read: me) were to be placed in the sole custody of one Georgia Ellen and Forrest Scott Foster.

They were about as cool as you'd expect a pair of grandparents-turned-parents to be. Of course, they were much older than all my friends' parents, but they never acted like it.

They attended every soccer game, and Pop was always the loudest one in the stands. He picked a fight with a referee once, and Golly yelled at him all the way from the concession stand to sit down and shut up. He listened, too. Golly always ran concessions with a mug of her hot chocolate—heavy on the Kahlua. She was a wild one.

Pop passed away a month after I left for Chapel Hill. His short but aggressive battle with glioblastoma left just Golly and me. Life around us became pretty quiet, and to keep things balanced, the two of us made sure that we were anything but.

At the end of my first year, Golly took me to the Virgin Islands for a three-month-long sailing expedition. The following Christmas, we spent four weeks touring Sicilian castles. When we missed our flight home, she sent an email to my biology professor taking full responsibility for my missing the first few days of class—including a paltry threat to make his life a living hell if I found myself dealing with any serious repercussions. I didn't, of course. But that didn't stop Golly from contributing to the whirlwind of chaos surrounding that same professor when he finally got caught dating not one but three of his students. Did you know that you can send an anonymous bag of gummy dicks as a gag gift? Golly did.

We got real good and smashed on Bourbon Street for Mardi Gras my junior year, and after graduation, we spent the summer surfing in New Zealand. We didn't know how to surf when we got there, so we signed up for daily lessons for beginners at sunrise. The instructors were the most beautiful men I'd ever laid eyes on, and we kept paying for lessons well after getting the hang of it. Of course, my instructor stopped charging me when I found myself waking up on the pillow next to him every morning. You could say our time in New Zealand was multipurpose and thoroughly enjoyed.

Life with Golly wasn't nearly as long as I wish it would have been, but it sure as hell was a full one. Full of adventure, full of love, and never lacking for anything—except for maybe sleep and wise decisions.

We lived a lavish but humble lifestyle. I always knew my grandparents were sitting on big money, but I never found a reason to go digging for an explanation about exactly how much or why. Golly always said it was just an accumulation of the generations of family wealth and trust funds, and that was enough for me. Suffice it to say, when I paid a few bills with her credit cards the week she passed, I got a peek into just how significant those trust funds were. The cost of dying was alarming but still no match for that AmEx Black Card.

Now, here I was on a Tuesday morning, front row at the Sacred Heart Catholic Church in Raleigh, listening to Father Paul eulogize the most prayerful, noble, refined, and proper parishioner he'd ever known. *If he only knew.*

And you know what's some more shit? What are the odds of becoming an orphan twice? Are you technically an orphan if you're an adult? I'd lost a lot so far in my life. I had a lot of living left to do, and it was starting to look like I'd be doing it all on my own.

After the funeral and a long enough-for-me appearance at the lunch reception, I grabbed the keys to her Mustang and made my way home. I kicked off the black wedges at the door and strung my purse straps over the banister at the bottom of the stairs. Up in my room, I sat on the edge of the bed, more than ready for a few good drinks and a long nap. I smiled as I noticed our framed photo on my nightstand—Golly and I with our collection of beads on Bourbon Street—sitting next to my journal. I opened the cover and fingered through the pages I usually wrote in each night before bed, and started to read the last journal entry.

Today really sucks.

Golly died today. I knew it was coming, and I thought that the time to prepare myself would be helpful—but it turns out that there's no amount of time to prepare for losing someone you love that makes it feel any more acceptable.

When they told us the survival rates of pancreatic cancer, I thought for sure that she'd be one of those five percent that survived. Those were slim and shitty odds, but Golly was never one to back down from a fight. I think that's why it surprised me so much when she declined treatment. Although, the five percent survival rate was *with* treatment. Without it, Golly was walking herself right through the pearly gates.

I was mad at first. I even stopped by the hospital to visit with the oncologist on my own one day. When I asked him how I could talk Golly into the chemotherapy regiment he'd proposed, he poured me a cup of coffee and went full-on dad-mode on me. The worst part is—I knew he was right.

There wasn't anything I could do to force Golly into the treatment, and I'd never forgive myself if I'd done it anyway.

Instead, he walked me through the process. I'd told him that I wanted to know everything, that I didn't want to wonder what was coming. I wanted to know what it was going to look like. And as any good doctor would, he supported his patient—and her family. He explained the earliest signs of decline, what we could handle at home, and what would require a hospital visit. He promised me he would do everything he could to keep her comfortable and support me along the way.

But none of that made it any better.

I lost her just as fast as he said I would. It's almost as if he's done this before. Hah. Ain't that something?

What do I do now? Where do I go? Next to Golly was the only place I've ever belonged. She's never left my side. Now she's gone, and I'm alone. I'm an orphan again. Is this still the place for me? How do you belong somewhere when there's nothing left of it that you recognize? I don't know if this place will ever feel like home again.

Maybe I'll add a little rum to my tea tonight. That's what she would have done.

Cheers, Golly.

I spent three weeks after her funeral trying my best to get back into the swing of things. I fought my emotions and tried to get back into my old routine: I'd leave the house— Golly's house, the place I was raised in—around seven each morning and drive to the Berkeley Brew for a table by the window and an oversized and over-caffeinated latte. I'd crack open my computer to a steady list of online orders to fill, send those orders to the shipping label printer in my office, answer each email, and polish off every drop of that latte before getting a refill to take into work for the day.

Tucket Teas started as a stand at a farmer's market one summer, where a few of us worked just enough to make sufficient beer money for the weekend. My organic tea blends slowly grew in popularity and eventually turned into somewhat of an east coast success. A year or so into the gig, I started paying rent at a shared commercial kitchen. With the room to stock more ingredients and prepare more teas, I made my products available online, and—well, it just took off. It was a lot of work, but it didn't depend on time. I was usually able to handle everything in my downtime between classes. Anytime we left town, or I needed a few days off, I'd just add a note about a shipping delay to my online ordering system and get back to it when I was ready.

I liked working for myself. No one was in my way, and I didn't have to rely on anyone else to ensure things were done right. I handled it all and listened to my favorite playlists on Spotify while I did it. Rather than work for the man, I *was* the man—or the *wo*man.

Other than the occasional drop-in visit from Golly, I was rarely interrupted. So I was caught off guard when my first morning back in the office was halted by a phone call from Alexander Elliot, Esquire—the attorney responsible for Golly's estate and the closest thing I ever had to an uncle.

"Hang on, Alex." I covered my phone and yelled, "Alexa! Pause the music!"

"Taylor Swift, huh?" He asked.

"You know your tunes, old man."

"I'm not that old, darling. Besides, a man with eighteen grandchildren tends to stay up to date on things like Taylor Swift and her heart-break warfare."

"Touché, Alex. Now, what can I do for you so bright and early in the morning?"

"Well, sweetheart, the paperwork is all finished, and I've got...well... many things to go over with you. Namely, your new, shall we call it..." He paused for a moment, and I could hear him scratching at his beard. "...financial status."

"Oh, just tell me, Alex. I get the house, right? The car? I'm not completely blind; I know I'm the only family she has. I mean, had." I wasn't sure I'd ever get used to referring to Golly in the past tense.

"It's not that simple, dear. Forrest left your Golly with several savings accounts and stocks. She took most of that and made some very wise investments. Not to mention...she's always been well ahead of things like payments and saving for future expenditures. Even with all of your rather extensive travels over the years—"

"Oh, Alex." He could probably feel my eyes roll through the phone. "We don't travel half as much as you and Louise. Where is it you're going next month?"

"Bali, dear. Louise has a whole itinerary planned out. We'll be visiting a monkey sanctuary; can you believe that? Are you sure you don't want to join us? I still have plenty of time to grab you a plane ticket."

"No thanks, Alex. I appreciate it, but I need to soak up some quiet time after all this chaos. I'll go see the monkeys with you next time."

"Fair enough, dear. If you change your mind, you know where to find me. Now…as I was saying." He paused, flipping through pages and clearing his throat. "Right, anyway. All that to say, Golly has left everything to you. I've also factored in the payments you received from the government after your father died and the life insurance from your mother—all of which have been saved all these years and accruing interest of their own. So, while you are now the owner of a mortgage-free home and that Mustang she just *had to have*, among other things, you are also nearly…six million dollars richer." I slid down the wall and collapsed onto the kitchen floor while my cheeks flushed and my head spun.

A girl with a newfound six million bucks would celebrate. A girl would call her friends and family and throw a party. Here I was, drowning in the biggest news of my life, and I didn't have a soul to tell. I guess they do say money can't buy happiness. You can't buy friends, either. Or parents and grandparents back from the dead.

Now I was lonely and rich. *How fun.*

"That can't be right, Alex." I leaned back against the wall in the kitchen. "I mean—there have to be things I'll need to pay off. What about my student loans?"

"Golly took care of all of that, sweetheart. I'll need to have you sign a few documents, but otherwise, it's all settled. Her things are yours. Every last dollar."

"Well, shit," I said.

"Language, dear."

"Sorry, Alex. Look, I can stop by this afternoon if that's all right. Louise is waiting on a restock of my honey-lavender blend, anyway. While I'm there, we can do whatever you need me to do. I'll just—I'll see you in a bit."

"All right, sweetheart. I'll see you later."

Alexander and Louise Elliot were longtime friends of Golly and Pop, so they didn't miss a beat when it came to taking care of everything when she passed away. Louise helped me with most of the funeral arrangements, and Alex handled what he referred to as *the particulars*. I just hadn't considered that the particulars would entail quite so much. It was a bit overwhelming to hear him lay it all out.

So, I did what any overwhelmed thirty-one-year-old would do in the middle of a rather stressful morning at work— I danced.

"Alexa," I hollered. "Play Cruel Summer."

ANNALEE THOMASSON

CHAPTER TWO
VAL

A month later, I tossed and turned until ungodly hours of the morning, unable to sleep a wink. I pulled my phone from the nightstand and opened up Instagram to begin the late-night scroll I'd mastered in recent weeks. Grief made a lot of waves in a person's life, and being slightly nocturnal was one of many unhealthy habits I'd developed since Golly's passing.

Seemingly everyone I'd ever been acquainted with was in Augusta, Georgia, for the Masters' Tournament, providing hours' worth of photos to scroll through before I came across an ad for Airbnb. *Getaway home!* The title phrase didn't make sense, but the crystal clear water in the advertisement photo was enticing enough to click.

The idea of traveling without Golly felt like a salt scrub in my wounded heart. As much as I wanted to get out of my mind and shake things up for a few days, I just couldn't imagine going anywhere and having any sort of fun without her. I'd spent the time since her funeral in near isolation—on my own accord. I'd declined a few invitations to go out with neighbors or some of the casual friends I'd made in recent years and more or less shrunk my life down to filling orders at Tucket Teas by day and binging Netflix at home all night. At the very least, I was overdue for some fresh air.

In the handful of times we'd met to go over those particulars, Alex had mentioned that I wouldn't need to "hustle my little tea thing" anymore...but I didn't see it that way. I never needed the money before, and I certainly didn't need it now, but Tucket Teas was never about the money. It was more of a desire to prove that I could do something of my own. It gave me something to do in college and reminded me that I wasn't completely dependent on my family's wealth. Now I was in desperate need of a distraction, and I was thankful for the business that provided it.

Golly and Pop didn't raise me to think that I might get anywhere by being lazy. I may have inherited enough money to fund the United States military for a hot second, but I had no intentions of living freely off inheritance for the rest of my life. I'd built my company by myself from the ground up, and I was damn proud of it. I wasn't about to let it all collapse just because I didn't need the income. If anything, I had my sights set on bigger things for Tucket Teas now that I would never have to worry about funding again. I had a lot of learning to do, too.

I knew better than to make decisions at such hours of the night, but before I knew it, I was booking a rental on Ocracoke Island without so much as a swipe through the photos.

At the very least, I knew Ocracoke to be a small, safe, and quiet place. If a bunch of college girls managed to get on and off the island without a single arrest, injury, or accidental pregnancy for four years, there was only so much trouble I could get into as a grown adult. Irrational? No, I was rarely irrational. Impulsive, maybe—but I had some time left to get away with blaming my choices on grief. Then again, even if I *was* being irrational, it's not like I had a damn soul to step up and stop me.

Booking a trip without Golly was like a punch to the gut, and the punch hurt just enough to drive me to do it. I'd have to do *something* on my own eventually, and a weekend in Ocracoke seemed like the safest place to start.

I hadn't been back to the island since college, but it seemed like a logical place to go: I was familiar with the area and it wasn't terribly far from home—or what was left of it. Would I ever feel at home again? Were grown orphans destined to become perpetual vagabonds? I needed to get away, but I was also desperate for a sense of peace that I didn't know how else to find. Ocracoke was the place. Peace filled my heart for the first time in a long while as I pictured myself there: in the last place I'd been that I didn't feel quite so lonely.

The booking confirmation popped into my email, and, while I was satisfied that I had something to look forward to, I was still wired for sound. Par for the course these days, sleep would be hard to come by. Instead, I followed another advertisement to the Realtor App. Golly and I used to settle into the couch for movie nights, only to spend hours looking at real estate listings in luxurious places just for the hell of it. We never had any actual plans to move, but it was fun to look at.

I cleared the filters from our last search and set my criteria to the entirety of Ocracoke Island—not that it left much of an area to search. The very first listing was an old run-down house on the edge of the island. I flipped through the pictures and confirmed my suspicions. The sale price was for the property; the house wasn't worth the cement slab underneath it.

You could do a lot with two acres by the beach, though. I wondered how long demolition took but quickly decided I didn't care. I had deep pockets and no plans for tomorrow. Why the hell not?

My brief internet stalking didn't lead to much about whoever lived there until the house went on the market three years ago, and the property records reflected small and steady price drops since the initial listing. Maybe I was the only hope.

The possibilities were endless. Maybe I was due a good mulligan. The world hadn't exactly dealt me an enjoyable game in recent years. I could build a new place and move. Or, I could build a smaller place and rent it out—automatic business. It didn't sound like a terrible idea. In any case, it didn't have to be a waste of money. I could make use of a place like that no matter what I did with it. There was safety in a good backup plan and a backup to the backup plan. Alex Elliot, Esquire, would have been proud of me.

Then again, with my life and everything as I knew it completely tossed up in the air, building a house by the beach and relocating seemed to be a reasonable idea. It was a chance to *grab life by the balls*—as Pop used to say—and make my move. I loved living with Golly and enjoyed my town and the existence I'd established there. But my business didn't rely on its location; hell, my business was just a business. It could probably survive without me—some college kid that was coherent enough to pack orders would do the trick. Or, I could work to keep things growing and chase the large-scale distribution ideas I'd been collecting over the years. I could set up a kitchen space to create and ship my teas just about anywhere.

The melancholy of life after death was putrid, and I was eager for an escape. While I typically willed myself never to chase overnight ideas, primarily because they were usually fueled by a lack of sleep and an overly-exhausted or less-than-sober conscience, this one had some merit...and I couldn't shake the idea.

The next morning, I set my navigation app to the Cedar Island Ferry, where I'd make my way to Ocracoke Island for a long weekend of staring at the tide, reading a stack of rom-coms, and brainstorming what the rest of my life might have in store. At the very least, I had nothing—and no one—left to lose.

I locked the deadbolt behind me and walked down Golly's cobblestone driveway to my brand new pearly white Land Rover Defender. The purchase was utterly ridiculous and financially irresponsible, but as clueless as I felt about moving forward with my life, the one thing I knew for sure was that I would not be driving Golly's Mustang. I barely fit in the thing to begin with, and I wanted the room to grow. That and Golly never did let me get a dog, and now that I was free to make my own decisions, I had every intention of finding one rather large rescue pooch. Maybe even two.

My mind raced as I drove. I found myself reminiscing on my college days...particularly back to the mid-fall of my first year when a few of us girls formed a study group to survive anatomy and physiology. A few exams later, the lot of us had become the best of friends and inseparably close. Not to mention, we were the source of a hysterical song that helped students memorize the names of bones throughout the body. To my knowledge, the stupid tune could still be heard in the lecture hall today. Truthfully, the song was a product of a few drunk college kids desperate to memorize enough to pass their next exam. Whatever—it worked.

Back when school was our only responsibility, we vowed to spend one long weekend each semester in Ocracoke. If nothing else, we wanted to allow our bodies a break and our minds a chance to reset. Girl-time and salty air without the pressure of work, assignments, and whatever stupidity the boys in our lives were creating; it was the stuff a college girl dreamed of. These days, it was harder to make such a commitment. Hell, I barely made the effort to pick up the phone and call anyone.

That spring of 2013 trip—just a few weeks before pomp and circumstance—was our last and the one where we all said goodbye: to college, to each other, and the end of an era. We went in six different directions after graduation to follow six different dreams. But deep down, we knew we always had each other, and we always had Ocracoke.

So, it had been quite some time. Nine years, to be exact. But that didn't make the ferry ride from Cedar Island feel any less familiar. I parked on the side of Western Drive and locked my new car, laughing at myself when I remembered that we never so much as locked our front door when we stayed on the island.

The fancy navigation system in my fancy new car announced my arrival just as predicted: I'd reached the offices of Coastline Real Estate at four fifteen, leaving me plenty of time to have a little chat with one of their agents about buying the property I'd found there on the island.

I stepped underneath the teal and white striped awning and reached for the front door when it opened for me instead.

A young man with a well-worn brown leather briefcase tossed over his shoulder stepped out and turned to lock up.

"I'm sorry, are you closing?" I looked down at my watch.

"Yep! Are you checking out of your rental? I can take your keys. That's no problem." The man reached out a hand and waited.

"Uh, no. I'm not here to give you keys; I'm interested in purchasing one of your listings." I looked at my watch again. "Google said your office was open until five." The man was the very definition of tall, dark, and handsome, which was wildly unfortunate for me; it made it harder to argue with him.

"Well, yes, usually it is." He paused to look at his watch. "But it's Friday afternoon, and I don't have another appointment until Monday morning. That, and there's an empty seat at the bar calling my name. So, unless you were having some sort of real-estate emergency, Miss—" He reached again to shake my hand.

"I'm Val Foster."

"Right, well, Miss Foster. Unless you are in fact having a housing emergency...I'd be happy to introduce you to my father, who would be more than willing to help you with your home search first thing Monday morning." The pleasant smile across his face made it very clear that he thought I would go along with his witty explanation and alternative suggestion.

"That's a terrible business practice," I said. "Closing up early to get to a bar? How exactly do you expect to sell houses that way?"

"Well, I don't sell houses; my dad does. I'm more of a background kind of guy. I just wrapped up with a settlement, so

27

my work for the day is done. Normally my father would be here, too, but he had to step out this afternoon to take my aunt to her chemotherapy appointment." The slightest reference to cancer had me swallowing a lump in my throat and folding my arms to hide the trembling in my fingers. Tall, dark, and handsome didn't seem to notice. "Without the real estate agent and the administrative assistant, a real estate office doesn't have much to do. So, like I said, I'd be happy to put you in touch with my dad first thing Monday morning."

"Don't worry about it. I'll just find another office if you don't have the time for me." I turned back to my car, leaving the man behind me.

"Good luck," he called. "By the time you catch the next ferry to Hatteras, you'll find their office closed, too."

"There isn't another real estate office here?" I asked.

"Have you taken a look around, ma'am? This island is about as big as a football field. There isn't much room for another real estate office; even if there were, they'd be bored out of their minds. There are barely enough houses on this island to keep my dad busy."

"Well then," I said as I stepped toward him again. "I'm sure your dad knows about the property on Lighthouse Road. And I'm leaving on Monday, so unless that barstool will die without you, I think you might be wise to take me up on my offer."

"Your offer?" He scoffed.

"Yes, my offer. I'd like to buy it. I can pay in cash. Or check. Or Apple pay. Or…whatever, I just want to go ahead and buy it. So, if you could help me get started with the paperwork, I'd appreciate it."

"Well, I hate to break it to you, but it's not that easy."

"It should be. The property records make it pretty clear that the house has been on the market for a little over three years—completely abandoned and all but collapsed from the looks of it. If you had another reasonable offer, I'm sure the listing would have been pending by this time on a Friday afternoon. So, that leads me to believe that you don't actually have any other offers, and the place is still fair game. Are you really about to walk away from a buyer ready to pay the full listing price? I'd think your dad would be excited to earn the commission on a place like that. He'd probably be a bit disappointed to hear that you turned away a cash buyer, wouldn't he?"

Tall, dark, and handsome grew wide-eyed and turned back to the door, unlocking it and stepping inside.

"You're tough." He said as I followed him over the threshold. "Welcome to Coastline Real Estate. I'm Jack. How can I help you?"

"Thank you, Jack. I'd like to buy a house."

ANNALEE THOMASSON

CHAPTER THREE
JACK

Terrible business practice? Who did this girl think she was? Our company was thriving. My dad knew what he was doing; he'd run the place for decades—with great success, I might add. I could see why this Val Foster might be frustrated to find me leaving the office early—she was clearly an out-of-towner with some business to tend to—but to accuse me of having a *terrible business practice?* Well, that was just rude.

Rude was pretty, though. She smelled nice, too. I held the door open for her, breathing in the bits of a citrus scent from her hair that seemed to reach out for me as she walked into the front sitting room of our office. It was such a peculiar thing to notice about a person, and the fact that I noticed—and liked it—distracted me from the problem at hand. Long waves of blonde hair fell behind her shoulders as she turned slowly, making a full circle to look around our office before turning back to me.

"So, what do you think?" She asked.

"About what?" I was still caught up in that citrus scent.

"The house on Lighthouse Road. What should I do? Write a check? Use a card? I'll need to find a builder soon if I want to get started. I think a new cottage would do well on the back of the property. I mean, you can set up a mortgage on auto-pay for me, right? I've been paying my power bill on Apple Pay these days." The girl was absolutely clueless, and I swear if she mentioned *Apple Pay* as a sufficient source of bill paying one more time... I felt my eyebrows lift and my eyes bulge as I put together just how much I would have to explain.

"Listen, Miss Foster." I sat down on the couch in the front sitting room, and she sat on the other end, crossing her legs at the calves. My sister had always said that's how the royals would sit. "It really isn't that simple. There's a lot of paperwork to process when it comes to buying a home. We could start by having you take a look at the property, but again, by the time I arrange a visit with my dad, it will probably be Monday morning."

"Well, that seems a bit silly since the place is just down the road, presumably uninhabited and just waiting for someone to take a peek." She had a point. I checked my watch...again.

"I'll tell you what. No one lives there, so I suppose we could make a quick stop at the property for you to at least walk around the exterior. But I won't have a key to get inside until Monday, not that I'd even suggest the idea. I don't know that it's safe to go walking around that house." I moved toward the door and turned back to her with an afterthought that nearly had me laughing. "While we're there, you can explain why you came here with the idea that you can buy a house with *Apple Pay*."

Her cheeks blushed, and it hit me: she wasn't just blonde and clueless; she was completely naive about buying a house. I knew the property she spoke of, and I have to say: Val Foster didn't strike me as a girl who'd ever built a house or even knew how to use a simple drill. This property was going to require a hell of a lot more than a few simple power tools.

Leaving the office, I rechecked my watch, irritated that my being a few minutes late was turning into an eternity.

"Follow me," I said. "It's just down the street."

I watched in my rearview mirror as Val climbed into a shiny Land Rover behind me with a satisfied grin. I'm not sure what that girl had in mind, but hopefully, her curious determination and ungodly confidence would be of some help. She couldn't possibly be prepared for such a project. She seemed fragile: like the type of girl who couldn't even fathom breaking a nail.

I barely had time to buckle up before we pulled into the driveway on Lighthouse Road, the property she supposedly wanted to own within the next ten minutes. I stepped out next to my car to wait while she did her looking.

"You can go ahead and walk around," I said. "No one's lived here for years though, so I'd be really careful if you go into the backyard there. It seems like the jungle might've taken over."

Val lifted her sunglasses to the top of her head, taking in everything from the bushes that were once meticulously manicured to the roof that seemed to have lost nearly every shingle and succumbed to a slight curve. She walked toward the remaining fragments of the front porch as my phone vibrated in my back pocket.

"Hello?"

"Dude. You dead?" Glenn's sarcasm poured through the line.

"I got hung up at work. I'll be on my way soon." I watched Val from a distance. She'd stopped to look at the mailbox that was miraculously still mounted next to the door. I didn't know how any bit of the place was still standing; we'd had enough decently sized hurricanes in the past few years. Without the necessary repairs, I was sure the wood stack would have fallen to the ground by now.

"Did you bring the cigars? You owe me two, and I'm grumpy. It's a good day for a cigar." I turned to peek at my front seat to double-check that I'd brought him the two cigars he'd swindled from me at last week's poker game.

"Uh…yes. I've got them. Look, I have to finish up with a client. I'll see y'all in a few." I hung up before he answered. When I looked back to the front porch, Val was gone. I hadn't intended to launch a search and rescue party for Miss Foster, yet here I was—heading toward the backyard that could eat a man alive.

I caught up with her on the side of the house that faced the bay.

"So, do you like the land?" I didn't want to be rude, but I was eager to leave.

"I do, but I've changed my mind. I don't want to tear it down. I think I'll play a little Chip and Jo. I think I'm going to fix it up." She stood firmly in front of me, shoulders squared and a smile plastered across her face. I might have been concerned about her general well-being if I knew her better. Truth be told, I was already plenty concerned about what Val Foster might do to my island.

"You'd really be better off building something new," I said as I followed her up the driveway. She'd changed her mind on the place so fast I almost wondered if I understood her correctly. I was sure she'd planned to demolish the old house and build a new one. How had she landed on renovations so suddenly? I blamed it on the only consistent trait I knew to be true about women: they were crazy. And the safest thing to do with crazy was to let it be.

"You can't just get rid of everything when it gets old," she answered. "Imagine how you'd feel if you got a little old and rusty, and every one said *to hell with him.*" The glare she gave me could have lit me on fire. Her eyes were fierce—an ocean blue that paired well with her long blonde waves. Beautiful, yes. But fierce.

"That's fair," I laughed. "So why *this* house?"

"Well, as you mentioned, there isn't much available as far as real estate here. And it seems to me that if this one's been passed on for three years, then I might be its only hope. It just needs a little...love."

"It needs a *lot* of love, Miss Foster. A *lot.*"

"Right," she said as she looked around again.

"Why Ocracoke?" I stood a few steps behind her, genuinely curious about the girl who showed up out of nowhere, hell-bent on buying this old heap. Her shoulders rose and fell as she took a few deep breaths before facing me.

"I love it here." She seemed to be deep in the traps of nostalgia and maybe even a touch of sadness.

"Care to elaborate?"

"This island has always helped me to...catch my breath. It's the only place I know where I can come and just...lay it all down. Everything heavy seems to disappear. It's like, when life gets tough, you can just...go to the beach." She'd stepped closer, and I saw a new redness in her eyes. "Back home these days...well, there's nothing left there for me anymore. So I figured, what the hell? There was always Ocracoke." The meteor of a human being that had arrived at my office just a short while before had softened into something more like sea glass— sparking a curiosity about her that I really didn't have the time or energy for.

"You know the island pretty well, then."

"Well enough," she said, turning back toward the house. "Enough to know that it's safe here, that it isn't lonely. Well enough to give it a chance."

"So, you're *not* leaving on Monday then?" I asked, caught on the way she bit her bottom lip and smiled.

"Okay, you caught me. I only booked a place to stay through Monday. I just kind of thought I'd wing it—take things a day at a time." She looked guilty, knowing full well that she'd just used a Monday departure as an argument for me to show her the house on the drop of a dime.

"Buying a house isn't exactly a wing-it type of thing," I warned. "It's more of a significant and permanent jump."

"I don't have anything to lose these days. I could use a good jump." She cracked an honest smile, the first I'd seen that didn't seem to have some sort of scheming demand behind it, and walked off across the front yard and back toward the driveway.

"An older couple almost bought the property last year," I started to explain as she looked around. "They were hoping to turn it into a bed and breakfast or something, but the inspection came back and scared them off. Too much work, I guess."

"I've got time."

"And money…apparently."

"Not that it's any of your business," she faced me with her arms squared across her chest, "but yes. The money isn't something I'm worried about."

"All right, tell you what. I'll text my dad and ask him to make the arrangements to take you inside first thing on Monday. It really is the best I can do on such short notice."

I pulled my phone out again to find sixteen missed text messages lining the lock screen, mostly the guys giving me hell for being late and one more from Glenn about those damn cigars. I sent my dad a quick message about Val and the house.

Relaxing against the hood of my car, I watched as her long and tan legs brought those blonde waves back to me. If I was going to waste some time this afternoon, at least the view was excellent. In fact, it was so good that the image of her would probably plague me later.

"Thank you," she said, reaching to shake my hand. "I know what you think, and you're probably right. But, I'd like to buy it. So...just tell me what to do. I've never bought a house before."

"Clearly," I laughed before she shot an accusatory glance back at my sarcasm. "Okay, I'm sorry." I raised my hands in front of me. "That was uncalled for. Let's start with Monday morning. You and my dad can get together first to discuss it. Maybe forty-eight hours will be enough for you to realize what a terrible idea this is."

"You're very encouraging, Jack. Thank you."

"Here, take my card." I reached into my wallet and pulled an old faded card from its slot. I couldn't remember the last time I'd handed out a business card. Everyone on Ocracoke knew my family, and we got most of the island's listings by default. Not to mention, everyone knew where we lived and where to find us at any given time. It wasn't uncommon to take on a new listing at a backyard barbecue, a surf competition, or church on Sunday morning. Val Foster may not have appreciated our laid-back, small-town methods, but I was pretty fond of the way we did things here.

"If I do go to your office at eight on Monday morning, will someone actually be there, or should I wait until nine? Ten, maybe?"

"We aren't lazy," I countered. She was assertive, and I didn't hate it. It was irritating but thrilling at the same time. "You know, you said you came here to let the heavy things disappear. It might do you some good to relax a bit...loosen up that tight ship you seem to be running."

"I'll see you on Monday, then," she nodded and strutted back to her luxurious ride. Such an expensive vehicle seemed to be a good match for her. If I had to guess, I'd say there weren't even a thousand miles on that car yet.

"Thank you, Jack." She toyed with the business card, slid her sunglasses back down onto her nose, and laced her fingers through her hair. She was still staring at the house as I backed out of the driveway.

I made a u-turn in front of the property and drove the mile past my office toward Howard's Pub. Dust kicked up as I pulled into the gravel lot and had barely settled by the time I backed into the corner spot underneath the live oak tree out front. I tossed my keys to the floorboard and went inside.

"About damn time," Hank grunted from across the pub.

"Sorry, fellas. I got held up."

"Who died?" Glenn asked.

"Dude, no one died."

"You mean to tell me you just willingly stayed in the office…" He paused to check his watch. "…an hour later than you needed to on a perfectly good Friday afternoon for drinking?" Glenn kicked his foot, moving a barstool out for me.

"For the record, I *was* out of my office with plenty of time to spare. But this girl showed up demanding to see a house, and well, here I am. I guess I survived. Did anyone order me a beer?" I plopped down into my seat next to him.

"I live to serve," Bailey said, setting a pint of Highland's on a napkin in front of me. "You're late."

"Y'all won't believe what I just dealt with." I sipped down half my beer before I continued. "Next time I say that the tourists are the worst, remind me about the out-of-town rich girls who get bored in the city and want an island retreat for a second home." My friends all looked at me with expressions of disbelief. "I was literally walking out the door when this crazy girl walked up, all but demanding that I turn around and let her in. She says she wants to buy the place on Lighthouse—and she's serious. She asked if she could use Apple Pay. *Apple Pay*, you guys." Hank laughed, and Glenn looked confused.

"I know, dude. I feel the same way."

"She must have been pretty, seeing as how you allowed her to distract you for over an hour." Bailey showed up with another round and set the glasses on the table. "Tacos tonight, guys? Scooter brought in some tuna; it's already on the grill."

"Hell yes," I said. "Thank you, Bailey."

"Me too," Glenn added.

39

"Tacos all around," Hank said, turning to me. "So, explain to me why it bothers you so much that some crazy girl wants a house?"

"First, she wanted to buy the property to demolish the old heap and build something new. She didn't even seem to care about how much time and work that would be. Then, it was like she blinked and shape-shifted into an even crazier kook. One minute in the front yard and she announced her plans to renovate instead."

"She sounds terrible," Bailey mocked.

"She was. Aggravating as all hell, too. She said that my leaving early was a bad business practice. She's completely entitled. Google said we were open until five, so damn it, she wanted to talk to me until then. She must be one miserable broad," I scoffed. "Life's too short to be so pretentious."

"I don't believe it," Bailey said, jaw-dropped.

"I know! I mean, what kind of person has the cranky audacity to criticize a man she doesn't even know?" Bailey walked out from behind the bar and tossed her rag onto the counter. A smile crossed her face before she sprinted toward the front door.

"Bailey?" I recognized the voice behind me that called in a high-pitched shriek to my friend.

"Val! What are you doing here?" *Shit.* I was right.

I turned around to see Bailey and Val Foster wrapped up in each other like long-lost sisters.

"Crazy girl wouldn't happen to be a tall, pretty blonde thing, would she?" Hank asked quietly.

"That's the one," I groaned, taking another long pull from my beer.

"Bailey sure seems excited to see her," Glenn said. "If they're friends, she can't be all that bad." Bailey returned to her side of the bar as Val sat in the empty seat next to me.

"I hear you've already met Jack," Bailey said, winking at me.

"Of all the bars," she said, smiling at me with a dramatic flair.

"As I said, it's not that big of an island, Miss Foster," I answered.

"Glad you made it to your barstool," she said. "Sorry I held you up."

"So, you were looking at the place on Lighthouse?" Bailey asked. "Tell me that means my girl is here to stay." She set some sort of fruity drink in front of Val and laid her hands out flat on the bar, demanding an answer.

"Your girl?" I asked, slowly realizing that I was nowhere near rid of Val Foster.

"Oh, we go way back." Bailey leaned onto her elbows, ready to tell a story. "Val and I went to Chapel Hill together. After graduation, she moved back to Raleigh." She turned back to Val and playfully slapped her arm. "You didn't tell me you were coming!"

"I didn't know you were here," Val answered.

"Where are you staying?"

"I rented a place down by the ferry. I'm supposed to check in around seven."

"Oh, that's got to be Cole's place," Bailey said.

"Cole? As in Cole Stewart, Cole?" Val leaned in for dramatic effect.

"The one and only. He inherited the marina about a year ago. You'll probably see him when you check in tonight."

"So you held up Jack here, and you're also the reason Cole didn't make it out?" Hank was taking my side, and I was proud of it.

"I'm sorry, I didn't realize that my being here was such an inconvenience," she replied boldly. Val Foster was quickly proving that she wasn't one to mess with. If I was right, and I was sure that I was, Val seemed like the kind of girl who got her way—and frequently. I'd have been willing to bet that anyone who argued with her usually lost. I mean...I had.

"Stop it, guys. Cole's marina won't make it without these rentals, and Jack, your office literally exists for people that want to buy a house. So why don't you boys just thank Val for coming and...oh, I don't know, make her feel at home?" Bailey was right. My family's business did revolve around welcoming people to the island and making them feel at home.

"Welcome back, Val," I said. "It's nice to meet you."

"Thank you, Jack." She paused and looked from Bailey to me with those slow-moving eyes that looked like she was putting pieces together in her mind. "Dixon."

"Yes?"

"Jack Dixon, and you work in real estate." She looked back to Bailey, who seemed equally as confused. "Etta's brother!"

"Oh!" Bailey said. "Yes! Okay, remember that one weekend Etta took us home for dinner?"

"Right," Val answered, raising a hand to her forehead. "Her dad cooked us dinner and sent us back to school with an entire car load of groceries."

"Sounds like my dad," I confirmed.

"Small world," Val laughed.

"Too small."

"Where is Etta, anyway?" Val asked.

"At home with Tate," I answered. "She doesn't get out much."

"I'll be right back, you guys." Bailey stepped back into the kitchen, and Val pulled her phone out and began to scroll. Minutes later, Bailey returned with a tray full of tacos, topped with Scooter's fresh tuna and some cilantro from the garden that Bailey technically did not keep out back. We ate and drank, and drank and ate, until thirty minutes later when the lot of us finally seemed to be full and content.

You'd never find yourself with an empty glass at Bailey's bar. She knew the way to a man's heart. Not my heart, of course. Bailey wasn't my type. I mean, it's not that I *didn't* like her. I loved her. It was just that the love we shared was more like a brother-sister kind of thing. She put me in my place, and I respected her for it. Growing up, I'd been close friends with her brother Robert, and she and my sister were inseparable. Recent years and a few significant life events gave me a closer friendship with Bailey Brooks, and for that, I was thankful. Every man ought to have a woman like that looking out for him.

"Fellas, what's on the agenda for the weekend?" I asked as we cleared our plates.

"I'm working," Hank said.

"You were working last weekend," Glenn said, irritated that his roommate and favorite fishing buddy was out for a second week in a row.

"Sure, my dude," I chimed in, seemingly needing to remind Glenn that I was in the room. "I'd love to go fishing this weekend." A fishing trip acquired through guilt was still a fishing trip I wanted to go on.

"We don't call you for fishing trips—my dude—because you don't believe in pulling your ass out of bed before the sun comes up." Glenn rolled his eyes.

"That's not surprising," Val said with a quiet snort-laugh. I looked at her and back to my friends.

"Maybe I would if you asked."

"Fine. Five fifteen tomorrow morning at the dock, ready to go." Glenn said. "With a bucket of live shrimp."

"I'll see you there." If history served as a good prediction, I would, in fact, not see him there. I'd be cozy in my bed until I got up for Saturday brunch with my parents.

CHAPTER FOUR
VAL

In all fairness, I'd been less than gentle when I met Jack that afternoon. When you pair that with my quick change of plans, I could see why he was slightly irritated with me.

When I first mentioned buying the property on Lighthouse Road, I told him I intended to demolish what was left of it and build something new. And I did, honestly.

That is until I stepped up onto the porch and noticed the mailbox. It wasn't the typical suburban street-side post box. Instead, the square tin mounted to the side of the door was old-fashioned and charming. I'd never seen a mailbox like that in person. I was toying with the lid when I noticed a light pink envelope inside. I pulled it out, surprised to find mail at an abandoned home. Rather than being addressed to a specific person or even a street address, the front of the envelope simply said, *hello there.*

The faded spots across both sides and tiny drops where I supposed rain might have stained the paper told me it had been there for quite some time. Curious and maybe snooping, I folded the envelope and snuck it into my back pocket when Jack wasn't looking my way.

Hoping he was distracted by his phone call, I snuck around to the backyard to open the envelope. The pages inside were just as soft and faded while surprisingly legible. Considering the note might have been sitting there for three or more years, I was impressed. So, I began to read.

To my new friend,

I hope you don't mind that I've called you my friend. I'm just so glad you're here. I suppose, if you're reading this, you must be my home's new owner. That, or you're doing a thorough once-over of the place before you officially buy it. You know, Lighthouse Road used to be nothing more than a dirt road from town to the water. These days, I find it to be more like a pathway to heaven.

I've spent nearly my entire life in this house. When we began building here, my husband was nineteen, and I was only seventeen. The land belonged to a family friend, and they allotted us a portion of it to build our home on. It was a generous gift to us, a gift for our future.

Oh, you should have seen it. My husband built this place from the ground up. He taught me how to frame a window, how to lay a level floor, and how to build a staircase. Later on, I returned the favor. I taught him how to toss a simple salad, hang curtains, and host like a proper southerner ought to. Although I still say you can't trust a man to throw a proper party. Everyone knows that the good Lord gave the man a woman to handle the details.

We never did get the chance to raise babies here. My love passed away before we even had the opportunity to live a full life together. Instead, my years in this home were spent loving my friends, my neighbors—you know, the family I chose.

I like to think that I helped raise all the babies of Ocracoke. Kids would stop by after school for a treat. The boys would play football in my front yard, and the girls would help me tend to the garden. As they all grew into teenagers, most of them would come to me at some point or another with stories of the new girl at school or the boy that broke their heart. Every now and then, I'd have the honor of talking through something with one of those babies before they went home to confess such a problem to their own parents.

It was an honor to be a home to so many. I guess the only reason I'm writing this to you is to share how important it was to me over the years that I kept this home so crowded. Your home isn't just for the babies you make, you know. The more seats you add to the table, the more love you'll be surrounded by.

So, if you're reading this, I suppose my home is about to become yours.

You probably haven't thought much about its history or the stories that have been told here. I guess all I can ask of you is…to do your best to continue the life I lived here. I certainly lived a good one.

If you aren't one for a crowded table, well, I'd just ask that you reconsider. The heart of life is good, my dear. And the only way everyone will come to believe that is if someone offers them a seat. It's an honor, indeed, to be the home to offer such a thing.

So, open up. Invite a few more. Maybe you'll get around to extending the dining area out back one day. I'd always imagined doing that. Can you believe that view? There's no better place to share a meal.

Blessings to you, my sweet friend. I've lived a good life here. I had everything I ever could have wanted and more. I had it all.

And now that I'm gone, I hope that my home can offer the same for you—for a long, long time.

All my love,

Betty Ann Highland

47

400 Lighthouse Road
Ocracoke Island, North Carolina

I wiped a few tears that had leaked from my eyes while I folded the note back into the envelope and slid it back into my pocket as Jack came around the corner. He'd startled me, which in all fairness, is easy to do when someone is snooping around. I tried to hide my nerves and quickly explained that I'd changed my plans. I wasn't going to knock down Betty Ann's home. I was going to restore it. He wasn't exactly excited about the idea.

Back in my car with some time to kill and an empty stomach, I made my way to Howard's Pub—the bar we'd spent most of our nights in when we'd visited back then. Nothing about the place surprised me as I pulled in to park. The same tire swing hung from the tree out front, and the same dust kicked up underneath my car.

What *did* surprise me were the people I found inside. Not only did I walk in to see that Jack had in fact made it to his barstool, but I also found Bailey Brooks—one of the girls I'd come here with all those years before. We never did keep well enough in touch, and I regretted it. Seeing her smile as I walked through the door felt like a sign that maybe I was where I belonged—maybe I wasn't destined to be alone, at least not yet.

I joined the crowd that knew each other well and kept close to Bailey as I met her friends. She brought out drinks and dinner and made me feel right at home.

Scooter's tuna tacos were incredible, and as much as I wanted to stay and catch up with Bailey all night long, a comfortable bed and a long hot bath in my weekend rental were calling my name. After making plans to call her the next morning, I said goodnight to my old friend—and my new ones —and left. In the parking lot, I thought about how long it had been since I had an impromptu dinner with friends before heading home for the night. I couldn't think of a single one.

Everything in Raleigh was so busy, and everyone had a schedule. If I wanted to have dinner with a friend, it needed to be planned out a week or two in advance. Not to mention the traffic.

I thought about the long weekends we'd spent here and how Monday mornings always came too quickly. The dread of packing up to head back to school was always a heavy feeling and was only ever balanced by the onset of excitement to come back the next semester.

I thought through my ideas as I drove. What if I lived here? What if I made a change and moved to Ocracoke? The thought of renovating a house seemed like a stretch, but how often does one find themselves with work to do and the pockets to fund it? I'd found myself at the helm of a great opportunity, and I had a mind to just go with it and see where it led. And the house, I mean *that house*, it had potential. It stood like a pile of neglected bones—but good ones, I could tell. Strong ones. At the very least, it was a very valuable plot of land. If I could turn the rickety old house back into a home, I'd be set.

All that waited for me in Raleigh was Golly's house and my small business. I was never locked into the idea of spending my life in the city; it was just convenient. I'd built a business once, and I could do it again. The whole thing could be relocated anytime, and no one would know—or care.

Except, of course for Alex and Louise: the only two people left in Raleigh who considered me family—by association, of course. They were friends of my grandparents, not actually blood-related family, but a girl like me had to find and keep a family where the good Lord gave it to her. He gave me Golly and Pop, with Alex and Louise. It would be sad to leave them behind, but if I never stretched these wings... Then again, it wasn't all that far of a stretch.

Still, they had plenty of family and friends around to look after them. I loved the Elliots, but they alone were not reason enough to stay in Raleigh and ignore my ideas and dreams. Hell, they'd probably love to visit me down here on Ocracoke. I'd be doing them a favor. Everyone loved a beach vacation.

I pulled into the Forsyth Marina and immediately second-guessed the address I'd typed into the navigation. I didn't see a single house or hotel or anything that looked rentable for that matter. It looked like a marina: boats and water.

I left my car in the gravel lot and moseyed toward the docks as I searched for the reservation confirmation on my phone. Before the email could even load, a familiar face stepped out from the first boat in the row, washing me with bittersweet joy and reassuring me that I had come to the right place.

"Can't be Cole Stewart," I said, winking when he turned to face me.

"Damn, baby!" He laughed as I ran to him, leaping into the big bear arms of my friend's ex-husband. Cole and Maggie couldn't work things out, but it didn't make me love either one of them any less. He was a good man.

I stood in line behind her on the day they promised their lives to each other and vowed to support them whatever may come. Unfortunately, they grew up and grew apart, and rather than figuring out the world and its hurdles together, they decided to go their separate ways. I always wished they'd tried a little harder or waited a little longer, but that was easy to do from the outside. Playing Monday morning quarterback with someone else's divorce was useless. The marriage was theirs, and the choice to end it was too.

"Bailey just told me this place was yours! I had no idea." He set me down on the gravel road and hugged me again.

"Damn, it's good to see you. Wait a second—Tucket Teas? That's you?" I forgot that I'd used my business card to book the trip. That card came with a long list of hefty spending rewards, and I used it every chance I got.

"That's me. I guess I never added my real name to the reservation. Sorry about that. But here I am, yours for the weekend."

"Well, let's get your bags; I'll show you to your place."

"I thought I had the wrong address…I don't see *any* place."

"The boat," he pointed to the slip next to the one he'd just emerged from. "I rent out a few of the boats here on the property. You booked it through Airbnb, didn't you?"

"I did. A boat, apparently." I put it all together and realized my weekend in Ocracoke wouldn't be exactly what I'd thought. This was a perfect example of why we don't take action on random late-night ideas.

"Come on, and I'll show you around." We walked back up the gravel driveway to my car while Cole filled me in on his new gig there at the marina. "My Uncle Frank passed away last year—Frank Forsyth. He left this whole place to me. There's the main house, a couple of guest cottages up the hill, and the marina down here, which, of course, came with all five of his boats. It's way more than I need, so I'm renting it all out until I figure out what I'm going to do with the place."

"And where are you living?" I asked, unlocking the Range Rover.

"That boat right next to yours." He nodded back to the first slip. "Nice car," he said as he reached into the trunk for my bag. "Some things change, I see." I never had a car of my own in college. I'd insisted on riding my bike everywhere, much to everyone else's entertainment.

"Uh, yeah...my Golly died, actually."

"Shit, I'm sorry, Val. I know y'all were close."

"Yeah, she was the best. She was also rich. I mean, I knew that; I just didn't know...how rich."

"Land Rover via death benefits?" I glared in his direction. "Too soon? Sorry."

"No, you're right. I guess my emotions got the best of me. I kind of...bought it impulsively a week or so after she passed away."

"Can't say I'd be too sad about it," he joked. "I mean, it's a Range Rover."

"So," I huffed. "I'm sleeping on a boat." I took the opportunity to change the subject. Talking about Golly had my eyes welling up and tears threatening to pour out any second. I didn't want to get any further into it. Not yet, anyway. "I found Bailey at Howard's, by the way. A few of your friends, too, I think. They seem like a...happy bunch."

"Ah, I know they seem like a hot mess. Bailey and Etta keep us all in line, for the most part. I promise you'll love them when you get to know them."

"I suppose I might have the chance," I said, taking his hand as he stepped onto the boat and led me right behind him. The whole thing wobbled in the water, and I moved to catch my balance. "I'm meeting with Jack Dixon first thing Monday to talk about buying a house. The land kind," I laughed. I wasn't sure I knew what to do with a night on a boat.

"Well, I'll be damned," he laughed. "You're moving here? To stay?" The smile that crossed his face at the idea nearly matched Bailey's, and I had a second rush of that feeling—the one that told me I had a home here on the island, whether I had to renovate the place myself or not. I was starting to think it wasn't about the walls around me as much as the people I was with.

"Well, I was thinking about it. Another impulse idea, really. But I figure I can't go too wrong. There's a house not far from here, actually. It's on Lighthouse Road—"

"I know the house. That place has seen better days." He pulled a chair out from the table on the deck and sat across from me.

"I suppose it has, but I saw the listing online, and I just couldn't shake the idea. Maybe there's a project down here for me. I at least need something to do for a while. Gotta shake things up a bit now and then, you know?"

"I think that's a great idea, Val. We'd love to have you back here."

"So what have you been up to? How's everything since —"

"The divorce?" He kicked his feet up onto the table and leaned back into his chair. His exhale seemed to be full of memories. "I'll tell you what. Maggie, she—she took a big piece of me with her, you know?"

"I think she left a big piece of herself here with you, too," I said. As with Etta and Bailey, I'd only kept in touch with Maggie here and there over the years, but she always seemed to be missing the island. She'd never admit to missing Cole, but I could tell she ached for him, at least in her own way.

"That may be, but it didn't slow her down any." Cole stared off into the water, and the memories began to seep back into my mind.

Cole Stewart grew up on a peach farm in Franklin, Georgia, and came to Ocracoke each summer to work for his uncle at the marina. On one of our long weekend visits, Maggie found Cole front and center of the karaoke stage one drink shy of closing time, and they ended up slurring the words to *Summer Nights* together. The rest is...well, it *was* a happy ever after, at least for a little while.

Even in college, Maggie never could keep up with her family's expectations, and eventually, I think they got the best of her. When her father offered—or really demanded she take—a position at their home office in Charlotte, she caved and took it, and Cole didn't go with her. We were all sort of shocked by the news, but Maggie adjusted to life at the firm pretty quickly, and Cole seemed to be living his dream here on the island. I hadn't done my best work at keeping in touch with either one of them, but my love for them hadn't faded at all. Their marriage may not have worked out, but everyone still loved them both. They were two of the best friends I'd ever known.

"I haven't been up to all that much. Just life, really." Cole started. "I was bartending with Bailey in the summers, but I've got this place now, and I guess it keeps me pretty busy... especially with summer approaching."

"Any special ladies in your life?" I had to ask.

"No," he laughed. "There never was, after Maggie. I don't imagine there will be...at least not anytime soon."

"You still love her." My heart throbbed. I wasn't asking. I just knew.

"I never stopped, Val. She left me—I didn't want her to. We were arguing one night, and she brought up the office in Charlotte. I told her if she was so unhappy here with me, to just go. I didn't think she would actually do it, but she did. She packed her bags and left. She never even called, you know. I opened the mailbox one day to divorce papers, and it was over."

"I'm sorry, Cole."

"It's okay." He said, turning his hat around as he stood and fidgeting with the handle on the back porch door while he cleared his throat. "So, this place is yours for the weekend!" We walked inside, and he flipped the light switch, highlighting a small but cozy living room and kitchenette combo and a cabin up in the front.

"You've got a half bathroom here to yourself, but the shower house is just at the end of the dock—the cedar shed with the metal roof. No one else is staying here this week, so you'll pretty much have it to yourself. It will get a bit tight in the summertime, but it's still pretty quiet for now."

"Thanks, Cole. This is wonderful." I laughed.

"What is it?"

"It's just...I booked this trip on my phone at some God-awful hour overnight. I don't think I even scrolled through the photos—I just didn't realize I was staying on a boat."

"Sounds about right," he laughed. "You always were a bit impulsive."

"You know, I prefer to think of it as *exciting* and *adventurous*. But, yes. I guess you could say so."

"I'll let you get settled in," he said with a smile. "It's good to see you, Val."

"You too. Goodnight, Cole."

He hugged me again and stepped outside, closing the sliding glass door behind him. I felt the boat sway again as he stepped back onto the dock, and I laughed as I thought through the irony of it all.

My entire life felt like a boat that had been tossed around in storm waters. I was just starting to feel like things might be settling down, which the trip to Ocracoke seemed to help in a way. And here I was, sleeping on a boat that jostled around you every time you so much as blinked a certain direction.

I changed into the pajama set I'd packed and climbed into the bed, noting every rock and sway as I moved. As I settled in, the rain started to pelt the deck above me, providing an excellent sound to lull me to sleep. I thought about that old saying about rain on your wedding day. Maybe rain on my first night in town was a good sign.

At the very least, maybe I'd finally get one good night's sleep. I closed my eyes and wondered what it might be like not to go to bed alone. Maybe one day. Maybe.

CHAPTER FIVE
JACK

I spent most of my free time on Saturday morning arranging the paperwork for Val's offer on the property. My dad couldn't believe we had another potential buyer. He was sure that a few good hurricanes would turn the place to rubble over the years, and we'd eventually just change the listing to a land offer. In all fairness, we were nearly there. I told him about Val Foster, her untimely, albeit entertaining, arrival, and even her sudden switch in plans from building to renovating. He didn't seem bothered in the least and told me to go ahead and handle the paperwork. So, that's what I did.

Buying a home could be complicated, especially when a buyer is planning to finance the purchase. But a cash offer on an "as-is" and otherwise abandoned property was pretty straightforward. Another perk of doing business in a small town was that—even on a Saturday morning—all the right people were just a text message away. After verifying her cash offer with my friend Scott Langston at Island Financial Associates, I sent a text message to Val for an update.

Jack: I'm pretty much finished with the paperwork for your offer on

*the Lighthouse Road
property. The listing price is
$675,000, which I think is
fair. The offer should be
accepted pretty easily. If it's
all right with you, I can
submit it first thing. Dad
gave me the keys, so if you'd
like to meet me at the house
Monday morning, we can
walk through and give you
one last chance to change your
mind.*

*Val: I won't change my
mind. I'll see you
Monday morning.*

She wasn't just crazy—she was confident, and those two things made for a lethal combination. The right amount of crazy paired with such confidence would have gotten me into a lot of trouble, but Val Foster seemed to be thriving.

I never did go on that fishing trip with Glenn, opting instead for brunch with my parents at a much more reasonable time in the morning. By the time Sunday evening rolled around, I'd prepared myself for the wrath of my best friends. They were good at giving a guy some shit, and I was known to provide them with plenty of opportunities.

Pulling into Glenn's driveway, I noticed the familiar white Land Rover parked between the usual stack of pickup trucks. That could have only meant one thing: Bailey invited Val, and I'd have to deal with the crazy girl at what was supposed to be a quiet and laid-back kind of night.

"Surf's up!" Glenn opened the lid to the grill, and a whiff of perfectly blackened shrimp lofted into the air. "Shrimp's done," he added.

"Fellas," I said, opening the cooler on the patio and adding the bottles I'd brought to our stock. "How is everyone tonight?" Fist bumps and bottle taps were met all around except for Glenn. The man always had his hands on the grill and his wide variety of cooking tools.

My friends stood in their usual circle on the patio. Cole, Hank, Brady, and Scott had taken their places, leaving just enough room for me to take mine.

Next to the grill, Cole Stewart stood with one hand in his pocket and another holding a beer. He stayed pretty occupied with his marina these days, but he always managed to pull himself away for our Sunday night gatherings. Ever since he'd inherited the place, he'd been less social and more addicted to working. I got the impression that he didn't want to let his uncle down, like he felt compelled to make the Forsyth Marina a grand success. In all fairness, I found it pretty respectable that he didn't want to live on his uncle's wealth but take the opportunity to turn the place into a positive cash flow. All of that, combined with the divorce, really took a toll on his social life.

Next to him stood Hank Miller, our secretly very tender-hearted tattooed grunt of a guy who worked as a trauma nurse at the hospital. He sipped his beer and listened as Brady recalled a recent trip to Jeffreys Bay in South Africa for a modeling shoot with the team at Roxy.

Bradford Hilton III, better known as Brady Hill, was a show-runner for Ford Modeling Agency in New York City. Rumor has it, he was home now because he'd gotten into a drunken bar fight a month or so ago. Brady told us that he just got tired of the chaos and wanted to move home, but I saw the articles. We knew he'd confess to the details and the drama when he was ready. He was staying at his father's place on the island for a while until he figured out his next move. Getting blacklisted by Ford seemed to be a heavy enough repercussion that I doubted he'd get any serious work any time soon.

Between Brady and me, Scott stood completely zoned out from the conversation as he scrolled on his phone, as usual. Scott was a banker and never could shut off his work mode. It usually irritated the hell out of me, but this Sunday in particular, I knew that he was working to help me with the sale of the Lighthouse property. As I said, small-town perks.

"Your girl's inside," Hank said, tapping his beer bottle to mine.

"You know, I think we should stick to calling her Val," I said.

"Looks like crazy might be sticking around," Glenn added.

"Crazy?" Cole asked, confused. He'd missed the conversation at the bar where I explained my first run-in with Val.

"Doesn't matter," I said. "Val Foster. It looks like she's moving to town, fellas, so let's be nice."

"Yeah, let's be nice," Cole said with pinched eyebrows. "She's a good friend of mine, and I expect you animals to treat her as such."

The guys all looked between Cole and me and back again, likely waiting for more of an altercation.

"Okay, okay. I'm sorry," I said as I waved my hands in defense. "I guess we just had a bad first impression. I'll give her another shot."

"All right then," Cole nodded, seemingly satisfied.

The door to the kitchen opened, and laughter poured out, followed quickly by Bailey and Val, who carried platters of food and drinks.

"There she is," I said, taking the tray full of pitchers from Bailey. "How was work today?"

"Quiet," she answered with frustration as she poured glasses for everyone—always the server. "It's all right. Summer's coming, and things will get busier."

"Or, you could let them find another bartender and get to work on building your cafe." My suggestion was short and sweet and had been made a million times before. Bailey always thought she'd gotten away with letting her dream of owning her own cafe fall quietly to the wayside, but I knew her, and I knew better.

"Cafe?" Val Foster obviously didn't know her friend as well as I did, which filled me with pride.

"It's nothing," Bailey said, arranging the plates on the countertop next to Glenn. "It was just an old idea."

"It was a damn good idea," Cole said, nodding to Val. "She's just too chicken-shit to do anything about it."

"To do what?" Val was so out of the loop.

"A while back," Bailey started slowly, "I was thinking about opening up a cafe." She looked at me, irritated that I'd brought it up again. "But starting a business is expensive, and I'm not really even sure where to begin, so I haven't done it yet. The guys can't seem to get it out of their thick skulls that sometimes ideas are just ideas. Not everything has to come to fruition." She handed Glenn a serving plate, and when he finished loading up the shrimp skewers and crab legs, she took the dirty dishes and utensils inside, leaving Val to the wolves.

"She'd be amazing with her own cafe," Val said, watching her friend walk off.

"She hasn't done anything for herself in years," I said. "And no one can seem to get her to reconsider."

"Why is that?" Val asked. The guys each took a drink, keeping silent and staying out of it.

"She was drawing up the business plans with her brother before—"

"Oh," Val said, obviously understanding. "Is he still…in prison?" The group remained quiet. None of them had stayed in touch with Robert since he was arrested, but I had.

"He is. It's been four years. Two years to go."

"Maybe she'll get back to it…one day, I mean." I seemed to have knocked the wind out of Val's sails.

"I've been trying to get her to do it; she just won't budge."

A rumble in the gravel driveway interrupted our conversation, and we all turned to find my sister's Jeep pulling in. I set my beer down, walked over to meet her and help wrestle my nephew out of his seat.

"Whose car is that?" Etta pointed to the Range Rover as I walked up to the open passenger window. In all fairness, it was kind of hard to miss.

"A friend of Bailey's is in town. Val—"

"Val Foster? No way!" She tossed me the keys and ran across the yard, just ahead of a squeal only a group of girls could produce. I shook my head and brought my attention back to the kid.

"Hey, Tater. Did you bring your football?" My nephew smiled and held the ball up in the air, ready for a game. "Let's go, dude." I struggled to unlatch his seatbelt. Those damn five-point harness car seats were locked up like Fort Knox. Safe, I guess, but annoying.

"Let's go, Uncle Shack!" The kid hadn't figured out the letter J yet, so sometimes Jack sounded more like Shack. I didn't hate it.

"Let's go, Tater!" I mimicked him as he jumped down into the grass and took off. "Go long!" I threw the ball across the yard, well ahead of him. I had one job with my sister, and that was to wear out her son. I took my assignment seriously, and I loved that little boy.

Etta did a damn good job at being a single mom. She worked as a Kindergarten teacher and somehow managed to have just enough energy each evening after a day full of crazy kids to keep up with Tate, too. The day that boy went to school might be the day she finally caught her breath.

Etta got pregnant while she and Jake Tuftly were engaged, and they were only a few months from walking down the aisle when he died. The rest of us stepped in and helped where we could, but I knew that nothing we could ever do would replace Tate's dad. Jake would have been a good dad, and I hoped desperately that Tate would grow to know that.

Tater was with me and ready to play with the big guys: just the way we liked it. We picked up a gentle game of "tackle" football while the girls hung out in the house, presumably catching up with Val about the years that had gone by.

"Tater!" My sister stepped out of the house an hour or so later. "Time to go, bud."

"One more beer, mama!" He answered. Etta threw her hands to her hips.

"Excuse me?" If a look could kill, my sister was one blink shy of murdering us all.

"Relax, Etty. It's just root beer," I said, wrangling my fingers over his head. I handed him the football and knelt down to tie up his loose shoelaces. "Night, buddy."

"Night, Uncle Shack." He hugged my neck and ran around the grass to fist bump each of the guys. He may not have a dad on earth to love him, but he sure as hell had a bunch of uncles—me as a real one and plenty of bonus ones—who would do their best to love him just as much.

I joined the guys on the patio to finish off our beers while discussing the stock market, the impending tourist season, and picking on Brady a bit more about what did or did not happen in New York. Finally, I took off, ready to hit the hay. If I was going to deal with Val Foster bright and early the next morning, I would need a good night's rest.

I said goodnight to everyone and waved to the girls through the kitchen window before climbing into my truck to head home. I was thankful for these Sunday nights. Life on Ocracoke was good.

CHAPTER SIX
VAL

At dinner that night, I listened as the girls filled me in on all the small things I'd missed over the years. I learned that Bailey came right back to Ocracoke after college and—other than the incident with her brother—seemed to have built a good life for herself. She and Jack seemed close, and for that, I decided I'd have to give him a second chance. The girls explained that Jack sort of felt the need to protect Bailey the way Robert would have if he were around. He always reminded them that the way he cared for them both was just *what a brother would do*. The girls really loved him, making it clear that my first impression of him was, in fact, very wrong.

Etta had driven through Raleigh a few times over the years and would try to stop for a brief visit, but like the others, we just hadn't kept in touch nearly as well as we should have. Happy Birthday messages quickly fell into the chaos of everything else in life, and Christmas cards got lost in the piles of mail on the counter. I regretted letting such good friendships fall away, but maybe life was giving me a second chance. I sure deserved to have friends since God or whoever had seen it fit to take everyone else I loved from my life.

I went to Jake's funeral and spent a little while with everyone there, but it didn't do as much as it should have to make me take my friendships more seriously. After he died, Etta mainly kept to herself. She raised Tate on her own and—as Bailey described it—did a damn good job. Etta spoke so highly of Jack. He was a good big brother and more than helpful when it came to her son. It was sweet, actually, the way he played football with Tate in the backyard. The guys all dropped everything to play with him, and I could tell that Etta was grateful.

In the living room, I explained my plans to buy the old house down the street. Etta was excited to hear that I would be around for a while and, much like everyone else, couldn't wait to see what I planned to do with the place.

Back at the marina later that night, the tide rocked me to sleep—but not before my mind filled with all the things I'd missed over the years. I'd barely been around for more than a wedding and a funeral, and I'd missed out on all the little moments in between. Life lately was reminding me that the little moments were actually the big moments. When you missed out on the day-to-day life with someone, you actually missed out on it all. I fell asleep thinking about how small—though wonderful —my world had become. I had Golly, and I was satisfied with that. But now that she was gone, I wondered what the rest of my life had in store. I wondered if the pieces of my past were going to shape my future.

If the lives of my friends were any example, there was so much more out there that I could be enjoying. Friendships, traditions, the little things, the nuances. I didn't regret the life I'd lived with Golly, but I wasn't done yet.

The next morning, I got up early enough to watch the sun rise up over the edge of the marina while I sat out on the deck with a fresh cup of coffee. Before I fell asleep the night before, I'd taken a few minutes to learn more about the boat I'd booked for the weekend. The old Sea Ray 240 Sundancer was small but offered plenty of room for at least a temporary stay. It was more than enough for a place to sleep. Any more, and it would have been cramped.

I grabbed a towel from the small closet and walked over to the dock house in search of the shower. Cole said I'd be the only one needing it this weekend, and I started to wonder what it would be like to share the place during tourist season. A bigger dock house with multiple showers would have to be put on the top of his list if it wasn't already there.

The shower and its contents made me laugh. The place was obviously only ever used by Cole—one very young and very single man. An old rusty razor sat next to a collection of empty bottles of ninety-nine-cent store-brand shampoo and nothing else. I figured I'd do the best I could for the day and make a stop at the store for some higher-quality products later on. Three days of that sorry attempt at shampoo would do more harm than good.

After a barely sufficient shower, I realized I'd only brought a towel to the dock house and not my change of clothes; I'd found my definition of roughing it. My dirty clothes were soaked from sitting on the bench in the shower stall, so with no other options, I decided to make a run for it back to my boat.

My imagination of the worst-case scenario looked like an unprepared Cole Stewart seeing me flee in a tiny towel down the dock; of course, that wasn't anything he hadn't seen before. Maggie's bachelorette party and its aftermath left little to the imagination. At the end of the night, Cole ended up having to track us down and bring us home. Unfortunately, that led to him seeing a bit more than he probably ever wanted to of his future wife's friends. It made for a good story, though.

Back down the dock and safely on the boat, it was only at the sliding glass door—which had apparently locked when I left—that I realized I'd left the keys inside. My phone, also inside and likely tucked somewhere between the bed cushions, wouldn't help. Desperate, I turned to Cole's boat and prayed he was still there.

My loud and rapid knock met with no answer confirmed otherwise. I stomped my feet in frustration before remembering one of my favorite parts about living on Ocracoke—having no need to lock a door. The habits of a small-town boy were going to save me.

I slid his door open, whispering thanks to God above that it was, in fact unlocked, and searched the place for a spare set of keys. He may not have felt the need to lock his own door for safety, but surely the owner of a marina and a handful of boats would have a ring full of spare keys to each one of them. I scoured over the countertops and on what looked to be a makeshift desk but found nothing.

Shivering and still dripping wet, I reached for the blanket on his couch to wrap around my shoulders. I turned around to leave, stunned to find Cole and Jack standing on the deck of the boat. Their presence alone scared the hell out of me, and rather than wrapping up in the blanket, I ended up dropping it—and my towel—giving them a show we all could have done without.

"Shit!" I squealed, naked as the day I was born. I hit the ground and reached for the blanket, wrapping it around my shoulders, still shivering cold.

"Damn, Cole. That didn't take you very long," Jack said. The boys were both looking at me with wide, satisfied smiles.

"I swear, man. She wasn't here when I woke up this morning." He laughed and crossed his arms over his chest, innocently entertained.

"Hilarious, Jack." I rolled my eyes as I shivered uncontrollably. A breezy spring morning on the water wasn't the most efficient time to get locked out of a boat with nothing to wear. "Cole, I seem to have gotten locked out. Can you please let me in?"

He reached into his pocket and pulled out a full key fob, jingling it in the air between us. "Come on, Val. You're shivering."

"It's okay. I'll stand under the hair dryer a little longer than I need to."

"Yeah, I'd prefer it if Val wasn't a popsicle for our meeting later."

"So funny." I walked past the boys and out onto the dock, tip-toeing as quickly as I could to the deck of my own boat. Cole followed right behind me, enjoying my misfortune with a quiet chuckle.

"Haven't had a naked girl on my boat in a long while." He unlocked the glass door and slid it open, making room for me to walk inside.

"Thank you, Cole. I'm sorry for the trouble."

"It's no trouble, really. Besides, you probably made Jack's day with that view."

"Well, that's great. I'm sure he'll take me very seriously at the house later now that he's seen my breasts."

"Worse things have happened. You'll be all right." Cole laughed and stepped back onto the dock. "Let me know if you need anything else."

"Bye, Cole." I laughed, irritated.

I dried my hair a good twenty minutes too long just to sit in the hot air as it filled the tiny cabin. When I finally stopped shivering, I got dressed, put on some makeup, grabbed my phone and keys, and walked up to the parking lot.

"I'm heading over to the office now if you'd like a ride." Jack's voice echoed behind me. My cheeks blushed at the thought of him seeing me naked, and I turned toward him, thankful to be fully clothed this time.

"Thanks, but I was going to stop on the way for breakfast and some coffee," I said. "And, I'm sorry, by the way. Sorry about that—"

"Consider it forgotten," he answered. "I know a place where you might find a cup of coffee. I also have heated seats." He nodded his head toward his blue 4-runner and smiled. I actually had to force myself not to give in and go with him. I had plans.

"Oh, Jack. I'd love to, really. But, I told Bailey I'd meet her this morning before I went to the house." He was trying to be kind, and I felt terrible turning him down. A piece of me even started to wonder if I'd get the chance again. "Can I take a rain check?"

"Sounds good. Tell her I said good morning, and I'll see you at the house in a bit." He smiled and waved before getting into his car and driving off. Maybe he felt the need to give me the same second chance I was mustering up to give him.

The Landing Cafe was the only place to eat at the docks where the north-side ferry arrived each morning from Hatteras, and it was appropriately packed.

"You would *not* believe what happened to me this morning," I said, slumping into the chair across from her. She'd gotten a table by the window with a perfect view of the ferry heading back out and north.

"You caught a fish?" She guessed.

"Hardly. I did flash the boys, though. Cole and Jack."

"I'm sorry, *flash?*"

"Nipples and all," I confirmed as my face fell into my hands. Bailey's hands flew to her mouth as she tried to stifle her laughter. "Thank you. I'm sure Jack will take me *very seriously* now that he has that view in his mind."

"Jack's a gentleman," she said, wiping tears from her face. "Don't worry about him. How exactly did you find yourself in this... *tit*uation?"

"Very funny."

A waitress interrupted, setting two lattes down in front of us.

"I went to take a shower and came back to find the door to my boat locked. I went to Cole's, but he wasn't there. So I went inside to look for a spare key." I took a sip of my latte and continued. "God, that's good. Anyway, I saw a blanket, and I was shivering. But the guys walked up and scared me half to death. I ended up dropping both the blanket and the towel, giving them a ripe close-up."

Bailey snorted behind her hands, laughter pouring out of her.

"I should just go back to Raleigh. Maybe that whole fiasco was a sign from God that this moving thing was a terrible idea."

"Who knows...maybe Jack liked what he saw." She sipped her latte, swallowing the last rumbles of her laughter.

"I bet he likes every set of breasts." I scoffed sarcastically. "Listen, I'm actually supposed to meet him in about half an hour. He put an offer together on the house for me, but he refuses to submit it until I've at least seen the inside. So, if I don't change my mind, I might own a house by this afternoon."

"That's wild!" Bailey said as she reached across the table for my hand. "I'm so glad you're here, Val. I've missed you. I hate that you lost Golly, but I really am happy to get to spend some time with you."

"I love it here," I said, sipping from my mug. "I like Raleigh, but there's nothing left there for me anymore. I can always go back, I suppose. But with everyone gone and work being...well, I'm the boss." Bailey nodded with a hopeful understanding. "I'm young. I'm single. No one's relying on me. Why not do something on my own? Something big? At least once, just to say I tried."

"I think that makes a lot of sense," she agreed.

"How about you? Are you happy here?"

"Here in town? Sure. Am I happy? Like with... everything?" She stared out the window for a few seconds before continuing. "You know, I love working at the bar. I make good enough money. But Jack was right…I can't shake the idea of a cafe of my own. This is the only cafe on the island, and I can't help but think that another one would do well down on the south side by the lighthouse. Especially in the summertime."

"What's stopping you?" I asked. She took a deep breath and smiled.

"My brother and I had all these plans, you know." Her eyes reddened, and she bit her bottom lip. "When Robert left— when he went to prison—" she cleared her throat, "it just seemed like our plans went with him. I don't know if I can do all of that on my own. I don't know if I want to or if I *should*."

"You can't stop living your life because of what happened to your brother," I argued.

"It's not just about him, though. It's about…Etta, and Tate. He will never know his father. Etta will never have her husband to help raise her son. How can the rest of us just move on like it doesn't matter?"

"It does matter," I said. "But how does your opening a cafe make any difference in their lives? Etta obviously doesn't blame you for anything that happened. At dinner last night, it seemed like the two of you were closer than ever."

"I just…I can't imagine going back and chasing the same dreams we all talked about before. It's a lot, you know? A lot has changed."

"Yes, it's a lot. But it might also bring a lot of joy into this town. A lot of joy that you—and Etta—might really need."

"You make a good point," she said, smiling.

"Well, speaking of new things. Let me get back up to the house and see what I can do with this idea. Maybe it's something you and I can do together."

"That would be fun," she said. "I'm catching the next ferry to Hatteras, so I'll have to catch up with you later. You can tell me all about it." We stood, and she hugged me like she was catching up on the years we'd missed. Bailey was always a hugger. It wasn't strange to find her hanging on a friend, or wrapping her arm around the nearest person, even if everyone was just sitting around. I'd missed her hugs.

As thankful as I was to be near her again, I couldn't help but wonder what all we'd missed out on over the years. They say that the truest of friendships can pick up right where they left off, and while I was finding it to be true, I still wished we hadn't left off at all. Bailey and Etta were wonderful friends in college. I'd let them go once, and I didn't intend to do it again.

I left the coffee shop sad that I'd never encouraged the girls to come spend more time with me in Raleigh. Golly would have loved them, and they would have loved her. If I'd learned anything from losing Golly, it's that you have to hold tight to the ones you love while you have them. You never know when things might change. Second chances don't come around every day and now that I had this one, I intended to make the most of it.

The thirteen-mile drive down the island to the end of Lighthouse Road gave me enough time to think about Bailey's cafe—and she was right. This was an excessively long stretch to go without another coffee shop or just a place to sit and spend time with friends. Another cafe near the lighthouse would make a killing in the summer season and probably stay just busy enough with locals the rest of the year. I really wanted to encourage her to chase the idea and see it through.

Pulling into the driveway, I saw Jack standing next to his car while he spoke to someone on the phone. To be fair, he was pretty good-looking. I hadn't noticed earlier that morning, but he was dressed for business—well, beach business anyway. He looked handsome in his slim dark jeans and a white button-up long sleeve shirt that was untucked and blowing in the breeze. Large tortoise-shelled sunglasses rested on his sun-kissed cheeks and brown leather sandals on his sandy feet. If there was an official beach-boy image, Jack Dixon was it. He looked devilishly stylish, but comfortable. If I didn't know any better, I'd say that my body was as attracted to him as my eyes seemed to be.

As I approached, he ended his call and slid the phone into his back pocket, reaching up to wave. I wished like hell that he hadn't just seen every inch of me, cold, perky, and shaking on the boat. Our first impression was less than pleasant but it least it was appropriate. Our second wasn't far behind. We clearly shared a group of friends that wouldn't be changing anytime soon, so if we were going to spend that much time together, I figured I'd better let go of the embarrassment.

"Hello again," he said, meeting me halfway down the driveway. "You look...warmer."

"Yes, a hair dryer and a hot latte do wonderful things for a girl in distress." We both laughed, and Jack unlocked the door.

"Here you go," he said, placing the key in my hand. "Let's go inside and see if you really want to make this place your home." He pulled the key back toward him. "On second thought, let me go inside first. Just…stay close behind me. I don't want you falling through the floor or anything." I felt my eyeballs nearly bulge out of my lids.

"Do you really think it's that bad?" Maybe all of his attempts at talking me out of this were valid. Maybe he knew more than I did about how much work I was jumping into.

"I guess we'll find out."

I followed a few steps behind as he opened the door and stepped into the foyer. He jumped lightly in place, testing the strength of the floorboards beneath him, and turned to face me.

"Well, so far, so good." My stomach twisted at the thought of us falling through the floor. There's no telling what might be waiting for us underneath the house. I'd always wanted a dog, but when it came to any other kind of animal—especially the ones known to live in the waterfront areas of the coastal Carolinas—I was on one-shot terms. There wasn't enough ammunition in the world to get me into a crawl space in a place like this, let alone coming back out alive.

We walked carefully into the living room, which took up most of the front of the house. I settled a few feet from Jack at a big bay window that offered a clear view of the falling tide. "This is wonderful," I said. "I could do a lot with a place like this."

"Yeah," he said hesitantly. "I mean, I still worry about how much it would take. But I could see sitting here with a sweet tea and enjoying the view." Maybe he'd be admitting that I was right after all. *One step at a time.*

"Let's go take a look at the kitchen." I turned to find him standing with his hands in his pockets, admiring the sight in front of him. I just wasn't sure if he was looking at the tide through the window or at me.

"Being abandoned will do some damage," I said. "It takes heart to be willing to stick around and put a place like this back together." Jack nodded as he circled the kitchen island, dragging his fingers through the layers of dust on top.

"Well, depending on how you put it back together, there's a formal dining room on the other side of that wall. But I have to say, it seems like the kitchen has more than enough space to eat."

Betty Ann's letter came to mind, and I remembered the suggestion she'd made about the kitchen. Jack was right, there was plenty of space as it was: easily able to seat a dozen or more. But if Betty Ann spent her entire life here, and wanted a larger space for everyone to gather, I felt like it was important to consider.

I looked up and around at the appliances—for placement, not functionality. If I were remodeling a kitchen, I'd put brand new appliances in it, too.

"I don't hate it, though. I mean the layout...it seems right."

"Think you could whip something up in here?" He stood against the countertop, leaning back into it with his arms crossed over his chest.

"I suppose I could," I said, letting his smile linger on me for a moment.

"Let's go take a look upstairs." Jack nodded behind him to the grand stairway in the foyer. I followed him up the stairs, distracted by the way his jeans fit just right. "The master suite is downstairs, but there are three more bedrooms up here—each

with its own bathroom. Big place for just one person."
Questions lied beneath his words.

"I never said I'd live here alone," I said.

"Oh! I'm sorry. Boyfriend? Husband?" He looked to my left hand rather indiscreetly. I mean, he didn't even try to hide his curiosity.

"No. There's no one. What I meant was, you know maybe roommates or something. One day." I'd been single for quite some time. It never really crossed my mind that I was looking at an obscenely large home for a single girl. On the other hand, I wasn't exactly used to tight living, either. Golly and Pop's place always had more than enough space. Even when visitors came, we were never cramped.

Sure, the house was a big place just for me. But it wouldn't be that way forever. Would it?

"Honestly, the whole place needs a total gut job," Jack said, looking around upstairs. "I can't imagine anything in this house is worth keeping."

"That's okay," I answered. "I'm up for a challenge."

CHAPTER SEVEN
JACK

The next day, I worked in the office at my parents' house to help my dad finalize the offer for Val's place, among a few other things he had waiting for me in a stack of pending paperwork.

"Daniel Dixon!" My mother hollered from the kitchen, loud enough that my dad and I both looked up to see what type of reckoning was coming our way. She stepped through the foyer and into the living room, waving a stack of papers. "How much money are you going to spend on that damn boat?" My dad closed his eyes tightly, hissing through his teeth—knowing full well that he was in trouble and prepared for whatever came next.

"You know what they say, dear. B-O-A-T...break out another thousand." He tried to add a charming smile, but my mom wasn't amused. "It was the cushion liners, dear. If we didn't replace them before this summer, those seats would start to scratch up your legs every time you sat down. We can't have that." My dad stood and romanced my mother into forgiveness with a sway back and forth to the music playing behind him. Within a minute or two, mom had tossed the credit card statement, and they laughed as they spun across the living room floor while Tim McGraw played in the background. My dad could convince my mom to do just about anything if he had Tim McGraw coming through the nearest speakers. Although, my mom would probably do a hell of a lot more for Tim McGraw himself.

"If you two could peel yourselves apart for just a second…" I pretended to gag at the display of affection. Truth be told, my parents had it all—more than anyone could ask for in a marriage. If I ever found love even half as good as theirs, I'd be amazed. "I have everything ready for you to look over, dad."

"Go ahead and print it all out, son. I'll be back in a few minutes." He took my mom by the hand and led her out of the living room and up the stairs. I knew exactly what they were escaping for, and the thought caused me to choke on a real gag.

"Gravy!" Tate's little voice echoed in the tall ceiling of the foyer and his footsteps pitter-pattered toward me across the tile floor. "Pop?"

"They're busy, bud." I offered a distraction, hoping he'd run into the living room instead of going upstairs to find his grandparents. Some traumas could never be healed; ask me how I know.

"Good morning," my sister sing-songed as she kicked off her flip-flops at the door.

"Hey, Etty." I hit print and shut my laptop just in time to catch my favorite four-year-old mid-air.

"Where's Gravy?" Tate barely got the words out as I tickled his ribcage and held him upside down.

"Gravy and Pop are working on something in the attic, and they'll be downstairs in a little bit." I flipped him right side up and set him down on the floor.

"Gross," Etta said. We'd always used "working on something in the attic" as code for "our parents are doing the deed".

"I was just about to get a snack. Y'all hungry?" I stepped into the kitchen just in time to catch a cue ball before it went through the window over the sink. "Tate! Dude! Below the shoulders." I rolled it down the hallway back to him as my sister collapsed into a stool at the kitchen island. "Why aren't you working?"

"Teacher workday. I skipped out on this one. He wanted to say good morning to Gravy, so I told him we could make a quick trip." She checked the time on her phone. "Then again, I might leave him here. He's exhausting, Jack. He's so exhausting."

She was joking, but also she wasn't. Little boys weren't exactly known for being calm. Tate was a top-notch boy, and I didn't know how my sister survived it, let alone managed to keep him even mildly under control.

"Etty, seriously. Why don't you just move back into town? You're going to make yourself crazy with all this back and forth."

"I know," she exhaled. "I think it's time I found a place right here by the school. I just…you know."

"I know." I winked and reached to squeeze her hand as I laid a tray of cheese and crackers on the counter between us. Dad and I had a habit of working from the house, and mom kept the pantry well stocked. She was on a charcuterie kick, and no one was sad about it.

"Why aren't *you* at work?" She countered with a mouth full.

"Dad wants to get Val's offer done, and he had everything we need here at the house. We just met here to finish it up and haven't left yet."

"How's it coming? Is she really moving back?"

"I guess so. She made a cash offer, so there's really no reason for it to fall through. If that's what she wants to spend her money on…" Most of me thought that Val was diving in way too deep for her first home renovation project, but the rest of me knew that the right contractors were just a text message away. We'd be able to help her out if it all got to be too much. And I couldn't ignore the fact that I was almost glad that the project would take so much work. It would keep her around for a while, and that was an idea I was starting to be interested in. She made my sister and Bailey happy, and that made me happy. Listening to Bailey and Etta go on about her had me believing that my first impression of her was wrong. I mean, I still thought she was wild. But there was more to her than I'd seen. Then we had our accidental encounter on the boat and…well, it wasn't terrible. I wouldn't be devastated to find her in the lineup when we all paddled out in the mornings. I'd give just about anything to see her again. In a bikini next time, of course. I'm not a total pig.

"What's left then?"

"Not much, really. I need to give her a call and schedule a time for her to sign everything. We've had the keys to the house for years. Betty Ann arranged everything with Dad before she passed away, so…the house is basically ready for her."

"Is she staying there during the renovations?" Etta looked a bit concerned, and I remembered that I really *was* the only one who had taken the time to think this whole idea through. Everyone was just going to let Val jump right into a shit storm. The least we could do was hand her a raincoat.

"God, I hope not." I hadn't considered that she'd actually be living there. Not that she seemed like the type to think things through, but had she even considered the possible mold? "Hasn't she found another place to stay?"

"I don't know that she was aware she needed to."

"She's going to have to crash with you or Bailey for a while."

"My lease is about to expire, so probably not at my place. And what if I do decide to move? Bailey is still living with her parents, so I doubt that's an option. I think Val was just planning on roughing it." Etta clearly didn't know how terrible the house had gotten over the years.

"Okay, I'll work on that. There's no way she's staying there. Not yet, anyway." I'd have to do some digging, but I knew I could figure something out. Maybe she could go back to the boat at Cole's place.

"You have a spare room, you know." Etta's less than subtle suggestion came with a devious smile.

"That's a terrible idea, Etty. She'd probably kill me. Or at least drive me to insanity. And then I might kill her."

"She's not that bad, Jack."

"Okay, no. She's not. She's just…she's something else." I raced to grab the last cracker from the plate, hopeful that my sister couldn't tell what I was really thinking about her friend at that moment.

"Get to know her. There's a lot more to Val than a pretty rich girl with ideas and nothing better to do." My sister had a point. She *was* pretty. A hockey puck flew into the kitchen, just over my sister's head, and I reached to catch it. "Dude! Pucks outside!" Tate followed with a hockey stick in his hand. Some days I genuinely wondered how my sister was still alive.

My dad came down the stairs and into the kitchen with a wide smile and some pep in his step.

"Feel better?" I asked.

"Well, I'm not in trouble for the boat anymore." He wagged his eyebrows with pride.

"Gross," my sister and I said in unison.

"Etty, baby. How are you doing?" Dad kissed the top of her head and opened up the fridge for a beer. "Where's Tater Tot?"

"I just kicked him out. He's got hockey sticks in the driveway."

"Ah. Time for my workout, then." Dad went for the door.

"What about the contract?" I hollered with my arms outstretched, irritated that my dad was leaving me to finish everything.

"Handle it, son. You know what to do."

"He's going to retire soon, you know. He's making you do everything because you're going to be responsible for the whole company one day. You need to make a plan."

"I know. I just…don't know if I want to keep doing everything his way." I'd known for years that my dad planned to have me take over the office when he was ready to retire, but truth be told, I just wasn't sure what to make of the opportunity. I wasn't going to let my family business crumble— I couldn't. But taking over things as they were didn't seem right for me either. Was this a quarter-life crisis?

"There's plenty of time to work out the details," Etta said as she walked our dishes to the sink. "Why don't you give Val a call? She said she'd be back in town whenever things are settled."

"Back in town? Where'd she go?" I hadn't realized that she'd left.

"Back to her grandmother's house. She went back until things came through on the house."

"Work? Isn't she the boss?" I seemed to care about Val's whereabouts more than I would have thought. "What's the company again?" I'd done all of the paperwork but didn't remember the details of her entire life.

"She makes and sells her own tea." I guess my confused look told Etta everything she needed to know. "You know…tea. Loose leaf teas. Tea bag and boiling water type of thing." Contrary to her opinion, I wasn't a complete idiot.

"Oh. She…she makes tea?"

"Basically. I mean, she sells it online, keeps a stock in stores, and supplies a few restaurants, too."

"Wow. That's…"

"Impressive? I told you. There's more to Val than you think." Etta winked and slapped my shoulder as she followed our dad outside. "Tater Tot!" She yelled as she walked out the front door. "Let's go!" I heard something shatter just before the door closed behind her, just before an "Oh, shit," from my dad. I cringed as I thought about what it might have been. Mothers were miracle workers.

I pulled my phone from my back pocket and sent Val a text.

*Jack: Paperwork is ready
whenever you are. Etta said you
left town.*

*Val: I'm back in Raleigh. Just
keeping up with work and lying
low for a while. Do I have a
house?*

*Jack: You will, but you do know
you can't live there...right? Not
yet.*

*Val: Oh of course I can. It has
power. And water.*

*Jack: Absolutely not. I'll work
on some temporary
arrangements for you. Just let
me know when you'll be back so
we can get together.*

*Jack: You know, for you to sign
the paperwork. For your house.*

*Val: And here I thought you just
wanted to spend time with me.
-shock-*

Jack: Just doing my job.

Val: Right. Thanks. I'll let you
know when I get there. Just give
me a few days.

Jack: See you soon. Drive safe.

Drive safe? I didn't need to be concerning myself with her driving—safe or not—back into town. But for whatever reason, a part of me instinctively worried about her. I was the same way with Bailey and Etta, but they were my sisters. That's definitely not how I felt about Val. Not that I knew exactly *what* I felt about Val. But sisterly protection wasn't it. I put my phone back into my pocket and grabbed my car keys from the hook by the door and stared into the mirror as I thought through the options.

Val wouldn't be able to stay with Etta or Bailey. Hank and Glenn shared an apartment and had a spare room, but they were also known to sleep with any girl that simply existed in front of them. The idea of Val being their next play-thing made me nauseous. My sister and Bailey had always been off limits to the guys for that exact reason. Surely, Cole would have a place for her to stay, at least for a little while. I wouldn't complain about her staying on the boats. Maybe she'd need to use that shower house. Maybe I'd be there. Maybe we'd...*stop*.

Gravy and Pop wrestled Tate into his car seat and I waved as I passed them, following Etta down the driveway. On the way to the marina, my mind circled back to seeing Val on the boat—seeing *all of Val* on the boat. Yeah, the boat. We could get her to stay on the boat.

"Sorry, dude. I'd all out *give* her a boat if I'd known she needed a place, but everything is booked up starting next week." He had a point. Summer was coming, and most places were booked six months out at a minimum. But I still wanted to argue. Staying at Cole's was the best idea. At least he wouldn't sleep with her. To my knowledge, Cole hadn't slept with anyone since his ex-wife.

"You hardly even advertise this place, Cole. How do you have everything rented out already?"

"Brady did a shoot for Google and dropped my name with someone. I guess they're doing company retreats or something this summer. They booked every boat and the whole house for an entire month. They have like a hundred people coming in." Cole stood taller after his explanation, and rightfully so. He'd been a mess over what to do with the place. The Forsyth Marina had a lot of potential, and Cole wanted to make use of it. To finally have the place booked up was a good sign. A sense of pride grew in me for my friends. Not only was Cole chasing big dreams for the marina, but Brady working on a project with Google was a big deal. He was crazy, but he was obviously successful; except for the part about the bar fight.

"Who'd have thought that Brady would be the man behind the business," I laughed.

"You're telling me," Cole said. "But I sure as hell wasn't going to turn down a month-long rental. From Google, no less. Talk about repeat business. That and...Google reviews."

"That's fair."

"You have a spare room, don't you?" Cole stopped hosing the dock long enough to turn to me, clearly wondering why I hadn't thought of the idea myself.

"Cole, I—nah."

"Oh, come on, man. Can't manage to let a female into your bachelor pad?"

"No. I—" Cole shot me a glare that was just chock full of judgement. "I just—"

"You saw her naked." He eyed me up and down as if I wanted to return the favor.

"Let's be adults, dude. She's pretty. And oops, I saw her naked. *We* saw her naked. Regardless, I don't think she'd want to stay with me. I mean, Tate stays over now and then. We have Uncle Camp, remember?" I didn't have a ton of excuses as to why Val couldn't stay with me temporarily, but Uncle Camp seemed like my best shot.

"I'm sure she wouldn't mind the occasional four-year-old on the couch, dude." Cole laughed at my attempt. He didn't say another word, but his face said it all. I was going to let Val stay with me.

Back at my car, I thought over the idea again, talking myself up to survive a few weeks with Val Foster. If we could just get a strong foundation, replace the roof, and get some walls up...yeah—a few weeks.

Jack: Cole's place is all booked up.

> *Val: That's fine. I'm sure Bailey or Etta can handle me for a few days.*

*Jack: Weeks, Val. It's
probably going to be weeks at
minimum.*

*Val: You make it sound like they
would die if I stayed there.*

*Jack: Well, it sounds like
everyone here is a bit tied up.
So, I just thought I'd offer.*

Val: To tie me up?

Jack: Jesus, no.

*Val: Wow, I really am repulsive,
huh?*

*Jack: God, Val. I'm sorry. I
meant I wanted to offer you a
place to stay. You know, if
you need one. Which you do.
You can't stay in that house.*

*Val: You sure are helpful for a guy
who couldn't wait to get rid of me just
a few days ago.*

Jack: Well, maybe I was wrong.

Val: You were.

*Jack: Fine then. Stay in my
apartment while you work on
the house. Make me
realize how wrong I was and
how much I want you to stay.*

Val: Challenge accepted.

I had a snarky comment to text back to her, but I decided against it. The last thing I wanted to do was make her think I was flirting right after I basically asked her to move in with me.

And God, I really had just asked her to move in with me, hadn't I?

Saturday morning came earlier than I thought it would, and my justifications for all the times I'd skipped out on early morning fishing trips with the guys only grew. It pained me to wake up so early, especially *by choice*. We lived at the beach. We could fish literally any hour of any day. Why did it have to be an ass-crack of dawn activity?

"Fellas!" Glenn walked down the dock with a cooler in each hand and a very large and very awake grin on his face. "About time we had a boys' trip," he glared at me, "with *all* of the boys."

"I'm sorry, I'm sorry." I raised my hands in defeat.

"You can sleep when you're dead, bro." Hank shook my head by a handful of hair as if I were a puppy.

"So I've heard," I said, rolling my eyes. We all climbed into Glenn's boat and took our seats as he got ready to drive us out to whatever destination he had in mind for the day. I never asked. Glenn knew best. Don't get me wrong, I was a man who loved his boat. But there was no one I knew that was better than Glenn at navigating the waters around the island and pulling in the fish. Hank and Cole sat on one side while I sat next to Scott on the other.

"Is it...can it be..." I brought my hand to my chest in shock. "Did Scott Langston put his phone away?"

"Shut up," he laughed. "If I didn't work so hard, your life wouldn't be so easy."

"That's fair," I said. "But you really should take a day off more often. There's a whole world out here, dude."

"Yes, I know." He turned his hat backward and lowered his sunglasses as Glenn picked up speed. "I just...I like what I do."

"We all do," Hank said. "But I like food, too. And girls. And fishing."

"And girls," Cole added.

"Don't judge me, you prude." Hank kicked Cole in the knee, starting a boy fight—or as much of one as you could have when seated on a moving boat. "Not all of us are divorced and sad." Hank squeezed in one more jab to Cole's ribs.

"I'm not sad, you brute." Cole wrapped an arm around Hank's neck and locked him into a chokehold. "I'm just not a man-whore."

"I resent that!" Hang grunted from underneath Cole's arm.

"Oh please, you're the exact definition of a man-whore," Scott confirmed. I just kicked back and watched. That is until I got called out.

"Tie-breaker, Jack." Scott pointed to me.

"Ehhhh, I think I'd rather stay out of it."

Cole let go of Hank, and Scott leaned forward as all three of them stared intently at me, suspicious and waiting for more.

"What?" I asked.

"You want to stay out of it?" Cole asked.

"You aren't going to give Hank shit for his most recent round of late-night visitors?" Scott looked thoroughly confused.

"Ah, I know why." Hank crossed his arms over his chest. "Because he has girl problems of his own, and he doesn't want us to know about it."

"I do not," I waved. "I do not have girl problems."

"Bullshit," Hank said. "Spill."

"Oh, you're talking about the breasts," Cole said, looking proud that he knew something the rest of them didn't.

"No," I started in defense, but he cut me off.

"The man got a full frontal view of some nice boobs on a beautiful girl, and now he can't get her out of his mind."

"Thank you for that, Cole."

"Wait, what?" Hank asked.

"Who are you seeing naked?" Scott followed. "And why haven't you shared?"

"Because not all girls need to be talked about like they're the tail of the week," I said. That was all they needed. I was keeping a girl from the man-whores, and for that, I'd get slaughtered.

"Holy shit, he's falling in love. Who is she?" Hank couldn't get enough. "Wait a second. You're not talking about the crazy girl, are you?"

"Are you?" "Is he?" "Are you in love with the crazy girl?" A collection of responses flooded around the guys.

"I thought we agreed to not call her that," Cole said.

"Her name is Val. And I never said I was in love."

"No, you just saw her naked," Cole added. I was going to kick his ass later for making this worse.

"Okay, for the record, I'm not the one who got her naked; she did that herself—on your boat." The guys laughed and diverted their attention back to Cole as they waved me on, eager for more. "She got locked out of the boat after a shower and went to Cole's for a spare key. We scared her, and she dropped her towel, that's all."

"She's gorgeous, ain't she?" Hank asked.

"Of course she is, but that's not the point." I was feeling defensive and wanted to keep her to myself.

"Okay, so you're totally into her," Scott suggested. "Is she single?" He turned to Cole. "You know her. Is she single?"

"Look, I—I mean she's beautiful but she's nuts. I mean you guys have no idea what she thinks she's capable of." They all looked at me as I paused, waiting for me to elaborate. "I mean she—you know, she...she's just crazy. She's got crazy ideas and the money to play with. She's just here to play Joanna Gaines for a while. She won't stay long."

"Oh, he totally likes her," Scott said.

"Regardless," I said as I waved between us all. "I might have made it a bit more complicated than that." I ran my hands through my hair. "I kind of…maybe suggested that she move in with me."

"Damn, that was fast," Cole said.

"It was your idea!" I argued back while Hank and Scott just laughed. Glenn slowed the boat to a stop.

"What did I miss?" He asked as he killed the engine and waited for a recap.

"Dude saw the crazy girl's tits, and now she's moving in with him." Hank wasn't exactly helpful.

"What the hell?" Glenn lifted his sunglasses to the top of his head and waited for more.

"Look, guys. Val needed a place to stay, and I offered my spare room. It's that simple."

"It sure *isn't*," Glenn argued. "We have a spare room, too."

"Yeah, and I know what you've done and who you've done it with in that spare room," I said.

"She's better than that, you guys. She's friends with Etta and Bailey. Can we not make her some toy to chase?" Cole seemed to be getting irritated, which surprised me because he started the whole conversation in the first place.

"All right, all right," Scott said. "Jack, other than serving as a very convenient housing option for our new friend…what are your intentions with Val Foster?" They'd cornered me, and they knew it.

"I don't know, man." A collection of growls and rumbles said the guys were unsatisfied with my answer. "Okay, look. She's attractive. Yes. Gorgeous, even. But I hardly know her. Can we just leave it at that?"

"Let's fish," Cole said as he reached out for a fist bump. I'd wanted to kill him, but now I owed him one.

CHAPTER EIGHT
VAL

"Are you sure about this?" I followed Jack inside, where I was shocked to find things looking slightly less bachelor-pad-like than I'd imagined. Two weeks had gone by since he'd offered me his spare room, and it looked as if he'd taken advantage of the time. His place was...clean. "I can stay in Raleigh, you know. It's really not that long of a drive."

"Yes, Val. I'm sure. It's not a big deal. I don't use my spare room anyway." He set my bags down in the foyer and took the duffel from my shoulder. "You'll have your own bathroom. I just washed the towels and sheets for you. It's all on your bed." For a young single guy who lived alone, he'd certainly taken care of quite a bit before I arrived. He stepped further into the house and began to give me a tour. "This floor is basically all of it: living room, dining room, kitchen, and the office is through the back there." He pointed through the kitchen to the office where a large sliding glass door led to a patio overlooking the marina.

"Your home is wonderful, Jack. Thank you." If I didn't know any better—and I did—I'd say that Jack's eyes hung on me a few seconds longer than they needed to. At the very least, I was impressed that he'd gone so far out of his way to ensure that I was comfortable.

"Uh, right. So—upstairs are the bedrooms and bathrooms. Like I said, each bedroom has its own bathroom, so you'll have all the privacy you need." This time I was sure that his eyes drifted back down to my chest—as innocent as he tried to make it look—probably remembering everything he'd already seen. A hint of desire peeked from his eyes as we stood there, and I'd be lying if I said I didn't like it. He was attractive and, aside from our first encounter, seemed to be a decent human being. While I'd been back in Raleigh, my thoughts had wandered around him more than a few times. I'd shaken it off to the best of my ability, but knew that it would be a bit more difficult while I was sleeping just on the other side of a wall.

"Well, just let me know what I owe you," I said in a quick attempt to change my train of thought. "You know… rent, bills, whatever it adds up to."

"Don't worry about it, Val." He waved a hand to brush off my offer.

"That's kind of you, but not necessary. You're doing me a great favor, Jack, and I appreciate it." *Damnit.* Now he was being chivalrous, too.

"Do you cook?"

"I can…" I watched his face as a plan came together in his mind.

"Tell you what. Make me your favorite meal before you go, and we'll call it even."

"Okay," I laughed. "That's easy. Completely unfair in trade value, but easy enough."

"Why don't we set your things in your room, and we can head over to the office to get everything signed? I have the keys for you, so you could be in the place by this afternoon. I'm sure you'll want to get in the house to start working on a plan. Or maybe burning it down."

"That sounds great, Jack." Again, it felt as though his smiling eyes hung around a bit too long. Certainly, I must have been misreading him. Jack Dixon couldn't wait to get rid of me when I first returned to Ocracoke, and I was sure that it wouldn't be long before he remembered that and wanted me off the island and out of his house, too.

I was shocked when I learned that not a single one of my friends had a space for me to crash while I got started on the renovations. I thought back to the extra bedrooms in the house. I might be moving into the place on my own, but at least there would be room for everyone. There'd always be a bed for someone who needed it. Then again, It was becoming more and more clear that I wasn't totally aware of how extensive the renovation process was going to be, either. Joanna Gaines always makes it look so easy on the show. One good commercial break and a house had a whole new roof.

I followed Jack to the office, where we sat around a large table to sign my life away. Okay, not *my life*, really. Just seven hundred thousand dollars of it. In the grand scheme of things, seven hundred thousand bucks wasn't a big deal— especially if I was spending it on real estate, which Alex always said was more like investing than spending. In the few short months that I'd been on my own, Alex and Louise had set me up with the safest accounts and the best investments. They taught me just enough to begin managing my own money and left the rest to chance—or whatever wisdom they hoped I had. I worried that Alex would have a heart attack when I told him my plans for the house, but overall he seemed to be rather

ANNALEE THOMASSON

impressed. His only stipulation was that I found myself a reputable contractor before I went 'blowing up walls'—his words, not mine.

"I've got to say, dear. If I were buying the place myself, I think I'd build a new home. I'm a bit worried about the renovation you're taking on." Daniel was a father, and I couldn't fault him for being cautious.

"That was my plan," I said. "But..." I looked to Jack, unsure if I should tell them what I'd found. "When we were there, I found something."

"What do you mean?" Jack leaned forward with his elbows on the table.

"When you were on the phone, I was looking at the mailbox. I'd never seen one like that before. I thought it was pretty." Daniel smiled, and Jack laughed. "It's charming," I added. "I opened the mailbox just...looking around. But there was an envelope inside." That was enough to surprise them both. I took a deep breath while they looked between me and each other. They were clearly curious for more. I leaned down to reach into my bag, pulling out the envelope that had lines where I'd folded it into my pocket that day.

"It's from Betty Ann. I suppose she left it in the mailbox before she died." I handed the letter to Daniel and watched as he began to read. Jack waited silently, though his eyes on me said enough.

"Isn't that something," Daniel said, looking back up to me with a curious expression.

"I can tell the home was important to her," I started. "I just...I couldn't help but to think, what if someone did that to

100

my home? To Golly's home?" Jack nodded as if he was finally starting to understand.

"You can't let it go," he said.

"Well, it's obvious that Betty Ann didn't want to."

"No, I suppose she didn't." Daniel looked devastated and excited at the same time.

"I figure, if it meant that much to her, it's worth saving. It wasn't abandoned. It's just been…in waiting." Daniel slid the letter to Jack who read through it and passed it back to me.

"Well then, I guess you ought to get to work." Jack seemed to hold back a laugh.

"Do you have any questions, sweetheart?" The way Daniel Dixon spoke was evidence of his nature. He was about as fatherly as they came. When he'd joined us at the table, he nearly cried tears of joy when he remembered who I was. He mentioned how much he'd loved us coming to the island during college and how he'd always wondered what had happened to the rest of Etta's friends since graduation. While she and Bailey stayed close, it was only the two of them on Ocracoke these days. At the mention of my friends, Daniel confirmed my suspicions that Jack wasn't the only one keeping such a close eye on Bailey.

"Well…I'm sure I will have questions at some point, but right now, all I can think is that I've just taken on a whole lot more than I know what to do with."

"Well, I've been telling you this was—" Jack started to argue, presumably that he'd been right all along, but his father cut him off.

"None of that, young man." Daniel waved a hand at his son, who was silenced faster than a kid in the principal's office. I found the obedience to be entertaining. "Sweetheart, this is one hell of a project—I won't lie to you. But if I thought you were making a bad decision, I wouldn't have helped you do it. Rebuilding or renovating, either way, it was a wise investment." Daniel slid the keys across the table toward me. "Don't let anyone—including my son—" he whacked Jack on the shoulder with a stack of paperwork, "get you down. If you need help, ask for it. When all is said and done, you stand to own one very valuable piece of real estate. There's only so much dirt, you know. God ain't makin' any more of it. So good for you, buying up a piece."

"It's a large piece," Jack said, earning another smack from his father. I couldn't help but laugh.

"Why don't I write down a few of my favorite contractors for you? Let me step into my office and get their phone numbers. Now, I'll tell them you'll be calling so that they know better than to mess with you. Don't you let them take your money. Pit them against each other and make them duke it out. I can help you look over their bids. You know...smart business." Daniel winked and walked away.

"There's no backing out now," Jack said with his hands up behind his head, reclining in his chair. "I hope you know your way around some basic power tools."

"I think you could be slightly more encouraging and less of a total downer," I said, standing to follow Daniel to his office.

"Val, wait." Jack stood and grabbed my arm, turning me back to face him. "I didn't mean that; I'm sorry."

"You didn't mean to insinuate that a girl like me couldn't possibly renovate a house?"

"Even Joanna Gaines has Chip, Val." He laughed as his brain caught up with his mouth. "Just take it slow, okay? One step at a time. Let's see if my dad has those phone numbers for you."

I rolled my eyes at how easy it had been for him to turn the conversation around. If he wasn't so painfully attractive, I might have fought him on the topic a bit more. Instead, I felt my ability to stand up to him dwindling bit by bit. I followed him into Daniel's office.

"All right, son. I've got three names and numbers here. I believe you know each of them. Make sure she doesn't pay too much for anything, you hear?" Daniel handed the sheet of paper to Jack, who looked through the list before his eyebrows met in the middle in frustration. He pulled a pen from his blue jean pocket and scratched out one of the names.

"What did you do that for?" I asked with a laugh.

"Lincoln Nicholson. Don't bother." He handed me the paper, which he'd narrowed down to two options.

"Why?" I asked.

"Son, Lincoln's probably the best contractor in town," Daniel added, equally as confused.

"Sure, just…there are better options. That's all." It was clear that 'better options' was in fact *not* all he was referring to. Usually, I would have jumped right into that discussion, digging for more. I was never known to take the high road. Golly taught me to take Aggressive Alley over Passive Parkway any chance I got, but something about Jack—or this particular conversation —had me hesitating.

"Sure," I said.

"Well, I have a few things to get to this afternoon. I'm going to get to it. I'll see you later then?" Jack stood and stuffed his hands deep into his pockets, looking slightly nervous. I didn't know what to do with that, but I knew for damn sure that I was about to hire a contractor.

"See you later, Jack." I stepped out of the office and walked to my car as I pulled out my phone to make dial the first number on the list—the only name I was interested in calling.

"This is Lincoln Nicholson."

"Hi, Mr. Nicholson. My name is Val Foster. Daniel Dixon gave me your number."

"Hello, Miss Foster. What can I do for you?"

"Yes, sir. Well, it seems I've just bought a house here on Ocracoke, over on Lighthouse Road. It needs…well…it needs everything. Quite a lot of it. And I hear you're the man for the job."

"Sure thing. I'll tell you what, I just finished up on a job site and was heading into town to run a few errands. I can stop by to meet you this afternoon if you have the time, or I'm happy to arrange for sometime next week."

"Well I don't want to rush you, but today would be great," I said. "It's 400 Lighthouse Road. I can be there anytime."

"Well, I'll be damned," Lincoln said. "You bought Betty's place! I thought that house would crumble before anyone bought her up."

"You and everyone else in town. Though, I'm not sure why. The property is absolutely beautiful." I was frustrated with Jack for being such a downer about renovating an old home. Now that a reputable contractor was saying the same thing, I wondered if Jack's repeat cautionary comments might have been worth listening to. Not that I'd ever back down, or admit that he was right.

"Oh, the property is incredible," Lincoln said. "It's the house you should worry about."

"Well, as I told the Dixons at the office, you can't just abandon everything that needs to be fixed up."

"I hope you mean that," he laughed. "I've got to make one quick stop, but I could meet you at the house in about thirty minutes."

"That sounds great, Mr. Nicholson. Thank you."

"Oh, just call me Link," he said. "I'll see you soon then."

"Thank you, Link."

Lincoln Nicholson seemed like a nice enough man. I hadn't noticed any immediate red flags, at least in talking to him on the phone. Jack seemed to feel strongly about my not working with Link, and I couldn't help but wonder why. I tried to shake it off, resting in the fact that Daniel wouldn't have recommended Link if he wasn't the man for the job. After all, I was moving onto a tiny island in the Outer Banks of North Carolina. One man's beef with another was sure to be just the first of many small-town dramas I was sure to learn about.

With a few minutes to kill, I decided to stop by Howard's to visit with Bailey. She'd felt terrible that she couldn't offer me a place to stay while I worked on the house. Apparently, her mother didn't handle Robert's sentencing too well, and moving back home with her parents was the only way Bailey felt she could keep everyone above water.

"We're closed," Bailey hollered as I walked through the door.

"I know," I answered, grabbing a seat at the bar. "I just came to see my friend." I stuck my tongue out at her as she turned around.

"Well, hey!" She leaned over the bar to hug me. I missed my Golly more than tongue could tell, but Bailey's hugs were a welcome reminder that I could make this place feel like home, too. Her personality was enough to make anyone feel at home, anywhere.

"I just finished with Jack and Mr. Dixon." I dangled the keys between us.

"No way!" Bailey gasped. "You really did it! It's done! That's it?"

"Yeah, that's it. Apparently, cash offers are easy."

"Huh. Who knew?" She tossed me a rag and I helped her to dry the rest of the glasses on the bar top. "So, what's next?"

"Well, I managed to snag a meeting with a contractor this afternoon." I stopped to look at my watch. "I actually only have a few minutes before I have to meet him at the house. Lincoln Nicholson, do you know him?" Bailey laughed without ever looking up at me. The way she shook her head told me plenty. Link was bound to be a handful.

"Every girl on this island knows Link," she said. "Terrible boyfriend material. Great contractor, though." Her exhale seemed to be a mixture of irritation and entertainment. There was a story there, for sure.

"What's so terrible about him?"

"That man sleeps with any woman who walks. He even manages to make a girl feel like she could be the one to settle him down, and then he leaves her high and dry. Usually, the girl with the broken heart has barely caught her breath before he moves on to the next."

"Hmm," I thought. "I wonder why Jack has such a problem with him, then."

"What do you mean?" Bailey looked confused.

"Jack told me not to bother with Link—said there were better options. He went as far as to scratch his name and number off my list."

"That's interesting. There's no better contractor in town. He's built or replaced every fence, porch, and kitchen sink on this island. Link will fix that place up for you in no time, and he'll do a better job than anyone else would."

"Good to know," I said, setting the last glass onto the dry rack. "I've got to get going, then. I guess I'll go see what Link has in mind for the place. I guess it's time to open up my eyes and see just how much I've gotten myself into."

"Have fun, homeowner! I'm proud of you."

"Thanks!" I grabbed my keys and started to head out.

"Oh, and don't think you get to avoid telling me all about living with Jack!" I pretended not to hear her and walked outside with a simple wave.

The cottage had obviously seen better days. This day, in particular, was sunny and beautiful—other than the half inch of pollen on every visible surface. The Azaleas were in full bloom, and the Bradford Pear trees were just starting to come alive and brighten up the streets. On the other hand, my property was an overgrown plot of a hot mess that would probably benefit more from a bomb before I stood a chance at that kind of yard work.

"Ms. Foster?" A tall and tanned man with tattooed arms and a backward ball cap climbed out of a muddy pickup truck in the driveway.

"That's me," I said, suddenly admiring how clean my Range Rover was. "I'm Val. It's nice to meet you."

"Hello there, Val. It's a pleasure." He removed his hat and nodded his head as if he were the leading gentleman in a perfectly hemmed black show-stopper of a tux at some lavish event. Rather than a typical handshake, he held my hand as if he were about to kiss the top of it. *Weird.* He lived up to the picture Bailey had painted of him: an absolute player of a man if I had to put my money on it.

"So, are you kin to the Highlands?" He asked as we stepped toward the front porch.

"The who?"

"Betty Ann Highland was the last one that lived here. She never did have any children. Her husband apparently died in Vietnam, and she lived here on her own for the rest of her life. She had some nieces and nephews visit a few times a year. Your parents, I take it?"

I wondered if I should tell Link about the letter, but he seemed to know her personally. I didn't want to spark any trouble.

"No, sir. I just…saw the property for sale online."

"Well, damn. I really thought the only way this place would sell was if someone kin to the property decided to take it on for the sake of nostalgia."

"Well, I hate to burst your bubble, but I'm just a girl with a few ideas."

"Good enough for me," Link opened the front door and motioned for me to follow him inside.

"Now, someone put an offer in on this house a while back. I did the inspection then, so I have a full report of everything that was wrong at the time. I'll have to make sure nothing's changed, of course—not that it could get too much worse. You're basically looking at a total gut job."

"Everyone makes that sound like the end of the world."

"It's not the worst-case scenario. It can be scary to a homeowner, but in my line of work…I like to think of it more like a blank slate. White snow. A fresh canvas—just waiting on your masterpiece."

"That's the kind of answer I've been looking for," I smiled. "So, what are you thinking?"

"Well, unless there's something major you had in mind, I think I'd keep the layout pretty much the same." I followed him through the living room and into the kitchen in the back of the house, remembering the way Jack leaned against the countertop when he'd brought me here the first time.

"I had a few ideas, but…it's your house."

"I'd actually like to hear your ideas if you don't mind."

"Let's see. I can put all the details into my proposal, and of course, we'll have to run the plans through the historical society to make sure we don't piss off any of our elderly island residents. But…informally?" He stepped up to the sliding door that led to the backyard. "This area could be a lot more open. The inlet is right out there. You should be able to see it."

"I agree," I said, standing behind him, waiting for more.

"I'd consider opening up this doorway so that the living room and kitchen are one and the same. That wall isn't load bearing; it's just for storage." He pointed at the wall between the kitchen and the living room. "There's the formal dining room, but it's decent the way it is. Huge, of course." I laughed when I remembered my plans to expand it.

"That's okay. I like to entertain." Link smiled, and I could only imagine where his mind went with my comment. I knew guys like him, especially in college. They could turn anything into a sex joke. "Dinner parties," I clarified.

"Of course." He walked around to the front of the house and looked up the staircase. I walked behind him and offered my biggest idea yet.

"So right now, the third floor is an unfinished space, probably used as an attic. I know it would be a lot of work, but I was thinking of possibly turning it into a bunk room. Whether I rent the place out or live here myself, I think a bunk room would be a great use of the space. There's plenty of storage elsewhere."

"I like the way you think, Val."

"Thank you." I'd managed to impress the contractor, and even myself. I wondered if Jack would ever come around to my idea for the house.

"The staircase needs to be completely redone. It's a bit wobbly at best. But other than standard updates upstairs, there isn't too much else I would do. I probably still wouldn't change the footprint."

"That's what I thought. I'd like to keep the layout relatively similar to the original." I drug my hand along the chair railing as I walked down the hall. "It seems like this house might hold some good stories."

"Oh, if Miss Betty were here to tell you her stories, I bet you'd be entertained."

"Why do you say that?"

"She was a hell of an old broad. She played cards with my grandmother, Doris. Betty Ann whooped up in blackjack; made a small fortune. Not that she needed it. Rumor has it, she always used her blackjack winnings to restock her margarita supply for the next week's game."

"My kind of gal," I said, making a mental note to celebrate with margaritas once I moved in.

He turned in a full circle with his hands on his hips, looking around at every nook and cranny he could see.

"Why did Betty Ann sell the house?"

"She died here, actually. She had cancer. There was a nurse here to take care of her around the clock. She always refused the suggestions for a nursing home. Apparently, she wanted to die in her own home by the water. Story goes, the nurse wheeled her out to the dock, went back inside to pour them some fresh coffee, and when she came back, Betty Ann was gone."

"Just like that?"

"Just the way she wanted, I think."

The idea of Betty Ann Highland spending her entire life here and dying on the edge of the water behind the house, made me want to fix the place up even more. Sure, at first I'd intended to level the place and build something of my own. But ever since I found her letter, I felt an uncanny connection to her home—maybe even to *her*. Before the purchase was even finalized, I felt like it had been my own. I couldn't understand how the entire town could just let such a place go—why no one would want to preserve it. Then again, I didn't know Betty Ann. Was I doing something wrong?

"Was there something wrong with her?" I asked.

"What do you mean?"

"You know. Was she some mean old lady? Did she piss off everyone else on the island? I just can't figure out why a place like this would be left to fall into such a mess. Seems to me that someone would want to keep it up." I thought briefly about the idea that I could one day be like Betty Ann, very much alone for the rest of my life. "It's sad. It's lonely."

"Well, she didn't have any family. And, it's not every day that someone has the kind of money it takes to buy a place like this." Home purchases were public record, so I had no misconceptions about keeping my purchase or the amount I'd spent to do so on the down-low.

"That's fair," I said. "I think I got pretty lucky, though. With a little bit of patience and a whole lot of your help, I'll make this house a home again."

"I'm happy to help." He reached to shake my hand again.

"What happens next, Link?"

"Let me build up a proposal for you. Simple summary? We'll spend about a week gutting the place, another week a new roof, clean up the slab foundation, and then it's just working from the ground up. We tend to prioritize full home projects like this, so I can likely have a team get started…well, actually right away if you want. I'm only juggling small projects right now. My next big renovation got pushed back last minute—the buyer's financing fell through. It's going to be at least a month before we can move forward on that one. Well, that and no one likes to do housework while they have renters all summer. So, I'm available!" It sounded as if his availability was two-fold.

"That would be great, Link. I know it seems fast, but I was thinking the sooner the better. I'm crashing with a friend until I can live here, and I'm sure he'd appreciate it if that arrangement didn't last too long. So I'd be appreciative of any work we can get done to get me into the house. Even if I have to live in a construction zone."

"Well, I can get you a new roof and new insulation and walls to make it a livable space within...oh...six weeks? As long as you don't mind us working around you to finish the project."

"Not at all. I look forward to it."

"Alright. I'll get a proposal to you by the end of the week. Do you have a designer in mind, or would you like me to call one?"

"The only designers I know are back in Raleigh."

"I have a friend in Hatteras. I'll give her a call and set up a meeting. What is your schedule like?"

"I'm all yours," I said, arms wide open. "This house is quite literally all I have going on at the moment."

"Great. I'll let you know when we can get together then. If I can't swing it by Friday, I'll plan on it early next week."

"Thanks again, Link." I waved as he climbed back into his muddy blue Tacoma. The man sure did match the vehicle, there. His boots and blue jeans were just as gross as the truck was, which I hoped was just a sign of a hard worker and not a sloppy man.

I slid back into my Land Rover, being careful to kick the extra dirt from my shoes first. My stomach growled as I started the car, and in an effort to be an appreciated addition to Jack's apartment, I pulled out my phone to see if he'd be home that night.

Val: Starving. Dinner plans?

Jack: None.

Val: Just met with the contractor. Looks like it's all going to work out. Can I buy you dinner? It's the least I can do.

Jack: You could, but don't worry about that. Happy to hear you're already moving forward with it all. Howard's? I'll be finished here at the office in about ten minutes.

Val: Do you ever eat anywhere else?

Jack: Is there anywhere else?

Val: Fair. See you there.

CHAPTER NINE
JACK

I finished with the paperwork my dad needed before his client meetings the following week and closed up the office to head over to Howard's. I wasn't going there just to have dinner with Val; I went to Howard's most nights with the guys. Of course, I wasn't planning on going there tonight in particular: Hank was on call and Glenn was out for a two-day charter, but it wasn't out of the ordinary for me to end up there after work. So this totally wasn't a date. It was just two roommates catching up over a good meal. Plus, I was excited to hear about the progress Val had managed to make on the renovation plan in a single afternoon.

"Hey, Jack!" Bailey waved from behind the bar as I walked inside, and familiar words came through the sound system.

"I love this song!" Val cheered, walking from the jukebox to join me at the bar. "You can never go wrong with Faith."

"This song is so..." Bailey rested her hands on the bar, staring up into space as if she'd completely zoned out.

"Romantic?" Val asked.

"Yeah," they said together, swooning over the song. *Girls.*

Taking my seat at the bar, I listened to the lyrics from Faith Hill's popular song, *This Kiss*. I had a sister. I knew the music.

> *You can kiss me in the moonlight on the rooftop under the sky.*
> *Or you can kiss me with the windows open while the rain comes pouring inside.*
> *Kiss me in sweet slow motion; let's let everything slide.*
> *You got me floating. You got me flying.*

I don't know what kind of kissing Faith Hill had been doing, but I hadn't been tangled up in a kiss or anything like that in quite some time. I'd be happy to, sure. The opportunity just hadn't...presented itself. I watched Val sing along in her own world, and caught myself with a stupid grin, admiring the hell out of her. I pictured myself kissing Val, and it wasn't hard to do. I tried to shake it off and hoped like hell that Bailey hadn't noticed.

"So, you found a contractor? Who'd you go with?" Bailey set a peach margarita on the counter for Val and opened a bottle of my favorite for me.

"I did! I already met with him and we even got started on a plan," Val started to recap her day as Bailey returned with a tray of shots. "Lincoln Nicholson." She turned to smile at me with a proud guilt, as if she'd incited a riot and knew it. My stomach turned at the sound of his name, but I tried not to let it show. I reached for a shot instead and raised it to the girls.

"You really hate him that much, huh?" Val asked, tapping shot glasses with Bailey before downing her own.

"Don't worry about it," I said, reaching for another. "He does good work."

"It seems to me like there's more to it than that." Val wasn't exactly prying, but I could tell she wanted more from me than the answer I'd provided.

"Don't worry about it," I repeated. "So, what's next?"

"Link said he'd put a proposal together, and we'll meet to go over it all next week. He thinks he could have it ready enough for me to move into at least a portion of the house within six weeks or so. Can you handle me for six weeks, Jack?"

"I can handle you, Val." The girls smiled at each other and then at me. "I mean, I can take care of you." Bailey's eyes widened, ready for more, as my hands instinctively covered my face in exhaustion. This wasn't the first time I'd gotten myself into a war of words around girls. "Yes, Val. Six weeks is fine. You can stay as long as you need," I groaned into my hands.

With three plates of burgers and fries, Bailey, Val, and I sat at the bar and talked through a few renovation ideas while we ate.

"Hell, we could have built you a whole new house for the money you're going to put into renovating it," I suggested. "Still could, you know."

"Didn't we already talk about this?" Val asked. "How would you feel if someone threw you away every time you got a bit frayed around the edges?"

"That house isn't frayed, Val. It's rotting. Crumbling. It would be better off leveled, and I bet even Lincoln Nicholson knows that."

"Maybe, but it also has stories to tell. It was someone's home once, and I can make it a home again. I can feel it in my bones. I want to find the charm that used to be there and…let it shine again."

"You're such a romantic," Bailey said. "It's sweet. I wish I was as hopeful about life as you are."

"It's not romantic; it's unrealistic," I interjected. "She's hopeful but naive."

"You'll see," Val said. "When I'm done with that house, you'll see the home it was meant to be."

My heart tugged in a new way—not as much about the house as the dedication Val seemed to have for it. An older lady lived there alone my entire life and probably as long as my parents were alive, too. Sure, there were probably a few generations worth of memories had there, but homes were torn down and built from scratch every day. Betty Ann didn't have any living relatives that had any attachment to the place—that's why we were selling it. It would have saved time and money to level the old cottage and rebuild it on solid ground. But for the little I knew about Val, I'd learned one thing for sure: she was a girl who got her way and probably had since the day she was born. I guess when you're playing with Daddy's money, being realistic and making the most of your funds isn't as much of a concern.

As irritated as I was with her apparent lack of care for her own financial security, I couldn't help but listen eagerly to her plans for the house. I worked with my father every day selling homes and filling rental properties. I'd never met someone as interested in a home as Val was in this one. I didn't understand it, but I was entertained and intrigued. Home design and construction and the business behind it all were intriguing. I hadn't had much experience with any of it. My dad and I worked more on the later side of homeownership: turn-key purchases and rentals and such.

We finished our dinners and Val promised to keep Bailey posted on anything she learned from the contractor. Bailey was excited to support her friend and probably would have encouraged her to do anything Lincoln suggested. On the other hand, I planned to keep a close eye on his work. I wanted to make sure that Val wasn't being taken advantage of. You know, not that Val was any more susceptible or anything, just that a man in construction could make good money off a girl without a clue. Lincoln Nicholson was a prime candidate—one of the least honest men I'd ever known. I may not have understood what Val was after with the house, but I knew that I could at least keep an eye on Lincoln. He'd been a menace in my life before, and I wasn't about to let him interfere again.

"I have some unpacking to do," Val said as Bailey returned our plates to the kitchen. "I'm going to head back." She stood and tossed a brown leather strap over her shoulder, letting her purse fall just above her hip, drawing my attention to the tight and dark denim that hid nearly every inch of the long tan legs I knew were underneath.

"Bailey, can you leave this for Etta's tab?" I set a few twenty-dollar bills down on the bar in addition to my own bill.

"She's doing fine, Jack. You don't have to keep taking care of her."

"I know I don't. I'm just helping out with Tate." Bailey leaned her head to the side and shot me a knowing smile—the one that said she knew what I was doing. "Let it go, Bailey. It's our secret, you promised." I struck my deal with Bailey a few years back to never charge my sister for a meal. To my knowledge, she'd held up her end of the bargain and my sister and nephew had eaten on my dime ever since. Etta quit trying to get the information out of Bailey after a few months and just chalked it up to a random gift from some nice townsperson who'd heard about her...unfortunate situation.

It wasn't about the money. My sister had everything she needed and more, and my parents had more than enough to help her out if she ever needed it—not that she'd ever allowed it. My deal with Bailey was more of an attempt to remind Etta that someone was looking out for her—and for Tate. At the very least, I just wanted to give Etta an extra reason to smile now and then.

When I got back to the apartment, I figured I'd only arrived a few minutes behind Val. Walking to the door, I began to wonder if she was settling in here, and feeling comfortable and at home. Moving from Raleigh to a place like Ocracoke was a big adjustment. As nice as it is to live at the beach, uprooting your entire life and starting over on a whim couldn't have been a simple feat. I wondered what all Val was leaving behind and why the sudden jump.

"Hey, I'm back!" I shouted upstairs as I dropped my keys on the table by the door and hung my old briefcase on one of the hooks on the wall. On the floor next to my shoes, I noticed hers—a tiny pair of sandals that looked barely big enough for an adult to wear. They were a shiny rose gold color —the same color as my mom's favorite jewelry. The sandals were...cute, much like Val. *Shake that off right now.* I immediately tried to replace my thoughts of her with something less intrusive, like finding a beer and seeing what might be on television.

"Hey!" Val came down the stairs and had obviously had time to change. She had changed into a blue and white two-piece bathing suit with a thin white sundress tossed over it and her hair up in a knot. "I was thinking about taking a walk down to the water. Would you like to join me?"

My mouth watered, and I nearly looked right through her. I cleared my throat and tried to speak.

"I uh—yes. Um, act-actually. Do you boat? I mean." I swallowed my sorry attempt at words, laughed, and tried again. "Sorry, do you like boats? I usually take a short ride on Friday nights when the guys aren't around. I was thinking about heading out for a bit. You know, if you'd like to come."

I was a stuttering and blubbering fool for a girl who drove me absolutely insane. But what was a guy supposed to do? She stood there in a basically see-through dress that did nothing to hide her figure—all tan and sexy, with the strings of her bikini just casually hanging over her shoulder. I would have done a lot of things to see what those bikini bottoms covered—or maybe didn't cover—on her backside. There was something about a girl's tanned hip bones that just made me...*damn it.*

"That sounds wonderful, Jack. Thank you. I might go grab something warmer, though. I guess it gets a bit windy?"

"It does. I would definitely suggest a sweatshirt." It pained me to encourage that she put a sweatshirt over that bathing suit. If anything, I was dying for her to take off that dress so I could see the rest of her—as any other cold-blooded man would.

I'd gotten myself into a terrible situation, letting her live with me. I was a gentleman, truly, but there was something about her that was making me weaker by the hour. I wasn't myself around her. At first, I thought it was just because of how frustrating she was. Now, I wasn't so sure.

She returned just a few minutes later wearing more clothes than I was hoping for. She'd probably lost the bikini entirely, trading it instead for some jean shorts and a plain white tee.

"So, tell me about living here. It seems we have a lot of friends in common. How did I not meet you in all of my time here in college?" Val dove right into the conversation as I untied the boat from the dock and got ready to pull out of the marina.

"Well, Etta and I grew up here. Bailey's been a friend of my sister's since grade school. I was in the same year as Robert, her—"

"Her brother."

"Yeah. So it's always been the four of us—and then Addy and Scott Langston...he's the guy at the bank who helped with your wire transfer. We've all known each other for most of our lives. Bailey tells me that y'all used to come down here for a weekend or so every semester?"

"Yeah. We wanted to get away once, freshman year. It was just supposed to be a quick getaway to celebrate passing a big exam, but it turned into...sort of a tradition. A home away from home." Val knelt down on the bench in front of me, resting her chin in her hand on the center console as I turned the engine.

"This is a good place to call home," I answered. "I think I must have still been away at school during most of your trips."

"Where'd you go?"

"I did my undergrad at NC State, but then I went to Duke for Law School." Val pretended to wretch all over the floor of the boat—dramatic but pretty standard when you admitted to belonging to the wrong school in the state of North Carolina. I was proud of my law degree from Duke, but discussion of my education sat quietly in the minds of everyone around me that bled Carolina Blue. If I knew one thing and one thing only, it was that you never challenged a Tar Heel. All you'd get was drama and a heckling. None of that mattered in court, though. I was good at my job.

"Gross," she added, with a smile from ear to ear. "I'm only kidding. That's impressive."

"Thank you. I suppose I was busy studying for the LSAT or slaving away as a paralegal in Durham while you were here on the beach, galavanting around on your long weekends."

"I resent that!" She adjusted her sunglasses on top of her head and leaned in with a scowl. "I studied my ass off, sir. *And* I graduated Summa Cum Laude after I finished all of that galavanting on the beach."

"I digress," I forfeited, bowing my head to the Tar Heel in defeat. "Not surprising, though. Etty always did hang out with the nerds."

"That's fair," she agreed.

"Sit down, Summa Cum Laude. Let's go for a ride." With a quick wink, my mind went from admiring my new roommate to wondering if she would one day be the co-captain of my boat. The *Muddy Marlin* could use another set of hands. My first impression of Val was quickly being replaced with... dare I say it, a hunger for her. A desire to know her better. *A whole lot better.*

She turned away from me and sat down on the bench right in front of the wheel as I pulled out of the marina. I slowly picked up speed, careful not to knock her off balance. I was better at driving a boat than most guys I knew. I took care of it like it was my most prized possession—which it was, for me anyway. But Val's hair flying back over her shoulder and the goosebumps across her neck had me anything but focused.

I had a white-knuckled grip on the wheel as I took us out past Teaches Hole and south toward the Inlet. The view of the sunset was best spent halfway between the southern tip of Ocracoke and Portsmouth Island: where there was nothing around to block the rays of the sun setting over the Pamlico Sound. It was the same route my parents would take us on for dinner cruises when we were kids and a ride I'd come to love as an adult.

When we got far enough out that all you could see was the marsh around us, I dropped the anchor and pulled blankets from underneath the benches up front, handing one to Val and sitting down next to her. I'd done this a hundred times on my own. Other than Etta, I'd never gone out on a sunset cruise alone with anyone else. Over the years, it was one of those things I liked to do to quiet down at the end of the night. It was the best way I knew to relax.

"Is this...Duke blue?" She put a great effort into looking disgusted, but the expression lost out to her laughter.

"Duke blue or shiver," I said with a laugh, spreading another blanket out over my own legs while she did the same. We leaned back against the console, kicked our feet up across the boat, and got comfortable on the bench.

"Do you like working for your dad?" I should have guessed that we weren't going to sit in silence. Val was a talker.

"I do," I started. "I guess…well, it's not like I have anything else in mind. I considered other things for a while, but when Tate was born, and—"

"Yeah…" Val seemed to know just enough about my sister's situation that I didn't need to elaborate. It was refreshing, and a bit of a relief in a way to not have to explain that part of my life to someone new.

"I guess when Tate was born, it just kind of reaffirmed for me that this is my home. That this is where I belong. So, what my dad has going here…it's waiting for me. Might as well go with it."

"You all are so close." I could feel the envy in her voice, and for a second I wondered how she must feel being on her own in this world. I wouldn't make it a day without my family. It was no wonder Val packed up and ran. I couldn't live in a place where I'd lost everyone I'd ever loved. For a brief moment, I found myself hoping that Val never found herself so alone ever again. If I didn't know any better, I'd say that my heart was already committed to ensuring it, and to taking responsibility for it all.

"We are. We always were, even me and Etta growing up. But then, Tate. I mean, I could never leave him."

"They're lucky to have you." I didn't even have to look at her. I could hear her smile in her words, and I smiled myself at the thought of it.

"What about you? Tell me more about Tucket Teas."

"Not much to tell; it's just a small business." I watched as she twirled her hands in her lap. "I started out with an idea, some cheap ingredients, and a tent at a farmers market. It just… I don't know. It just worked. Once I started making some

125

money, I started to get picky with shopping: looking for organic, fair-trade, and even locally sourced ingredients. One day I started working on a website and online orders started to come in faster than I could manage. Turns out people will pay a pretty penny for locally made, organic loose-leaf teas."

"It sounds like you have a budding empire on your hands." I was more than impressed.

"Maybe, but even if it just keeps going the way it is now, I like it. I like having my own thing and being in charge. That and…I don't know. You don't fix what isn't broken, right?"

"Would you rather be doing something else?" I asked.

"I don't know. It's not that I want to do something else. The tea business, it just always worked. I've always lived with my grandmother, even through college. I didn't need the money or anything, but I've learned a lot by building a business from the ground up. And Golly always seemed so proud of me." I turned to look at her as she stopped, and watched as her smile grew wide enough to force the tears that had pooled in her eyes. She took a sleeve to her eyes quickly before she continued. "She always told me that Pop would have taught me the ins and outs of the business world, so I just kept at it. She gave me everything I ever needed, you know. But I think she still wanted me to learn as much as I could. She still wanted me to be…self-sufficient." Just saying *Golly* out loud brought a smile to her face. She must have been an incredible woman. Val might have been a bit wild, but that Golly must have been something special to raise a granddaughter who was so…capable. Val had a lot to learn, but she was more than competent.

"When did you move in with your grandmother?"

"I've lived with her my whole life." She cleared her throat. "My parents passed away when I was really young. So, I've always lived with Golly. And Pop, too, of course—until he passed away."

"That's a lot..." I ran my fingers through my hair as chills seeped through my scalp. She'd been through a lot more than most people our age. Maybe she and Etta understood each other on that level: having a shitty deck of cards handed to you and still figuring out how to play the game.

"A lot of death." She exhaled and took another deep breath, and I started to feel guilty for forcing her into such a stressful conversation. "Sure is. But Golly? Growing up with her was...perfect. I had a good life with her. She took care of me just like I always imagined a mom would have. She was my best friend."

"I'm sorry," I said, turning my head to face her. I caught a glimpse just in time to see her wipe a few more tears from her cheeks and force a smile.

"Ah, don't worry about me." She seemed to shake it off, while I felt more responsible for her—her living arrangements and her happiness in general. Now that I knew where she was coming from, I couldn't possibly let her hop from place to place or friend to friend. She needed a place that felt like home. Everyone deserved that.

"Val, my apartment...I mean, your room. It's yours. As long as you want it." She smiled and hung her head as if I'd embarrassed her. "I mean it. You can stay as long as you need, or as long as you want. House or not. Don't rush over there just to get out of the apartment."

"Thank you." Her eyes lingered on mine for an extra beat before she looked back out to the water. "This really is one heck of a sunset."

"There's no better place to watch the sun go down," I answered. "In a month or so, it won't be quite as chilly when it gets dark."

"Thank you for bringing me here, Jack."

"Anytime, roomie." When I nudged her with my elbow, we both looked down, as if neither one of us had realized how close we'd been sitting. We looked up at each other again with a look of mutual acceptance, sitting silently as the sun set just below the horizon and lit up the sky with shades of yellow and orange before fading into a deep pink as it disappeared altogether. We continued to float there as it got darker until I heard her teeth chatter.

"Shit, Val. I'm sorry. You're freezing. Let's get home." I stood, and she reached up to grab my arm.

"I'm okay, Jack! This is wonderful, really. I don't want to leave." Her eyes were begging me to stay, and I was starting to feel myself falling into their trap. Too much more of those eyes and I'd be falling at the chance to give her anything and everything she wanted, anything to see the joy that she had right now.

"Well, we can come out here anytime you want," I said. I knelt down in front of her and laid my blanket over her, hoping that a second layer would keep her warm. If I'd noticed this chill in her anywhere else, I might have wrapped myself around her. But that would have been too much. At least for the time being.

"Promise?" The sincerity—or maybe it was a sort of desperation—in the way she asked had me weak at the knees. I decided right then, on my knee in front of her, that I'd drive her out here for the sunset every week for the rest of my life—hell, I'd bring her out here every night if she'd let me. That was the moment I realized that there was nothing I wouldn't do to bring her joy. I'd let myself go a whole lot farther than welcoming a new roommate to my apartment. I'd let this girl break into my heart in ways I wasn't at all prepared for.

"I promise. Let's get home and warm you up." She adjusted in her seat as I stood and tucked the blanket around her shoulders. She grabbed onto the corners, holding that Duke blue fleece tight to her chest, and looked up at me. We were close enough that I could feel her heartbeat. That, or my own heart was damn near busting out of my chest. *Or both.*

"Thank you," she said with a quiet voice. My hands nearly reached toward her all on their own, rubbing up and down on the outside of her arms as if it would actually help to warm her. If I had the guts, I might have kissed her—I sure wanted to. As much as I thought about pulling her in and touching my lips to hers, we didn't have that kind of relationship. We were just roommates, with a brand new friendship. There was no reason for me to throw self-control to the wind and get wild with her. I squared my shoulders, cleared my throat, and stepped around to the wheel to drive us back to the marina as quickly as I could without wind-blowing her into an icicle.

At the dock, I tied up to the cleats and stepped out of the boat. I turned to reach for her, offering a hand as she followed me. She laid her fingers in mine lightly, gripping me as she climbed out of the boat. I noticed every millimeter of her movement, and every part of her that touched me or nearly could have. I hadn't been so close to a woman in a long time. I didn't hate it, being near her. In fact, it felt good. It felt right. I couldn't recall the last time a girl had me so weak in the knees, but Val had me feeling things I'd never felt before. It wasn't just that she was gorgeous—which she was. It was that I'd had the chance to get to know her a little bit, and I was enjoying it. I was enjoying *her*.

I wanted to comfort her, to hold her and remind her that she wasn't alone. I wanted to keep her close and show her that she was cared for, and protected. *I* wanted to protect her.

If she wasn't so appalled by my *terrible business practices* and my affinity for the incorrect shade of blue, I might have thought that things had changed on that boat ride. If it wasn't just the boat ride, stepping out at the dock made it clear. Her eyes lingered on mine again while her fingers rested for a few extra seconds in my hand—which I didn't mind. I could have stared into those milk chocolate eyes for a long, long time.

CHAPTER TEN
VAL

When he held my hand to steady me as I climbed out of the boat, I could have sworn that Jack Dixon was attracted to me. He was definitely looking, and I didn't mind. Earlier that afternoon, I'd planned to go for a walk by the water and had even put on a new bathing suit to get some sun while I walked. A girl can't live at the beach and be as pale as I was. I wanted to have that island glow, and I knew I'd need to spend a few minutes in the sun each day to get it. Standing in that bikini in the house was the first time I caught him looking at me—really looking. The man had already seen me completely naked, but something about that bikini got his attention in a different way.

After our boat ride, I found myself processing a whole slew of feelings I didn't know I'd been suppressing. We'd spent one evening on the boat, sitting together while we watched the sun set down over the water. One boat ride, and for the first time since I met Jack Dixon, I felt as though we both enjoyed our time together *entirely*. It was almost as if I wasn't just some rich girl, and he wasn't just some real estate guy who was eager to finish his business with me.

Thinking back to college and the here and there I'd kept in touch with Etta over the years, I recalled her having a brother and that they were pretty close. But I'd never met him—at least not that I could remember. I was starting to wish I had and wondered what might have come of us if I'd known him sooner.

The next morning, Jack left early to surf with the guys, and I got in the car to head back to my office in Raleigh to fill orders and check on things at Golly's house.

After a few hours in the office, I met Alex and Louise for dinner at Sullivan's. The steakhouse on Glenwood had long been Golly and Louise's favorite lunch spot. We ate lunch there at least once a month for a girls' day out, and Alex took us all for dinner at least once or twice a month too. It wouldn't have surprised me if we'd earned some kind of stock in the place over the years; I might have started out on kid's mac-n-cheese, but I'd grown to love the pricey plates. Lord only knows how much money we'd actually spent there.

I listed off my updates and ideas to Alex, who took notes and made suggestions where he felt appropriate. I took a few notes of my own—on my phone, which he hated—and promised to keep him in the loop when it came to any more large financial decisions. He didn't seem bothered by the car purchase or the house—which he said was more of an investment than a purchase.

I quickly and quietly mentioned my temporary living arrangements, making sure to blend Jack in with the large group of friends who were also on the island. I didn't want either of them to focus too hard on the boy part of my life. Louise always pestered me, and I always told her that there was no one special. If I'd let onto anything with Jack, she would have hounded me about it until I caved and nearly married the man. She had that kind of way about her.

After dinner, I went back to Golly's house. I closed the front door behind me and hung my keys and purse on the hooks in the foyer. I took a few steps into the house and flipped the light switch. This house—my home—had never felt so distant…so unwelcoming. I didn't belong here without her. This was Golly's house, *our home*, and without her, it didn't feel like mine. It didn't feel right. Alex had explained briefly when he went over my financial adjustments that all I had to do was maintain the tax payments on the house, keep it cooled enough in the summer to prevent mold, and warm enough in the winter to prevent frozen and bursting water pipes. I reminded him quickly and clearly that I had no intention of selling the place. Even when I left for Ocracoke and told him about the fixer-upper I'd be working on, I never intended to sell the place I'd grown up in.

I brewed a pot of my chamomile blend and pulled a bottle of dark rum from the liquor cabinet in the dining room. I added a heavy splash to the mug—Pop's favorite Air Force mug. It was a speckled navy blue, and it was extra large. He liked the size of the mug because it was comfortable in his large hands. I liked it because it held more coffee, or in tonight's case…more rum.

I pressed play on *Sleepless in Seattle* but fell asleep on the couch before Tom Hanks even spoke a word. Not that it mattered; I knew every bit of the entire movie. It wasn't my favorite, but it was definitely in the top five.

I woke early the next morning and got to work on a few of the chores I had on my list: cleaning out the pantry and the refrigerator, washing the sheets on all the beds and putting them all back into the linen closet, washing all the towels and blankets that had collected dust since I'd been gone. I wanted to keep the house nice and ready for me to come back anytime, but I didn't need to maintain it as if I was living there. Putting things away seemed like a small and slow alternative to packing up and selling the place.

I vacuumed the carpets, mopped the hardwoods, set the thermostat to seventy-eight, and got ready to head back to the island. Leaving the house this time was a bit easier. I reminded myself that I'd always have the place here to come back to; that nothing was changing, and I was simply adding possibilities to my life—not permanently closing any doors on my past.

The trip to Raleigh wasn't really necessary. I could have figured things out from the island. But I was glad I went. I spent a bit of time with Alex and Louise and relaxed at the house. Still, it wasn't hard to leave the house that time. It wasn't hard to leave Raleigh behind. Noticing that feeling almost encouraged me, and made me feel like I was doing the right thing. I drove toward Ocracoke, eager to get back—eager to get *home*. I loved that feeling.

I listened to a new book on audible all the way back to Ocracoke and pulled into the driveway at Jack's place just as Connor Arrowood took his girls apple picking. Corinne Michaels was one hell of an author. Her books could make me laugh, cry, and fall in love all at the same time. I'd listened to a lot of her novels since Golly passed, mostly as a way to break the silence. I think her way of bringing people together was something I hoped to feel for myself. Corinne's stories had me believing that a family was possible for me yet.

Inside, I tossed my things on the bed and grabbed my computer for a second attempt at *Sleepless in Seattle*. I opened up the browser I'd been working on to run new ads for the following month and got back to work. I listened to the movie and worked on business for an hour or so before Jack walked into the living room, dressed to leave. I hadn't even realized he was home. Whatever he was doing, he'd been eerily quiet.

"You look nice. Where are you off to?" I set my laptop to the side and reached for my wine glass.

"Oh, dinner at Glenn's. Didn't Bailey tell you? It's kind of a weekly thing. Sunday nights, usually." Jack rolled his keys around his fingers like he didn't know what to do with himself. "Unless you didn't want to go."

"No, I...I just forgot. She told me...but it's been a few weeks, and I just...forgot."

"Well, why don't you change? Come with me. I'll wait."

"Oh, Jack. You don't have to wait for me." I waved him off and readjusted the blanket over my legs. "I can just go next week."

"No way. Everyone will want to hear about your week. You've had so much going on. What are you working on now?" He sat down on the other end of the couch, facing me, resting his head on his hand like he was ready for a story.

"Well, I still have my kitchen in Raleigh—the one I use for Tucket Teas. I filled orders before I left, but I've gotten a whole new list of orders since I came back. I'll need to go back to Raleigh for a day each week or so to fill orders and all. I was just doing a bit more work online."

"Couldn't you just move Tucket Teas here to Ocracoke?"

"I suppose I could. I mean, I thought about it. I just didn't really...put a plan into action."

"Well, I could help you. We could drive up one morning, pack up everything you need, and bring it here."

"Well, that's sweet, Jack. But where would I put it? I'd need to find a kitchen first."

"I'm sure we could find something. Hell, maybe you can talk Bailey into opening that cafe. Y'all could probably share a kitchen, right?" I hadn't been giving Jack enough credit. He really had a mind for business, and I was impressed.

"That's not a terrible idea, actually."

"You're welcome." He stood with a proud smile. "Now that we've settled that, why don't you go upstairs and get ready, and we can head over to Glenn's."

"Are you sure? I don't want to…crash."

"Val, I'm sure. You're part of the crowd now—or, again —get used to it."

He reached for my computer on the couch, closed it, and set it on the coffee table before nudging his head toward the door in a way that said *put away your work and let's go*. Bailey and Etta had welcomed me back to the island with open arms, but Jack talking me into their group dinner made it feel like I was the new neighbor they were all glad to have. Somehow, his actions felt different.

"Okay, give me ten minutes." I ran upstairs, flipped through a few outfits in my closet, and found myself wondering what my new roommate would think of each one. I hadn't given a single thought to what a man thought about me in so long that the idea of it really threw me off. I wanted to flirt with Jack, and I'd taken my chances as they came since I moved into his apartment. Sure, in the beginning, it was just fun to torture him. But now I was interested. I just wondered if anything could really come of us. My friend's older brother? The real estate attorney who helped me buy a house? The man I ended up living with during renovations? I mean, really, what were the odds?

I settled on a snug pair of deep navy skinny jeans and my Carolina pullover—just to frustrate Jack. I tossed some dry shampoo through my hair and touched up my mascara before slipping into my favorite sandals: the old faithful leather flip-flops.

"Remind me to kick you out of this house before the next basketball season." Jack nodded at my sweatshirt, but I just straightened the shoulders and smoothed out the wrinkles. I looked good in that sweatshirt. Carolina blue was my color.

"Alright, roomie. Take me to dinner." I opened the front door to find Bailey on the other side, arm straight up like she was ready to knock the door down. We scared the hell out of each other, screaming simultaneously as Bailey slid down to the floor against the doorway and I jumped back into Jack's arms. He hadn't startled, but he sure did catch me with ease. Bailey and I screamed until we fell into laughter.

Just as I stopped screaming, I noticed how closely Jack held me against him. My hair fell over one shoulder, while Jack rested above the other. He was close enough to smell my hair, kiss my neck, or anything else—all of which I would have been absolutely okay with, if Bailey wasn't standing right there, of course. At the very least, the way his strong arms wrapped around me caught my attention. He didn't let go nearly as fast as he could have.

"Oh my God," Bailey leaned onto her knees. "I can't breathe!"

"That was the best thing I've seen in a long time." Jack laughed as he unwrapped his arms from around me, dragging his hands over my hips before he stepped between us. "Come on, girls. Dinner time."

"I realized I'd forgotten to remind you about dinner," Bailey said as we caught our breath and followed Jack outside, arm in arm. "I see he took care of it." She nudged my arm.

"Oh, stop it. He was just being nice." It was *really nice*.

CHAPTER ELEVEN
JACK

"Morning, Dad." I walked into the office with a box full of cinnamon rolls and a hot cup of coffee first thing in the morning.

"Did you do something I need to fix?"

"No…"

"Break something I need to pay for?"

"No, sir." I set the cinnamon rolls on his desk, concerned with his assumption and quickly running my mind through the weekend's activities to make sure that I hadn't actually done anything wrong.

Come to think of it, I was *extra* proud of myself for how mature and professional I'd kept things with Val. It ain't easy to come home to a beautiful woman on your couch, looking all lovable and comfortable underneath a fleece blanket, and a glass of wine in her hand while she worked on her computer. That kind of view will make a man's heart just about explode. Ask me how I know.

Instead, I asked her to come to dinner with me. Not a date, but our friend's group dinner. On the way out the door, Bailey and Val scared the hell out of each other at our door, giving me a very welcome opportunity to pull Val close and hold her against me. The way her back molded against my chest had me so turned on that I had to let her go and walk in front of them to clear my head. I'd been a complete gentleman.

Later on, I even brought her drunk ass—one that's easy to look at, I might add—home and put her to bed. I'd like to think I was well past the activity of my college days. Not that I'd ever slept with a woman who was less than capable of making such a choice, but I'd have a few too many myself most nights and wake up at some point in a bed I hadn't seen before.

"You look like you need to make sure of that." My dad mumbled with a mouth full of breakfast.

"I did." I nodded. "I'm sure. I think. I've been a gentleman, scout's honor."

"It's just that usually when you butter me up with something along the lines of a sugary breakfast and an indecently large cup of coffee, it's because you've done something you need my help to fix. I'm not saying I won't do it...I'm just saying." He sipped his coffee and leaned back into his chair with another cinnamon roll in his hand. My dad was easy to please.

"Okay, stop it. I haven't done anything wrong." I rolled my eyes. My dad was quick to pick on us kids.

"But?"

"But I do need your help with something."

"There it is." He sat up, set his treat down on a napkin on his desk, and wiped his hands on his blue jeans. "What are we working on, son?"

"So, you know how Bailey and Rob—" My dad raised a hand to stop me. He never wanted to hear Robert's name so much as mentioned, let alone discussed in depth. "Sorry, dad." He nodded for me to continue.

"You know how Bailey had those plans to open a cafe a while back?"

"I do. I was really excited about that. It's one hell of a hike up to the north end just to meet a client for a decent cup of tar."

"Right. Well, I've been trying to encourage her to get back to the idea. You know, pick up where she…left off."

"How can I help? Does she need some cash to start up? Cosigner for a loan?"

"No, she's already got the money." My dad raised his eyebrows, impressed as I explained. "When Bailey moved back in with her parents, she started setting aside every dollar she made. She was never sure how she wanted to…move forward… but she knew she didn't ever want money to stand in her way." Dad nodded, and I knew that he was feeling a sense of pride. He'd always worried about Bailey. She and her brother were so close. As much as my dad hated Robert for what he did, he knew that Bailey shouldn't have had to deal with the aftermath. "I thought that you might be able to help me find a commercial space…one down here on the lighthouse side that she could build into a cafe. You know, Val, she—"

"Ahh, I was wondering when I'd hear more about that pretty roommate of yours."

"Dad, she's Etty's friend. I'm just trying to help."

"Mhmm." He took another bite, smiling while he listened.

"So, Val has money of her own; you know that. I mean, it's family money, but she also runs a business back in Raleigh. She's been talking about relocating her company here, but she would need a commercial kitchen."

"Two birds, one stone."

"That's right," I said. "I've been thinking a lot about it, and I've looked into the logistics and the financials. It's a no-brainer if you ask me. Bailey dreams of running a cafe; she's just too nervous about making the jump." I noticed that I'd started to pace across the floor. Business ideas always got me up and running, but an idea that could be so good for Bailey and Val had my bones damn near rattling with excitement. "Val is planning on driving back to Raleigh every week to pack orders in her kitchen. It's ridiculous, Dad. If we found one good place, the two of them could...hell, they could build a...a little island empire."

My dad laughed and brushed the crumbs from his hands. A useless task, since I knew he'd reach for another roll in just a minute.

"Tell you what, son. Give me some time to look into a few things and see what I can find. There aren't many commercial spaces around here, let alone available and ready for building. But I'll see what I can do. Maybe I can get an idea of buildings that might come available in the near future. In the meantime...why don't you figure out if that roommate of yours has any plans Friday night."

"What's on Friday night?" I knew exactly what I wanted to do with her on Friday night. I was going to take her back out on the boat. I needed to; I needed to see that joy in her again. I wanted to be the one that caused it.

"Your mother and I have been talking about going out on a dinner cruise. It's been a while. We haven't done much of that since you kids were in high school. I know you usually take yourself out for a ride on Friday nights these days, but we were hoping that you and Etty might join us for a good old-fashioned family dinner. Seems like Val might enjoy some family time…don't you think?"

My dad had paid more attention than I'd thought. Val made it pretty clear that she didn't have anyone left in Raleigh. When she met with my father and me at the office, she'd mentioned how moving here would give her the chance to have a close crowd of friends again, a makeshift family even. I hadn't really thought about that too much, but the more time I'd spent with her the more clear it had become: Val had no one. Ocracoke was her home now. It was *us*.

"I'll ask her, Dad. That's, uh…it's very cool of you."

"Good deal, son. Now, if you don't mind, I have a few of our rental properties to check on this morning. So I'll be heading out. Aunt Cora will be here in just a few minutes."

"Sounds good, Dad. Thanks."

I left his office and went into my own, stuck on the idea that Val had up and moved so easily. I couldn't imagine living life without anyone around me, let alone anyone to miss if I'd left. She was brave to make such a move, and now I could sort of understand why it was so easy for her to buy the place on Lighthouse Road. She had a house that didn't feel like home and had found a home on the island that used to be everything a girl could want. It was no wonder she wanted to fix the place up. All she wanted was a home again.

The bells at the front door chimed, and I stepped out to find that beautiful roommate of mine standing in the lobby with three cups of coffee.

"Hey," she said with a shy grin.

"Hey," I replied, reaching to help her with the cups.

"These are for y'all," she smiled. "I hope your Aunt Cora likes the same coffee as you."

"I'm sure she'll love it." She followed me inside and to my dad's office.

"Hey, Mr. Dixon." I couldn't help but enjoy the way she and my dad both seemed excited to see each other.

"Well, good morning, sweetheart. Are you here for that jump drive?"

"Yes, sir. Alex says thank you for making him another copy. I'll be sure to get it in the mail to him today."

My dad handed her the jump drive in question and explained its contents. "Every document pertaining to your home purchase is loaded onto here. We have paper copies, of course, but this is just another backup. I usually suggest leaving something like this in a safety deposit box, but giving it to a trusted friend is just fine."

"Sure thing, Mr. Dixon, thank you."

"Of course, dear." My dad quickly returned to his desk and picked up his phone. "Sorry... I've got them on hold."

Val and I returned to the lobby. "So, if you don't have any plans on Friday night, would you want to join us for a family dinner cruise? With Etty and Tate and my parents?"

"You and me...and your whole family?"

"Yeah. It was my dad's idea, but I think it's a good one."

"I wouldn't want to impose on your time with your family..."

"You're never imposing." One day I'd make her believe that.

"I have to run up to Raleigh today," she cleared her throat. "But I think I'll be back in time for dinner."

"You can't keep driving all the way back to Raleigh just to work, Val. Promise me we can talk about getting you a kitchen here on the island."

"Sure. I didn't realize it bothered you so much." I hadn't realized it either.

"I just want what's best for Tucket Teas." That wasn't true, but I felt like I needed a good excuse for caring so much about her travels. "A company needs a well-rested owner. We just need to make better use of your time." I knew exactly what I wanted to do with her time. Maybe if she was in town more and traveling less, I could actually spend some of that time with her.

"We can talk about it," she agreed. The affection in her stare said a lot: it seemed we were on the same page as far as the two of us went. I didn't have to tell her out loud that I'd be waiting for her to get home, and she didn't have to tell me out loud that she was eager to get back. The physical tension between us spoke volumes. "I'll see you later, Jack."

"See you later, Val." It was physically difficult not to reach a hand out to her and tousle her hair with my fingers, or grip the back of her neck and pull her into me. My dad sitting on the other side of the office was just enough of a buzzkill to keep me away from her.

I sat down at my desk after she drove off and tried to clear my mind. My thoughts returned to Robert and Bailey. I missed my friend. My father never allowed anyone to talk about Robert Brooks or the accident. He loved Etta's fiancé, and aside from losing Jake, he never did get past the fact that Robert's decisions cost his daughter the man she loved and the father of her child—his grandson.

I never felt the need to remove Robert from my life, at least not like that. Etty and I talked a lot about it all in the days after the accident. She always said that it could have been any one of us who'd had too much to drink. We were all known to put down a few too many. The only difference that time was that Robert threw a punch, and Jake took the hit.

I still remember that night, minute for minute. In some ways, I felt like I could replay it all in slow motion and feel as if I was still standing right there.

I'd gone over to Etty and Jake's place to hang out that night. We'd just finished dinner with my parents, and she was relaxing in the living room with her feet propped up. When she was pregnant, her ankles would swell so badly; the only thing that helped was lying on the couch with her feet up on pillows.

We'd all settled in with bowls of ice cream and had just pressed play on Top Gun. Jake had seen the movie a hundred times, easily. He could recite it word for word. Still, when it was his turn to pick a movie, he always chose Top Gun.

We'd only gotten a few minutes into it when Robert called. As usual, he'd been out drinking at the beach bars and had put down a few too many. He needed a ride home and, at the very least, had the wherewithal to call for a ride rather than try to drive. As soon as I answered, he forgot why he had called. But after he'd asked me to come out for drinks enough times, I realized what he needed was to come home. He couldn't tell me where he was, but Jake was able to talk to him just enough to get a few details and piece together where he'd ended up. If Robert had gone to the beach bars, he'd refuse to go home without a slice from Georgia's Pizzeria. That night, he'd complained that they were burning his crust. We knew exactly where to find him.

Etty always wanted a sober friend to go pick up anyone who needed a ride home. She never really trusted the drivers in the many Ubers and Lyfts—she thought they were out to take advantage of tourists. She always thought everyone should have a friend with them, anyway. So that night when Robert called, she told us to go find him and bring him home.

She even set up some sheets and blankets on her couch and put a snack, a glass of water, and a bottle of Gatorade on the coffee table and a trash can for him to puke in on the floor right next to the pillow. My sister was a momma long before Tate was born. She had the heart every man dreamed of finding in a woman. Maybe that's part of why I never settled down, myself. I've always held girls to high standards—the standards my mom and my sister set for me.

The problem was that when we finally got to him, he didn't want to come home anymore. A few officers had an eye on him on the street because he was starting to get rowdy, and in an effort to try and keep him out of jail for being drunk and disorderly, Jake grabbed his shoulder hoping to lead him back to the truck. They wobbled a bit as they walked down the sidewalk, but for the most part, we were all heading in the right direction.

I clicked the button on the key fob to unlock the truck, and it almost seemed like the flash of lights reminded Robert of what we were doing.

"It's too early to go home, dude." He spoke slowly and struggled to get the words out in the right order.

"It's not too early, dude. Etta has the couch all set up for you. We're watching Top Gun. Come on, man." Jake slapped him on the back like guys do, but I guess Robert's drunken perception of it was different. He took it as more of a first punch. Drunk people never made wise choices, and with one swift right hook, Robert swung at his best friend—the one who was just trying to get him home safe. When they both fell to the ground, Jake slammed the back of his head into the curb. He never woke up again. He never even saw it coming.

Robert was arrested on site, more because of his actions after the punch than the punch itself. The charges racked up over the next few days and in the end they hung him up for involuntary manslaughter—among other things. He was denied bail, pled guilty at his first appearance, and was almost immediately shipped out to the Neuse Correctional facility in Goldsboro.

Etty never blamed Robert, but she also hadn't had a sip of alcohol since then either. She didn't harbor anger toward him, though it was clear that even the thought of him brought on a lot of emotional pain for her. She chose to forgive him immediately, although she always reminded us that accidents didn't require forgiveness. She always insisted that when he came home, we were to welcome him back just as we would have before the accident. He was our friend, and he'd need to feel loved and supported when he came home. We all knew that, but Etty was adamant about it.

My dad was still working to reach that same kind of peace and understanding. As far as he was concerned, Robert Brooks was responsible for the death of his son-in-law—future or not—and so far it seemed as if there wasn't anything Robert could do to get back in my father's good graces. I always hoped that with time and healing, Dad might be able to forgive him, too.

My sister was grace in human form. After Tate was born, we all realized that as much as she hated the idea of being a single mother, she was good at it. She'd worked every day to raise Tater with the same grace and love and forgiveness that she gave the world, and it worked. Tate was about the sweetest boy this side of the Mason-Dixon.

It didn't hurt any that he had a whole bunch of uncles looking out for him. Hell, even Brady Hill had some qualities worth passing down to the kid. Between all of us, Tate had it pretty dang good. None of us ever believed that we could take the place of his dad, but we worked hard every day to love that kid to the ends of the earth.

As for me? Well, it took over a year in therapy, but I'd learned since the accident to allow myself to think through the things that bothered me rather than try to push the thoughts away and ignore them. The accident was a turning point in my life, and enough work with the therapist had me able to think about it, mourn one friend, miss another, challenge my sadness with forgiveness, and go on about my day. Before I'd learned how to put all of those steps together, I was just angry. It was the anger that eventually earned me a spot with a therapist. After a few too many sleepless nights, I found myself on the wrong side of law enforcement and nearly losing my job working for my own family. I fought it for a while, but eventually, I came to appreciate Dr. Regan and the things he helped me to understand. When all else failed, I'd repeat the same phrase over and over until I believed even an ounce of it.

It wasn't my fault. It was just an accident. It's okay to miss them both.

I caught up on paperwork over the afternoon, and by four fifteen I was ready to head home. Influenced by the island's newest resident, I considered staying until five just because Google said so. But Aunt Cora assured me that she'd be there well past five answering emails and that I could go ahead and take off.

On the way home, I stopped at the market to grab a few things for dinner. Having a roommate—especially a female—had me making a bit more of an effort at home. I was picking up after myself, keeping things a bit cleaner, and even keeping better groceries in the house. A single man can live on beer and bar food, but I figured Val would feel a little more at home if I acted like a grown-up now and then. That was one of the earliest clues that I was more interested in her than I'd intended to become.

I took a quick spin around the store and filled a cart with fresh fruits and vegetables, eggs, and bread. Then I went to grab my usual supply of toaster pastries, frozen waffles, uncrustables, cereal, and canned soup. What can I say? I said I was trying.

Walking into the apartment, I couldn't help but notice a certain smell. A whiff of lavender and clean laundry was in the air but not overwhelming.

"Val? You home?" I set the grocery bags on the kitchen island before she answered. My mom would have been so proud. She liked to pop into my house now and then with meals.

"Hey, Jack! Be right there." I started to unpack the groceries until I heard her come down the stairs and into the kitchen. I turned to greet her, but instead, I found myself speechless. She stood there on the other side of the island, looking like she'd just stepped out of a photo shoot. Her hair was long and wavy, and she reached up to tuck a loose strand behind her ear. She was wearing makeup, but it looked softer than usual—almost natural. A faded v-neck tank top covered all the parts of her I desperately wanted to see again, barely meeting the hem of her cutoff blue jean shorts.

I pictured Val on the boat, in that brief moment between her dropping a towel and covering back up with that blanket. Things had changed since we first met, but I would have done anything to find her in that moment again—to touch her and feel her skin on mine. I was thankful to be standing behind the island, keeping certain excited parts of me out of her line of sight.

"How was your day?" I asked, unloading the rest of the groceries.

"Good. I got back a little while ago and was just getting ready to run some laundry. I'm about to wash my towels if you want to toss yours in." She rounded the island, and I did the same—keeping myself and *myself* out of her view. When she reached into the cupboard for a glass, her shirt lifted up just enough to reveal the bare skin between her rib-cage and her hips—skin I wanted to wrap my hands around as I pulled her in close to me.

"Oh, uh, yes. I'll run upstairs and grab mine." I took the excuse to remove myself from the room and ran upstairs before she could say anything else. In my room, I wished like hell that I was home alone and could step into an ice-cold shower. Instead, I had to get back downstairs to the girl who was setting me off in the first place. I didn't stand a chance.

I thought about everything I could that might kill my mood, and after a few minutes, I went back downstairs and met her in the laundry room, where she'd already started the washing machine and was leaning into it to reach the buttons. She wasn't the tallest, and I appreciated watching her struggle just a bit.

"There you are," she said with a smile that had me locked in. "Hey, did you have plans for dinner? That's a lot of groceries you brought back." She took my towels and tossed them in before closing the lid—and for just a minute, I saw what could have been a typical night. Running laundry and fixing dinner together seemed so normal, like something a couple would do. As much as I wanted her, and as much as she hadn't been keeping her own distance, we weren't a couple. She was just my roommate, and it was only temporary.

"I didn't have any specific plans. I just thought now that you're here, I could get more than just beer and waffles at the grocery store." She walked into the kitchen, and I followed, trying my hardest to come up with an offer for dinner that she couldn't refuse. "Maybe I went a little overboard."

"I passed that fish market on the way in. What if I went to grab some shrimp and made us a scampi?" The girl was an angel—now I was certain.

"I don't know what I did to deserve you, but I'm going to soak it in while I can."

"Is that a yes to shrimp scampi?" She folded her arms over her chest and stood before me, waiting for an answer.

"That's a hell yes to shrimp scampi," I said. "Let's go to the market."

We grabbed our keys and phones and went outside.

"Hop in. I'll drive." I could have sworn that her smile changed from curious to excited as if she'd just gotten what she wanted. I couldn't see why; my 4-runner paled in comparison to her Land Rover. She didn't seem to care, and it had me thinking back to my initial observations about her being nothing more than a rich kid who bought whatever she wanted just because she could. I felt guilty for assuming so much—or rather, so little —of her through a first impression.

Now, she was just the beautiful girl in the seat beside me, riding with me to the market for some of the day's fresh catch so that we could go home and make dinner together. If I didn't know any better, I'd say I was falling in love.

CHAPTER TWELVE
VAL

Riding in the car with Jack, I couldn't shake the feeling that I didn't want this to stop. Our living arrangements were temporary, and I had no reason to change that plan. Once my house was in a livable condition, there was no reason for me to be taking up space in his apartment. The last thing I wanted to be was a burden, especially when I was enjoying being his friend so much. I wanted our friendship to continue. I wanted it to be more than a friendship, too.

Scooter gave us a hell of a deal. We got a few days' worth of shrimp for the price of a half-pound. Back in the kitchen, my fixing shrimp scampi for Jack turned into more of a cooking lesson. He paid attention and followed directions to learn how to make the dish himself, all the while talking through easy conversation.

"So, what's the update on the house?" Jack started by filling a pot with water and grabbing noodles from the pantry.

"Link has everything ripped out now. Today they took the dumpster out of the driveway. I'm not sure if they'll bring back an empty one or if I just have a whole entire driveway now." It really was the little things. I laughed at the joy I'd found in celebrating a dumpster removal. I'd turned into a real-life Joanna Gaines.

"How'd you end up with Link Nicholson, anyway? I thought you were going to call the others?"

"I never said that." Was he jealous? If he was, I liked that. "*You* suggested that I call the others, but I never agreed to it. Your dad said Link was the best, so I called him. And so far, he's done great work." Jack looked defeated, pouring pasta into the boiling water with a scowl on his face that I couldn't quite define.

"Well, he's a good contractor. I'm sure he'll do a great job on the house."

"Something tells me the house isn't what you were concerned about," I said. He stirred the pasta, nodding with a smile. I was right. "So what was it then?" He shrugged, seeming unsure if he should say what was on his mind.

"Link is just... He isn't a great guy. He's a good contractor, but he isn't...an honorable man. He's more interested in who he can get into bed with and less interested in who he hurts in the process. He can build incredible things, but he's single-handedly one of the biggest players I've ever met."

"So it wasn't the house you were looking out for; it was...me." I poured the shrimp into a colander in the sink and began to peel and devein each piece as I processed the idea of Jack looking out for *me*. A man who couldn't have cared any less about me when we met certainly had stepped up to the plate recently. He was a gentleman, and he was only impressing me more each day.

"I didn't mean to overstep..." He set the spoon down on the counter and hung his head as if he felt guilty. "I just... Link isn't known for treating a girl right."

"I appreciate you looking out for me, Jack." I blushed at the idea of Jack trying to take care of me the way he worked to take care of everyone else. He was so protective of Etta and Tate. He was always encouraging Bailey to chase her dreams. He loved to be around the guys, cheering them on when they'd fight over who hooked the biggest fish. He helped me, a complete stranger, to buy a house even though it wasn't his job. Then again, I didn't exactly give him much of a choice. But, other than the first day where my untimely arrival seemed to catch him off guard, he'd done nothing but support me all the way.

"So, what happens next?" He seemed to be making an effort to change the subject, and if what he said about Link was true, I could understand why he wanted to talk about something else.

"Next, we're going to need a frying pan."

He laughed and pulled a frying pan from the cabinet below. "I meant with the house, but here you go." The smile I'd come to love returned to his face as he set the pan on the stove.

"Next on the house is a few days of work on a new roof. Next on the shrimp scampi is a stick of butter in that pan, with some olive oil, some garlic, a bit of white wine, salt and pepper, crushed red pepper, and a lemon." As I listed off the ingredients, he spun around the kitchen to grab each one.

"You're like a younger, nicer, prettier Gordan Ramsay," he joked, setting a lemon and a knife on the counter.

"That's quite a compliment," I said, totally smitten.

"Sorry, I didn't mean to—" We couldn't find a balance with each other. We both seemed to be exploding with nerves, all colliding between us.

157

"No, I appreciate it." He reached for the lemon at the same moment that I did, his hand landing right on top of mine. When neither one of us moved, I realized that I didn't want him to. When I looked up at him, I noticed the way his chest rose and fell as he took quick breaths. I pulled my hand away and took a step back—not because I wanted to separate myself from him, but because I was overwhelmed.

"I'll be right back," I said as I walked away and up the stairs. In my room, I closed the door behind me and ran into the bathroom, noticing the redness and the tears in my eyes as I got to the mirror.

The mixture of emotions felt heavy, and it certainly didn't feel right. Was I really crying because a man touched my hand? If anything, I was glad he did. I'd been dreaming about touching him, about kissing him. I'd been desperate for another night out on his boat to watch the sunset. I'd accepted the fact that I had a major crush on Jack Dixon, and I didn't know what to do with it. But crying obviously wasn't helpful. I was being stupid.

A knock on my bedroom door pulled me out of my train of thought, snapping me from the anxiety, and I realized that I needed to shake it off or I'd risk finding myself homeless. I couldn't blame a guy for not wanting an overly emotional girl in his apartment. I'd kick that out, too.

"Val? I-I'm sorry." His gentle voice was muffled on the other side of the door. Behind it, I wiped my eyes, pinched my cheeks, and forced a smile.

"Don't," I said as I opened the door. "Don't apologize. I have no idea what happened." I forced a laugh, trying to get out

of my own head. "Maybe I-I think I was just thinking about...
cooking with Golly."

"Listen, Val—"

"No, Jack, really. You didn't do anything wrong. I just...
I think I just got overwhelmed for a second."

"Overwhelmed? By me?" He took a step backward, and
his shoulders fell. He looked devastated, and it crushed me. I
wanted him closer, happier, and as near to me as possible.

"No..." I tucked my hair behind my ears. "I think, I
just...when Golly died, I mean a lot changed. You know, she
was my last piece of family. I just got to thinking, all of a
sudden I'm cooking dinner with you, and it's...it's exhausting.
Not the cooking, I like this part. But the back and forth in my
mind. I'm constantly missing her and enjoying something with
you here. It's like I'm...I'm learning how to be an orphan, and
how to be completely surrounded at the same time."

"You're not an—"

"I am, though, Jack. It's been a long time since I've had
dinner with my family. I don't get to cook with my parents, or
play football with my brother, or meet my friends at a bar, or go
for dinner cruises on Friday nights. I'm an orphan. It's just me,
and no one cooks with me. No one calls my name when they
walk into the house. No one asks how my day at work was. I
mean, I know it hasn't been that long, but it was only a few days
after Golly died that I kind of...accepted that my life was going
to be lonely. I realized that I was alone and just kind of came to
terms with it."

"And now, every day, I'm asking you about the house,
bringing you groceries, suggesting business moves, and...asking
you to join my family on the boat." I didn't know what to say.

None of what he did was wrong. It was great, perfect even. But yes, it was a lot to think about. "God, Val. I'm sorry." He stepped forward but stopped himself before he got close enough to touch. "I know I'm not your family. I shouldn't have pressured you with all of that."

"Yes, you should have!" I laughed and cried at the same time. "Do you know how much it means to me? I had no one, and I figured I'd just make the best of it. But then I got here, and everyone just…I mean y'all didn't just welcome me to town; you basically celebrated that I was here. You invited me into your home. It's like you've been waiting for me. You cook dinner with me. You…"

"Give you my laundry?" I laughed again, thankful that he could crack a joke when a girl stood in front of him in tears.

"And, you smile at me, Jack. And I don't know what to do with it. I just…I like it when you smile at me. I like it when you keep me away from playboy contractors. I like going out on the boat with you. I like cooking with you."

"I like touching your hand," he said, taking a half step closer to me. I was confessing my crush on a man who was confessing his back to me.

"I like that, too." My tears were gone now, and I'd been filled instead with nervousness I couldn't settle. My stomach tossed and turned until he reached to tangle his fingers in mine, pulling our hands up between us and laying a kiss on mine.

"Shall we? I think that butter is probably melted." I laughed and followed as he led me down the stairs and into the kitchen. Not another word was spoken about the tears I'd just cried to him. Instead, we continued fixing dinner like all of it was as normal as could be.

"I can't do much in the kitchen, but I know what to do with a fresh catch." Jack poured the shrimp into the pan full of butter, wine, and seasonings and began to sauté the shrimp on each side.

"All that's left is to mix in the pasta and stir it up." I reached for the tongs and stepped over to the pot.

"What kind of drink do we pair with shrimp scampi?" He walked toward the liquor cabinet in the living room and opened the doors, turning to face me as he waited for an answer.

"I think a fancy restaurant would usually suggest a Pinot Grigio or a Chardonnay. But would *you* like either of those?" I joined him at the liquor cabinet, standing hip to hip as we looked at the bottles.

"I wouldn't choose it for myself. Can't say I have a bottle of either one, actually." I looked into the cabinet and noticed a complete lack of wine in general. "Would you mind a cocktail instead?" He asked.

"Sounds perfect. What did you have in mind?"

"I'm pretty partial to a Toddy."

"A Toddy? You mean a Hot Toddy?" I'd never heard of just a Toddy without the *hot*.

"Yeah. Instead of the hot tea and all the fixings, it's just sweet tea and rum. A Cold Toddy, I guess."

"You can't really go wrong with sweet tea or rum," I said, remembering my go-to late-night mix with my own hot teas.

"I'll fix us some drinks." He pulled a dark rum from the cabinet and returned to the kitchen. The view from the living room caught my eye, and I walked onto the back porch to catch my breath and get a better look and try to catch my breath.

A few minutes later, I heard the sliding door open behind me. Mortified that he'd see me cry twice in thirty minutes, I wiped my tears as fast as I could.

"Are you ready to eat?" His voice from behind was soothing, washing over me like summer rain in a drought. I tried to swallow my emotions, but before I could turn around and answer him, a hand settled across the small of my back. I looked out to the water, unsure of what to do next while my breaths came quickly and my palms began to sweat.

I turned to face him and found him closer than I'd realized. My chest pressed against his as he closed in, pinning me between his body and the porch railing. With one hand still wrapped securely around my lower back, the other found its way into the hair above my neck, pulling me closer to him before he pressed a kiss to my forehead and eased back just enough to look into my eyes.

"You'll never find yourself alone again," he said quietly. "If you'll let me, I'll spend the rest of time reminding you that you aren't alone. You'll never be an orphan if you stay here with me." His promise was like a key to my heart, opening the gate that had slowly built throughout my life, one loss at a time. I thought I'd gone and locked that gate permanently when I buried Golly. I came to Ocracoke because I knew it to be a safe place to be alone. Instead, what I found was a home waiting for me and a man who apparently not only noticed my greatest insecurity but cared enough to help me defeat it.

"What are we doing, Jack?" I whispered as I leaned my face into his grip, desperate for his lips to touch me again, for his fingers to hold the back of my head the way they had before, and for him to tug on my wavy hair while he kissed my neck.

"I'm not sure," he said as his other hand reached up to slide a thumb across my face. "But I'm sure that I'll be here with you when we figure it out."

I didn't know what to say, but he knew what to do. When I looked into his eyes, completely speechless, he reached down to my thigh and lifted me up to sit on the porch railing. He stepped forward, putting his hips between my knees and his hands back into my hair, staring at me with a soft smile on his face.

"I like not being alone," I said as the tip of his nose traced lightly across mine. "I like being with you." He moved to kiss my cheek.

"I like being with you, too." He reached a finger underneath my chin and lifted my face until my eyes met his. "I'm really glad you came here, Val Foster."

His lips sealed to mine in a way I desperately wanted and in every way I needed. He leaned in, pressing against me and pulling me into him at the same time. My hands gripped his forearms as he held me close and tugged at my bottom lip with his teeth. His kiss was thorough, but tender.

"Let's go eat before our dinner gets cold." He stood there with his nose resting on mine again, making it extremely difficult to agree to walk inside. "Maybe after shrimp scampi, we can have dessert."

I laughed, thankful again that he'd managed to lighten the mood. The nerves I'd been feeling about him and the way I wanted to be with him faded away in an instant as he grabbed my waist and lifted me down from the railing. He tucked my hair behind my ears, kissed my forehead again, and winked at me before leading me inside.

At the table, he pulled out a chair for me and lit a candle between us before plating up the dinner we'd cooked together. I'd left Raleigh two short months ago with no family to speak of, and suddenly, I felt like I had a family of my very own and even a home. At the very least, I had Jack Dixon.

CHAPTER THIRTEEN
JACK

We ate in an oddly enjoyable silence; her cheeks a bright pink, fully blushed from our kissing on the porch, and myself completely satisfied having finally gotten to put my hands on her skin and kiss her lips. Every few bites, she would look up to me, putting a smile across my face that I couldn't control.

"You mentioned desert?" She set her fork down after clearing her plate and looked at me with a smile that melted me to the core. I'd been referring to a different kind of dessert earlier, but I figured I could play along.

"I usually keep a good stock of ice cream; it's one of my favorite food groups. I've got chocolate, vanilla, cookie dough, and mint chip. I have waffle cones and sugar cones, sprinkles, and chocolate syrup, too. You name it; I usually have plenty."

"Ice cream...sounds amazing," she said, standing with her dishes and walking into the kitchen. I followed closely behind her with my own dishes, reaching around her to set them in the sink. When my arms surrounded her, she leaned into me, pressing those denim shorts back into my hips and driving me wild, stirring up the energy I'd fought to settle while we ate.

"You're going to miss dessert, Val."

"No, I won't. I just had another dessert in mind." A quiet grunt mixed with a laugh escaped me in one swift movement that surprised us both as I spun her around and lifted her up onto the counter in front of me. She wrapped her legs around my waist and grabbed at the front of my shirt, pulling me close enough to kiss again.

I pressed my lips back into hers, tasting the Toddy that lingered on her tongue. "Are you sure this is okay?"

"More than okay," she said with a smile. "So...very okay."

After a whole lot of making out on the kitchen counter and eventually on the couch, I poured us each another round of drinks and took her back out onto the porch for a breath of fresh air. I laid down in the hammock and invited her to join me. Wrapped up in each other and cozy underneath a blanket, we swayed in the breeze full from dinner, relaxed from drinks, and absolutely smitten with each other from all the kissing we'd done. It hurt like hell to keep my hands where they should have been, but I was a gentleman. I wasn't about to take things too far that fast. I was going to make her mine, and I was going to do it slowly and respectfully.

"I get the impression that you aren't a kiss them and move on type of guy," she said after a few quiet minutes.

"I'm not," I laughed, thankful that she was aware that my intentions were greater than quick fun. "What makes you say that?"

"I'm just wondering what tomorrow might look like." I rubbed my hands along her back, tracing my fingertips over her bare shoulders.

"Tomorrow, you're getting a new roof, and I'm going into the office for the morning to finish up a few contracts for my dad. Then, if you still want to, we can go out on the boat with my family and catch another good sunset—I hope."

"That sounds perfect," she said. With her head resting on my chest, I couldn't see her smile, but I could feel it. "And what about this part?" I reached up to lay my hand on top of hers as it rested on my chest.

"Making out in the kitchen and cuddling in the hammock? Definitely more of that. So much more of that." My laughing jostled us, and she shimmied around me, stirring me up again.

"Jack, you know that's not what I mean." She moved around to resettle on my chest.

"Well...what do you think tomorrow looks like?" I asked, raking my other hand around her hip and sliding my fingers into her back pocket.

"You know, in college, I would have run to Bailey and Etta to tell them about this cute boy I met. I'd tell them about how he made me dinner and that when I cried, he dried my tears. Then I'd tell them all about making out with him in the kitchen and on the porch and climbing in close with him in a hammock."

"But?"

"But instead, I'm worried about telling my friend that I'm falling for her big brother. I'm worried about wanting to date a guy in a town I just moved to...and that if it didn't work out, things would be weird, and I might lose the only people I have left."

167

"And if we did tell her about you and me, and it did work out?"

"That would be…something special," she said.

We laid, swaying in the breeze until sometime overnight when I carried her up to her bed and tucked her in. The next morning I woke up alone in my own bed, sad that she wasn't next to me but also thankful that we hadn't taken things too far the night before. I knew what I wanted—I wanted Val; I wanted every inch of her and all to myself. And I knew for sure that the only way to make her mine was to do it right, and that meant letting her take the lead. That night wasn't enough for me, although I was starting to think that nothing with her ever would be. I desired her in the most sensual way—a way I'd never wanted anyone else before. Everything about her left me wanting more.

The next morning, she left early to meet the roofers at the house. They were getting started and planned to have it finished by Monday. The rate at which Lincoln Nicholson completed projects was curious at best. She was hoping to meet them there with a big breakfast and an endless supply of coffee.

I loved watching the way she stayed involved at the house. She was excited about her renovation and eager to live in a house that she'd worked to turn into a home. The place had so much history, and she was certain that there was more to come.

The thought of her renovation coming to an end sort of stole my joy because at the end of it she'd be moving out of my apartment. I'd come to enjoy having her so close—I needed it. I needed *her*, and there wasn't a single part of me that wanted her to leave. In all fairness, she could only get so far on a fourteen-mile island.

I stopped for breakfast at the ferry dock and found my sister and Bailey at a table on the porch.

"Morning, ladies." I slid into the bench seat beside my sister and took a sip of her coffee.

"How many shots are in that?" I choked on the tar she called a latte.

"Rough night," Etty said. "Tater climbed in bed with me last night and asked if we could go to Heaven to visit daddy." A silence fell across the three of us, equal parts sadness and guilt drowning each one of us. I wrapped my arm around my sister and kissed her forehead.

"I'm sorry, Etty." Bailey wiped a tear from her cheek. I reached across to grab her hand, thankful that I could be there for my sister and Bailey on a tough morning. I loved those girls more than I could even understand, and it killed me that I couldn't take it all back and make their pain go away.

"Why don't I take him out for some Uncle time this weekend?" You girls should go have an afternoon to yourselves. Do the mani-pedi thing. Get a massage." The girls laughed, and I was proud of myself for putting a smile on their faces. "You should take Val with you. She's been working so hard on everything this week. She could probably use a spa day with y'all." Bailey and Etty shot each other a conspiratorial glance with heightened eyebrows before looking at me.

"How are things going with Val?" Bailey asked, resting her chin in her hand.

"Great." I tried to answer nonchalantly, but their stares made it difficult. I cleared my throat. "I mean, it's fine. You know, she's good. She seems to enjoy working on the house."

"And you? Are you enjoying…her working on the house?" Etty waggled her eyebrows at me. "Or should we delay the project a bit…"

"What are you talking about?" I knew exactly what she meant.

"It just seems like you and Val are getting along much better than you thought you would." My sister waited impatiently for my reply.

"Maybe first impressions aren't everything," Bailey added.

"Okay, so maybe we got off on the wrong foot," I admitted.

"Of course you did," Etty said. "I knew you'd see the other side eventually."

"I'm sorry, what?" I didn't understand.

"Oh, come on, you totally have a crush on her," Bailey said as the waitress approached. Lennon Stafford had worked at the cafe since we were sixteen; her parents owned the place, and she was planning to take over for them within the next couple of years. Until then, she was working on her degree at Chapel Hill and waiting tables in the cafe every free minute she had.

"Hey, Lennon," Bailey said. "Don't you think Jack and Val would make a cute pair?"

"Bailey, stop it," I said. "Lennon, can I get some pancakes and a coffee, please?"

"Of course," she laughed. "But I want to hear more about you and Val Foster."

"You know Val?" I asked.

"Mostly through the grapevine. I know she moved back here recently. I heard she bought the house on Lighthouse Road."

"She did," I answered.

"Jack helped her buy it," Etty said with a dramatic voice and a wink.

"Y'all need to stop."

"And he offered Val his spare room while she renovates," Bailey added. The three of them hit me with a stare at the same time.

"Okay, enough. I was just being nice. God, sometimes it feels like I have seven sisters." My eyes could not have rolled any farther back in my head. "Cole's place was booked, and I had the room. She's leaving soon, anyway."

"Yeah...to move all the way down the street from you," Etty said. "Do you think maybe this is the good Lord giving you a gift?"

"Okay, that's a bit much." It wasn't, though. The Lord had indeed given me the gift of a lifetime.

"I'll go put in that breakfast order, Jack." Lennon shook my shoulder and went back to the kitchen.

"Since when are the two of you so interested in me and Val?"

"Since I stopped by last night to visit with Tater before bedtime and saw you making out with her on the kitchen counter."

"You, what?" I thought through the night before: the tears, the kissing, the way I held her in my arms and never wanted to let go. And my sister had seen it all? What an oddly delayed cock-block.

171

"Tater wanted to visit, so we stopped by. You're lucky I peeked through the window before I used my key to walk right in. Then again, I would pay good money to see you explain that one to Tate."

"Okay, hang on just a second," I blushed and tried to gather my thoughts. I knew we'd have to explain ourselves to everyone at some point, but I hadn't considered it would be right away.

"Look, Jack. You've put your life on hold for me—and Tate. You need to put yourself first for once. Stop worrying about what anyone else thinks and just...kiss her. Go have your fun."

"Just don't mess with her. Don't kiss her and leave her. She's not that type of girl," Bailey added.

"I'm not that type of guy," I shot back. "I'm not kissing her just for fun."

"We know," Etty said. "You're one of the most stand-up guys on this island, and everyone knows it. Val deserves a guy like you, and you deserve a girl like her. To me...this seems kind of perfect." Etty finished off her latte with a satisfied grin, knowing full well that she'd caught me red-handed; an act a sister loved more than anything.

"Okay, listen. I know what you saw, but can you just... you know. Can you keep your distance for a while?" The last thing I wanted was to ambush Val. She was already feeling so overwhelmed with everything. I wanted to be her safe place, her place of rest. If she was worried about everyone else knowing, she'd shy away from me.

"Yes, but she's going to tell us eventually."

"Let her. Don't bother her about it. She's been through enough recently. That and she was worried about you herself last night."

"Relax, Jack. We aren't going to scare her off."

"Yeah, we only do that to the girls we don't like," Etty said. "And we like Val."

Lennon returned with my breakfast and sat down next to Bailey. "So, did we figure everything out?"

"We're going to let Jack and Val do their thing. And we're going to let Val tell us when she's ready." Bailey stole a bite of my pancakes.

"There are way too many girls in my life," I huffed.

"You love us," Bailey said.

"I do. That I do."

We sat together and shared the plate of pancakes for a few minutes while I listened to the girls cackle on about Tate, work, dreams, and even boys. The girls had no boundaries when it came to talking about their lives around me. Thankfully, neither one of them had any recent activity to speak of. There were certain details a guy just shouldn't hear about his sisters. I pretended not to care when they got into a discussion about the newest *toys* available at Target. Seriously, no boundaries whatsoever.

"Jesus, you guys." I rolled my eyes.

"Hey, not all of us have a live-in play-thing." Bailey was always quick with comebacks.

It was sort of weird but also a bit of a relief. I prided myself on how close I was to them. Etty deserved it, and Bailey needed it. I loved those girls more than anything and would give my life to make theirs better. Seeing them ease up and enjoy themselves was a relief. It wasn't common in recent years. It almost felt like Val had brought a piece of life back to them that they'd been missing all this time.

I got the last bite of pancakes just before Bailey stabbed a fork at it, and laughed victoriously. Lennon stood and gathered our dishes.

"Lennon, I've got the bill."

"A gentleman," Bailey said, reaching across to pat my cheek. "I have to get to the bar. Lunch special today, kids."

"Oh, thank God," Lennon groaned. "Dad's been groaning about those shrimp skewers since last week."

"Tell your Dad I'll have a plate ready and waiting for him. I'll see you all this afternoon, then." Lennon returned to the kitchen, and Bailey got up with her purse to leave. "Thanks for breakfast, brother-man."

"My pleasure," I said, leaving cash on the table.

We watched Bailey walk out the door, and when Etty and I were the only ones left, I knew I had more coming.

"So, you really do like her, huh?"

"Etty…would it bother you if I…you know, was actually interested in your friend?"

"Why would that bother me?" She reached across the table to squeeze my hand.

"I just…I never want you or Tate to think that anyone else is more important than you are."

"Jack, you've raised that boy with me like he's your own son. You never had to do that."

"I did," I coughed. "And I'll be there his entire life. He got the raw end of a shitty deal, and I'm partly to blame."

"Is that really what you think?"

"It's what I know, Etty."

"I'll say it until the day I die, Jack. If I could do it all over again, I'd send you two out to get Robert every time. You boys pick fights even when you're sober. The way that night ended... it was a mistake. It was an accident. It wasn't your fault, and it wasn't Robert's fault. It just...happened."

"But it happened, and I can't fix it. But I can help make up for what we took away."

"No, Jack. You can't. You can't make up for Jake being gone. What you can do is show Tater how much his uncles love him. And part of that job description is showing him what love looks like—what happiness looks like, even when life gets hard."

"Etty," I started, but she cut me off.

"No, Jack, listen to me. Do you think that Jake would want Tate to spend his whole life alone because he's too busy taking care of his broken-hearted mom? I don't. I think that you show him every day what it means to love your family. But you can also show him what it means to have your own happiness; you can show him what love looks like. God knows I won't get the chance to teach him that."

"You never know, Etty,"

"What I know for sure is that you are the best man in Tater's life. He may not have his dad, but he has the next best thing. And his dad would have wanted him to know love—true love—and you can still show him that. His dad would have wanted him to understand that you can't spend your life only thinking about what you've lost. He'd want Tate to believe that you can move forward, and keep adding to your life. That you can love others without replacing the ones you lost. He'd want you to know that too."

"So, you wouldn't mind if I...maybe took Val out on a date?" I was desperate to lighten the mood.

"It seems to me that you two have already gone quite a ways past a first date," she laughed.

"Okay, I'm going to need you to forget what you saw," I said. "If you're really okay with it...can you...maybe give me some advice?"

Etty laughed. "My brother is asking me for dating advice?" She threw a hand to her chest for dramatic effect.

"I know how to date a woman, thank you very much." I rolled my eyes. "I just thought maybe you could give me a hint or two about your friend. You've known her longer than I have."

"Val is...she's loud, and she comes across as confident, but deep down, she's actually an incredibly cautious person. She acts like a firecracker—and don't get me wrong, she is—but she's...she's really sensitive, too. And vulnerable. She's lost everyone she ever had. She might seem rich, and wild, and demanding, but she's just...taking care of herself the best way she knows how. She's like an onion. Once you peel back those layers, you'll find a girl who just needs someone to take care of her heart; someone to remind her that she doesn't have to."

"Thanks, Etty."

"Be thoughtful. Put her first. Peel back her layers. Let her have her emotions. Be there for her when they get the best of her because they will. Really, just...be you, Jack, and you'll win her over in no time." She winked and stood from the table. "If all else fails, just watch *How To Lose A Guy In Ten Days* with her." She glanced at her watch. "Time for school. I'll see you later."

"Love you, Etty." She stood and kissed the top of my head and while she walked out to her car, I sat and thought about what she'd said.

I knew that Val was vulnerable. The way she offered her broken soul to me and told me about everything that had beat her down over the years, it showed me that she trusted me with her vulnerability. Now I just needed to show her that she was right to do it. Val and I were off to a good start, save for our first impression. I was in deep for that crazy girl.

ANNALEE THOMASSON

CHAPTER FOURTEEN
VAL

"Link!" I hollered up to the man on the roof as I walked closer to my front porch. "You said three days, but it looks like you're almost done!" I stood on the ground below with my hands on my hips, wondering how in the hell the man had managed to put an entire roof on my house seemingly overnight.

"You'll never believe it, but I had another job finish up early yesterday, and I sent the guys over here to get started. Someone gave them some coffee—or maybe some cocaine because this morning I got here to find that the shingles were the only thing left!"

"Link, please tell me there's no cocaine on my new roof."

"Relax, preppy. It was a joke."

"Preppy?" I didn't know whether to be offended or laugh.

"Oh, come on. I know you came from Chapel Hill. You wore pearls and heels to football games, am I right?" He pointed my way with accusatory fingers. "That's preppy."

"Are you judging me?"

"Never!"

"Come down here, and I'll show you just what I can do in heels and pearls, Link." I laughed and walked inside, hovering over the kitchen island where Link's build plans were sprawled out across the countertop.

"So, what do you think?" He asked as he walked into the kitchen. He set a water bottle down in front of me and cracked open his own.

"Link, this is incredible."

"I'm going to need some design choices pretty soon. We're going to put up new insulation and drywall this week. The floors are fine, and they fixed the foundation last week. It's amazing how fast a dollar can make a team move."

"Was that a low blow at my bank balance?"

"Of course not. I'm just saying. Most projects don't move that fast. When you pay cash up front, they'll do damn near whatever you want."

"I'll take what I can get," I laughed. "So, after the drywall, we're good for the kitchen install, right?"

"That's right. Think you can get me some final plans tomorrow?"

"Of course." I wasn't as confident as I'd tried to sound.

"Thanks, girl. I'm heading back up there," He finished his water and tossed it into the recycling bin at the doorway. "Call if you need?"

"Will do," I smiled, blown away at the progress he and the crew had made in such a short amount of time. "Thanks, Link."

Looking over the build plans again, I couldn't help but think I wanted to expand just a little bit more. I still wanted to work to keep the layout of the house the same, but the more I looked at it, the more I realized we could add a few more seats to the house if we made just a few small changes—just as Betty Ann had suggested in her letter. I pulled out my phone and sent a group message to the girls.

Val: Hey, ladies. I want your thoughts on the next steps in the house. Can you guys meet me here this afternoon?

Bailey: Sure thing. I can be there around three.

Etta: Three fifteen? I'll have Tate with me if that's okay.

Val: Of course it's okay. I'll see you then. Thanks, girls.

The house already had charm. All I wanted to do was make sure that I kept it all. The place still had a lot of stories to tell, and I wanted to create a space to allow it. Later that afternoon, just as planned, Bailey and Etta arrived around three fifteen with Tate in tow.

"Tater Tot!" Link called from the roof.

"Don't you dare let him get hurt, Lincoln." Etta shot a mom glare up at the crew on the roof.

"Never! Can I put him to work while you're here?" Tate looked up at his mom with wide eyes and an impossibly large grin.

"Please, momma? I want to learn to work!"

"Be careful, please."

Link saluted Etta with a wink, a silent promise that he'd watch out for her boy. Everyone gave Lincoln Nicholson a lot of crap, but if I could trust my gut, he'd take good care of Tate.

"Go on, buddy." Tate dropped the football in his hands and ran over to the bottom of the ladder. "Wait for Link to come down, please."

"Come on in," I laughed. "You think he's okay with Link?"

"The man might be reckless with his manhood, but he isn't a complete dumbass," Bailey said.

"He's good with the kids," Etta added. "He's been coaching for the Little Groms Flag Football League for years now. They'll be fine."

"So, what are we working on?" The three of us settled around the papers on the kitchen island.

"The roof is about done, and then they're going to finish off what's left inside. If all of that goes well, we get to start installing the kitchen next."

"Oh!" The girls shrieked together, giddy at the news. "Show me your design plans!" Etta clapped.

"Well, that's what I needed some help with." I pointed to the drawings on the counter, and the girls settled in, ready to get to work. "This is what the original layout was. I want to keep it similar, but I also want to open the space up just a bit more. I was thinking…what if we turn this wall into a giant sliding glass door and make the screened-in porch out the back of the actual dining room?"

"Oh my god," Bailey started. "There's enough space in here to host a wedding."

"That's kind of what I was thinking..."

"A wedding?" Etta glared at me.

"No, Etta. Jesus. I meant that I was thinking about creating a large space for entertaining. You guys have your weekly dinners. And Etta, y'all spend so much time with your family. I just...I love having friends here. I want to create a space that is open for everyone. I want to give everyone a seat at the table."

"I love it," Bailey said. "There's plenty of room here."

"That's my hope," I said quietly, emotion tickling my throat.

"So, can Link do that? Piece together a few sliding glass doors?"

"I was thinking like...a sliding glass wall."

The girls gasped and looked in the direction of the wall in question. "Oh my God, Val." Etta walked to the window in place. "Can you just imagine?"

"Call me crazy..." I leaned on the kitchen island and hesitated, wondering if I really should offer up the idea I'd had recently. "Just hear me out, okay?" The girls looked at me, concerned but eager for more.

"Bailey, I know you've been living with your parents, and you've said you're doing just fine there. And Etta," I turned to face her. "You and Tate...well, you mentioned that your lease is up, and you were thinking about moving closer to the school."

"Right," Etta said slowly.

"What if…I mean, when the renovation is done, what if we all moved in here, together?" The girls stood silent for a moment, looking between themselves and me.

"Val, I couldn't even begin to afford the rent in a house like this," Etta said, a bit disappointed.

"No, no rent. Consider it Golly's gift from the grave."

"I couldn't possibly," Etta stepped backward, waving her hands between us, dismissing the idea.

"You could," I argued. "You *should*. You deserve at least that."

"She's right," Bailey agreed. "The rest of us can make up for the rent. You and Tate deserve a safe place to live. Put your rent money toward his college fund."

"No, I meant *no* rent," I clarified. "I paid cash for this house and for the renovations. I won't have a mortgage. All we'll have is utility bills and taxes. We can split all of that equally if you really want to fight me on it, but no rent. This is just… home."

Tears slipped from Etta's eyes as she looked around, processing everything we'd just thrown at her. Bailey stood with a hand over her mouth.

"Are we doing this?" Etta wiped her cheek. "Are we moving into this house together?"

"I think this place deserves to be more than just a house. It's just been waiting on another family to call it home again," I said, looking around the open walls.

"Home it is." Bailey agreed.

I nodded, satisfied and eager to see what the future might hold. "Time to get real good and crowded."

CHAPTER FIFTEEN
JACK

When I parked in front of the house after work, I paused before getting out of the car to think about what I was going to say when I walked inside. Most of me wanted to toss her into my bed and have my way with her, but I hadn't stopped thinking about what my sister had said earlier that morning.

She was right—I'd spent the past four years putting myself aside and putting Etta and Tate first. I didn't regret it, and I'd do it all over again. Truthfully, even if I did shake things up a bit and date someone…it wouldn't be at the expense of my family. It couldn't. I'd have to figure out the balance, but until then, I couldn't let go of either of them.

I pulled the key from the ignition and walked inside. Val's car was already there, which means she was already home after a day at her place. I didn't expect her to be home already, and that could be narrowed down to two possibilities—either everything at her house was going well, and she was home early after a day full of work accomplished, or—more likely—Lincoln Nicholson had screwed something up and was going to need a good talking to.

I opened the front door and was immediately met with a new smell. It was overwhelming in a good way.

"Val?"

"I'm in the kitchen!"

"What is that smell? And can I bathe in it?" I tossed my keys onto the hook at the door. Her laugh made my stomach churn in all the right ways. I walked into the kitchen and found her standing behind the counter, almost completely covered by boxes and bags.

"Don't kill me," she started with her hands up in surrender.

"Of course not," I laughed. "What are we doing?" I could feel my eyes bulge from my face. I wasn't worried, just curious.

"So, the other day, I placed an order for Tucket Teas, and—" I stepped up behind her slowly, resting my hands around her hips, and kissed her cheek. "When I arranged the shipping, I had it all sent here instead." I touched my nose to the nape of her neck. "I figured, if I can see just how well I can organize and condense my supplies, I could maybe find a storage unit to get started in. At least until I find a more…" I pulled her hips into mine. "…permanent solution."

"That's amazing," I said, pressing my lips to her neck again. "But Val, my house *is* a permanent solution. As permanent as you want it to be."

"I know, Jack. But even if I stay here with you a while, my business needs a commercial kitchen that's approved by the state."

"Fair enough." I met her smile with a kiss. "Did you get everything you need?" Being away from her all day was like torture. I'd stared the clock down all day long, waiting impatiently to get home to see her again and pick up where we'd left off the night before.

"Almost," she said. "I have some equipment in the kitchen in Raleigh I'll need to get." I interrupted her with my lips again. "Would you like to join me for a road trip?"

"I sure would." She smiled as if she was surprised at my answer. "How was everything at the house today?" She wrapped her arms around my torso and tossed her hair over her shoulders.

"Amazing. You wouldn't believe how much work Link has gotten done already. He says it's the power of a dollar." She laughed into my chest.

"That's a lot of power."

"I also had a chat with Etta and Bailey." The tone in her voice moved from excited to hesitant, and my stomach flopped.

"About what?"

"So, I've been thinking. When the house is finished, and it's ready to move into…well, I invited Etta and Bailey to live there. I was thinking back to when I first got here, and it seemed like I'm not the only one who might be in need of some new living arrangements. I kind of figured…lots of birds, one stone."

I did my best to hide the disappointment from my face. I didn't want her to think I didn't like the idea—I did. I loved that she was bringing Etty and Bailey into the house with her. It just reminded me that she would be leaving me sooner than later.

"I think that's a great idea," I said, trying to sound more confident than sad. "Etty will love that. She's been on her own for so long now. She's always so brave about it, but I know she'd love the company."

"No one should be alone," she said. Ironic, isn't it? The very problem she was solving by moving in with the girls would create the same problem for me.

"Bailey's been such a homebody ever since—" I stopped myself. "You know. It will be good for her too, to have you girls around and to enjoy herself for once."

"So why do you look so down about it?" She tightened her grip on me and leaned her head back to get a better look at the expression I was trying to hide. The way she looked into my eyes—like she knew something was on my mind—pulled me in like glue. Val spoke to me in a way I'd never experienced with anyone else before.

"Ahhh," I groaned, embarrassed that I already felt this way and unsure of if or how to share my feelings with Val. "Don't worry about it."

"I'm absolutely going to worry about it. Where'd you go? What's going on?" Her stare was a mixture of pity and desperation, excitement and curiosity.

I released my hold on her and leaned back into the counter behind me. I crossed my arms over my chest, unsure of whether or not I was about to ruin a really good thing—one of the first things that felt so good in years. She looked as if she didn't know what to do with the distance I'd put between us. She leaned into the counter across from me, looking like I was about to break her damn heart. I knew I wasn't—if anything I was about to overwhelm her with just how much I wanted her around. But the unsure look in her eyes still hurt.

"Val, I really like having you here." She smiled and tilted her head, pleased but ready for more. "I guess I just...I didn't expect to like having you here as much as I do. The closer you get to finishing things over at the house...I guess I'm kind of bummed that you'll be moving out." I held my breath, scared to death that I was taking things too far too soon.

She stepped forward and leaned into me again, raising a palm to my cheek. "Heartbreaker has a girl crush," she said with a wink.

A heavy blush crept up across my face, and my heart pounded in my chest as it occurred to me that I'd never walked in these shoes. I wasn't cocky about it, and I didn't have an ego problem—but I was usually the one doing the heartbreaking. Here she was, just a few weeks from breaking mine. Being in such a vulnerable position—being the one who was putting their heart in someone else's hands—was new for me, and I wasn't sure how to deal with it.

"Why was it so hard to tell me that, Jack?" She reached her arms up around my neck, tangling her fingers in my hair.

"Because...this girl showed up in my office like a firecracker and about drove me off this damn earth. And then she ended up living with me. And now I don't want to let her go."

"Who said I was letting go?" She looked bewildered at my assumption.

"Okay, I'll bite," I said. "What's a guy gotta do to keep you around?"

"Maybe the guy should try actually dating the girl in the first place."

"That's fair," I said. "I'm absolutely going to take you out on a real date. But come with my family and me on the boat for dinner first. Then you and I can go for ice cream and a walk somewhere downtown."

"An evening with you and the family…" She wasn't hesitating, just thinking.

"Yeah, you know. Girl meets family. Family meets girl. Bullshit in Bayonne type of thing." I leaned down to kiss her neck, wondering if she'd catch my reference. Thanks to Etta, I'd done my research.

"Well, Benjamin Berry. That's one hell of a first date."

"I'm trying."

"Family time," she said, nodding in agreement.

"Will you go out with me, Val Foster?" I figured a gentleman ought to ask, no matter how much kissing had already been done.

"I thought you'd never ask."

CHAPTER SIXTEEN
VAL

Early the next morning, I pulled onto Lighthouse Road, proud of myself for getting up early enough to get iced coffees for everyone working on my future home. I assumed I'd be the first one there, but when I pulled into the driveway, I found a lineup of dirty pickup trucks and a whir of generators and power tools already buzzing. I was shocked and also a bit concerned that I wasn't setting a good first impression with my new neighbors. There had to be some sort of rule about noise and general chaos so early in the morning.

"There she is!" Link stood on the roof and followed with a whistle.

"Lincoln Nicholson, do you sleep?" I stood with a tray of coffees in each hand, looking up at the man on the roof.

"I can sleep when I'm dead," he yelled.

"That scares me," I muttered under my breath. "Well, at least come down here and caffeinate before you pick up another power tool." He slid down the ladder in one smooth move and met me beside the front porch.

"I was just up there doing a last inspection of the roof. We're getting into that kitchen of yours today."

"Good! The cabinets are all in the living room. Countertops are being delivered this morning, and I'll be off to order appliances later today."

"You and I make a good team, Ms. Foster. Want a job?" He nudged my shoulder as he sipped down his coffee. "We could be the island's new Chip and Jo."

"No, sir," I laughed. "As a matter of fact, I'm in search of another kitchen, too. Commercial."

"That's above my pay grade," he said. "But I'd be willing to bet Mr. Dixon could help you out with that."

"Yeah, I suppose he could." I didn't care to elaborate about my dating life—least of all with the general contractor.

"Rumor has it you two have gotten to know each other quite well," Link suggested.

"I don't suppose that's anyone's business, Link."

"I just want to know if I can ask you out on a date or not."

"Not," I laughed. "Sorry, Link."

"Eh, it was worth a shot," he said. "Thanks for the coffee. I'll meet you in the kitchen in…" He pulled his watch up to his face—not that he could see it. Both his glasses and his watch were covered in grease, mud, and what looked to be dried-up specs of cement. The man genuinely looked as if he hadn't stopped working from the day before, or maybe even since I showed him the house the first time. "Give me twenty minutes?"

"Deal." We cheered our coffees and I laughed as we went our separate ways. The man was entertaining at the very least and, just as Daniel Dixon had suggested, proving to be the best contractor on the island. I couldn't imagine that there was a more efficient man out there.

I walked into the kitchen and sat down on the open windowsill overlooking the backyard. I pulled out my notebook with the printed kitchen plans and began to look through them. After verifying that the cabinets in the living room were correctly ordered and delivered according to the plans, I began to unpack the boxes to help Link and the crew get started. Part of me was starting to regret passing on that interior designer that Link had suggested. I'd stockpiled so many ideas that I was certain I could handle it all myself, but now that I was knee-deep in cabinetry and knobs and faucet finishes, I was rethinking my decision to pass on hiring a designer. I'd taken a look at a few portfolios online when I bought the house and quickly fell in love with Sarah Scott Designs. The company was based out of Wilmington, but I was willing to pay her to travel. I couldn't believe the work she'd done. Part of me wanted to call her and see if there was still time to get her on board, but I was sure she'd have a waitlist three years long.

I set my Spotify playlist to shuffle and tore into the boxes until a knock on the door surprised me. I paused the music just a minute or so into Montgomery Gentry's *My Town*, which I found quite fitting for the occasion.

"Anybody home?"

I popped up from in between the stacks of cabinets and boxes when I heard the voice I'd come to crave. I blushed at the deep tone of his slight southern drawl.

"What are you doing here?" I asked as Jack stepped inside and closed the door.

"I had a few minutes before I needed to be at the office. Saw your car and thought I'd stop by. How's your morning?" He kissed my cheek without hesitation—like we'd been doing the same thing forever.

"Great! I'm just unpacking the kitchen cabinets. The guys want to get started on them today." Jack looked around the room to see what guys I might have been referring to but found no one in sight. As soon as he noticed that we were alone, he pressed his lips to mine and walked us backward with shuffling feet until we ended up hidden in between the box towers.

"Jack!" I squealed as his hands touched my back beneath my shirt. "There are people all over this house!"

"Ain't nothing wrong with a man kissing his woman," he said before he kissed me again.

"You're crazy," I squealed. Just then, Link walked through the door as if he could sense a scene waiting for his interruption.

"Woah, sorry to break it up. Although if you guys would relocate your activities, I could finish up in the house and get you a nice master suite to continue in," he said, making a beeline for the kitchen.

"Nicholson, good to see you," Jack reached out to shake his hand.

"Always a pleasure, man. Thanks for the referral. Are you here to get to work?" Link swung his hat around backward and rolled out his blueprints on the makeshift table in the dining room.

"No, sir. Heading into the office. Just wanted to stop by."

"Can't imagine why," Link said without even looking up.

"Tell you what, Val. I will catch you later. Are you still up for dinner tonight?" Jack grabbed his keys from the top of another box.

"Wouldn't miss it," I said with a wave as he winked and walked out the door.

"Getting to know each other, indeed." Link stared intently at the blueprints.

"Can it, Link." I joined him at the table. "Everything looks good. The cabinets are all here exactly as ordered."

"Perfect," he said as he finally looked up at me. "We'll have this all done in a jiffy."

"You've set the bar high, Mr. Nicholson."

"I live to serve."

I grabbed my phone and my keys and headed toward the car. Lincoln Nicholson was a trip, but Daniel Dixon had been right all along—the man did great work. Later on, at the home improvement store, I triple and quadruple-checked my appliance order.

"Let's see, Ms. Foster." The older gentleman who'd helped me narrow down my choices adjusted the glasses on the bridge of his nose and scrolled on the screen in front of us. "I'll just review your order one last time. I have one under-the-counter microwave, two sets of double wall ovens, a full-size refrigerator, a full-size freezer, a forty-eight-inch electric cooktop, and a commercial production ice machine."

"That sounds right to me," I said, realizing how fortunate I was to be able to put it all on Golly's Black American Express Card. It was a good thing she never gave me access to that card in high school. We'd still be paying off the mistakes I would have racked up.

"And we're sure this is all for a house and not for Ocracoke's next big restaurant?"

"I'm sure. I just want to be able to feed...everyone."

"Ms. Foster, I don't believe you'll have a problem with that."

We went through the details for delivery and installation, read through the warranties, and shook hands before I left. "Best of luck to you!"

I pulled into Howard's Pub and felt that small town feeling again. I was planning to meet Bailey and Etta there for lunch, and when I told Bailey that I'd be heading home to get some work done on the computer, she offered to let me sit on the porch at Howard's instead. Hanging out to get work done at the local bar while they're getting ready to open for the evening was such a small-town cliche.

"Hey, girl!" Bailey was already behind the bar, knee-deep in whatever her daily list entailed. She moved in such a way that showed she could run the place with her eyes closed. It was a no-brainer that she would be building a place of her own one day.

"Let me know when you're ready to eat," I said as I settled into a table at the front. Fresh air and morning sunshine made one hell of a work environment.

The first thing on my to-do list was to let my landlord in Raleigh know that I'd be closing up shop sometime soon. I hated to leave him; I'd rented the space for years, and he'd never once raised the rent on me or given me a single problem. He emailed back immediately with condolences for losing Golly and well-wishes on my new endeavors. He was a sweet old man.

I opened a new tab on my screen and began a search for commercial properties on the island. I knew that I could easily replicate what I'd built in Raleigh; it wasn't a big show, just a small and well-oiled routine. But I couldn't shake the feeling that this was another opportunity to try something new. I'd had ideas here and there about how I might be able to grow the business, but I never made the jump. If I was relocating, I might as well do what I wanted—especially since the finances weren't exactly a concern.

The island wasn't full of strip malls and shopping centers like I was used to in the city. Instead, the bunch of mom-and-pop shops and stores that had been built decades before offered little room for imagination. The only available space that would meet my needs was a bit more than I'd had in mind.

I'd imagined leasing a space as I did in Raleigh, but the options were proving to be just as scarce as I thought they'd be. The one available commercial property was a historic bungalow that had been home to Albert's Diner since 1975 and his family since the forties.

I'd just bought a house with cash and set aside another couple hundred thousand dollars for the renovation—not to mention the brand new car. I was starting to feel foolish when it came to my inheritance.

Then again...was it foolish to invest in your business? I could keep everything as is in Raleigh and drive back once a week to fulfill orders. But would that get me anywhere? Would that allow Tucket Teas the growth it was capable of? I decided to drive past the bungalow later that day to take a look. An idea like that deserved at least a short conversation with an educated real estate agent. Daniel Dixon would have valuable input.

It didn't take much for me to zone out completely. The search for commercial property led me down a rabbit hole to a complete overhaul of my brand. I loved spending time in a creative zone. Designing logos and labels and imagining a new kitchen had me entirely removed from the bar, only brought back to life when Etta and Bailey stood in front of me, hands on their hips like they'd been waiting forever.

"Woah, sorry," I said. "In the zone…"

"No shit," Bailey said. "You ready to eat?" She pointed over to the bar where she had three plates already out with drinks.

"Absolutely. I didn't realize how hungry I was." I followed the girls over to the bar and settled in with a big whiff of the fresh blackened tuna sandwiches and slaw.

"I'll never get used to eating like this," I said.

"Perks of island life," Etta laughed. "As long as Scooter keeps fishing, anyway. So how goes it on the home-front?"

"Amazing," I mumbled with a mouthful. "Link and the guys are already finished with the roof, and they're installing kitchen cabinets today. I ordered appliances, and now I'm actually taking a bit of a house break to figure out what to do with my business.

"Oh yeah, what's the plan there?" Bailey asked.

"Well, I could keep everything the way it is and just drive back to Raleigh once a week to fill orders. But that seems a bit…"

"Ridiculous?" Etta shot.

"Yeah, a little." We all giggled. "I've been thinking about relocating the business here, giving it a good rebranding, and maybe work on growing it a bit. It's already profitable, and I don't put much work into marketing. I suppose if I did, I could grow the business substantially...with the right moves and a lot of work, anyway." I'd even thought about expanding into lemonade blends. Not to mention, a pushcart on the beach or a summer stand by the pier would make a killing.

"I think it's brilliant," Etta said. "Bailey, have you had any more thoughts on your cafe?"

"Actually...that's something I wanted to talk to you about." I sat back, unsure if I should bring up the idea before I had a single answer. "There's this old bungalow down the road, the old diner?"

"Albert Spencer's place," Bailey confirmed.

"Right, well, it's for sale." The girls looked at each other and then at me. "It would make a really nice cafe, Bailey."

"You're right; it would." She seemed to be considering the idea, and although I didn't want to press it, I went on. "I was thinking, what if we built you a cafe, and I shared the kitchen space with you to run Tucket Teas?"

The girls sat in silence for a few breaths, which made me nervous. "What do you think?"

"It's a great idea, Val, but we don't all have the money to just buy buildings and renovate houses and build businesses." My suggestion had offended her; she didn't need to say it.

"I didn't mean—" Bailey stood from her chair and took her empty plate back to the kitchen.

"I don't think it's actually about the money," Etta said.

"I mean, I didn't mean to sound like—"

"You didn't."

"I guess, you know, I've never had to worry about money. I just want to use what I have wisely. I just want to help."

"I think it has more to do with her brother. Bailey would get a loan for something like that in the blink of an eye. I think it's about moving forward with the cafe without Robert. That idea is hard for her to grapple with."

"She doesn't have to do it without him," I said, hesitant to say the next piece in my mind. "It seems like everyone will be glad when he gets home."

"I think so. Everyone except my dad, anyway."

"Why is that?"

"You know, I've never held the guys responsible for what happened. My brother carries his own guilt—not that he should. And Robert, I mean, he's always felt guilty. The first time I went to visit him, he told me that he felt like a murderer. He can't get past the idea that his hands caused his best friend's death. But even the courts didn't see it that way, not the judge, not the jury. He was charged with involuntary manslaughter— but everyone, including the judge, knew it wasn't intentional. Robert loved Jake." She was tearing up and wiped at her eyes before continuing. "I just want everyone to let Robert come home and move on with his life. He deserves peace. He deserves a future." I reached a hand across the table to my friend.

"Maybe your dad will come around. I'm sure it's just hard to see what you went through. It must feel impossible to watch his daughter suffer."

"Yeah," she sniffed. "Jake would have wanted it that way. He would have wanted everyone to give Robert grace—to forgive him and love him and stand by him as he moved on with his life. I just wish Bailey felt that way, too."

"You're a saint, Etta."

"I'm not, but I'm honored that you think so."

We finished our lunches and took our dishes into the back, where we found Bailey in the office, distracted by the computer.

"Sorry girls, I got into a beer order and got sucked in."

"Working yourself into the ground? I don't believe it," I scoffed.

"Sorry about that," she said. "About earlier, I mean."

"Shake it off, girl." I winked and smiled, thankful in part that I had friends who were honest enough to share life with me, the good stuff and the hard stuff. Everything would be better if we did it together. I always had Golly, and when she died, I felt like I'd lost that: the sharing life. I was lucky to have been blessed with another chance at it all.

ANNALEE THOMASSON

CHAPTER SEVENTEEN
VAL

I spent the rest of the afternoon on the couch with a fresh cup of coffee and a bowl full of strawberries as I finalized the rest of the paint colors for the house. Link was able to patch a few places in the hardwood floors, and I'd chosen a natural seal to finish them. I wanted to keep the house light and airy with pastels and soft whites to make use of all the light we'd get from the big new windows and my sliding glass wall.

Satisfied with the list I'd prepared to place my paint order the next day, I searched the internet far and wide to start reading about commercial properties. The online listing for the bungalow for sale mentioned cosmetic upgrades but no major renovations needed, which I hoped was true. Either way, I was starting to believe that there was nothing Lincoln Nicholson couldn't fix.

I didn't need the entire place for my own company, and the more I thought about it, the more certain I was that the bungalow would make a perfect cafe, complete with enough kitchen space to house both of us. I wanted Bailey to chase every dream and have everything she ever wanted. This building would be a great home for that.

Money was a tricky concept, and while I never wanted my recently deepened pockets to be a source of tension in my friendships, I couldn't help but think that money was best used in a way that helped others. Sure, buying the car and the house might have been a tad selfish...but I reconciled it all with the idea that I could continue to use the money to help others as well. It's what Golly would have wanted. She was more than generous, and I wanted to be the same way. She always tipped the full amount of a bill at a restaurant. She paid the cleaning ladies well and made sure they had gifts on birthdays and holidays. To my knowledge, there weren't any regular places she donated to—other than the Sacred Heart Catholic Church and anything Father Paul got her into. Instead, she made gifts here and there and everywhere, blessing people whenever she wanted and however she felt it was needed.

When I offered rooms in the house to the girls, it was never out of charity. I briefly considered that it could be perceived that way, but I didn't want that to stop me. My ideas for the bungalow felt very much the same. At the end of the day, if Bailey refused to join me, that was her decision.

The property was everything Bailey had mentioned in her idea for the cafe. It was on the south side of the island near the lighthouse. On the main stretch of road, it would be easily accessible to tourists and locals, and was even on the path to the local school. It was near the house we'd all soon live in and was already outfitted with a restaurant that had long been up and running. I imagined the place could use some updating, which the listing mentioned. But if Albert's diner was in working order, there couldn't possibly be any major flaws.

"Hey," Jack said as he walked through the door. "How was your day?" I felt myself shake with excitement as he walked inside. I was as giddy as a high school girl who'd just been winked at by the star quarterback on game day.

"My day was good; how about yours?"

"Busy, but good. Rentals are picking up a bit this week —the beginning of summer, I think. 'Tis officially the season for drunk college kids and unforeseen home repairs," he joked as he sat down at the table across from me. He undid the top few buttons on his shirt and rolled up his sleeves to reveal perfectly tanned arms that were muscular and toned in all the right ways. I'd been thinking about those same arms wrapped around me on the boat, in the house, in my imagined tea kitchen, and in every dream I'd had since he first kissed me. Jack Dixon was seeping into my bones by apparent osmosis, and there was nothing I could do to stop it; nor did I have any intention to do so. Although, I would have to address the idea with Etta sooner or later.

"I actually have an idea I wanted to talk to you about, or maybe your dad." I still didn't really know the difference between Jack and Daniel's jobs.

"Need another house?"

"Very funny," I said.

"Okay, sorry. Tell me everything."

"So, I found this bungalow…" At my introduction, his eyes widened, and he sat back in his chair. "It's Albert's Diner, do you know it?"

"Of course I know it. Albert was friends with my granddad, his daughter is friends with my mom, and they have twin sons a few years older than me." He rattled off the details about them just as he did everyone else in town.

"I'm not sure I'll ever get used to the small town thing."

"Front porches and first names…just the way it is," he laughed.

"So anyway, the bungalow is listed for sale online."

"Albert's place? For sale?" He was surprised, but I could have sworn there was a disappointment in his eyes as well.

"Ah, so the local boy doesn't know everything after all." I waggled my eyebrows at him for flair.

"That's…interesting. I'll have to ask my dad about that."

"Well, maybe we could ask him tonight. I wanted to get your—and his—thoughts on buying the place. I thought we could turn it into—"

"A cafe." He finished my thought, and a smile knocked the concern from his face.

"She's on her way, Jack. She'll get there. Sometimes people just…need a little encouragement."

"I've been encouraging her for years," he answered, seeming defeated.

"Can we talk to your dad more about it tonight?"

"Sure we can; he'd love that."

"Will it earn me any bonus points? Chatting commercial real estate with the island businessman?"

"You don't need any bonus points, Val." He smiled and stood from the table. "I'm going to change. Whenever you're ready we can head out to the marina."

"Oh, well, what should I wear?"

"You could try on a few outfits and let me be the judge…" He took my hand and pulled me from my seat at the table, led me up the stairs and into his room. It was going to be a while before I tried on any of those outfits.

An hour or so later—exhausted, showered, and dressed —we left the house for the Forsyth Marina. I hadn't been back since I'd stayed on Cole's boat my first weekend here. This time when we arrived, the parking lot was filled and left barely any space for us to park.

"What is happening here?" I unbuckled my seatbelt and looked out the window at the multiple travel buses, vans, and the crowd on the dock.

"Our friend did some work for Google a while back and managed to get their annual retreat transferred here from Charleston. They have a few hundred people coming into town over the next few weeks. The first round got into town just after you stayed on the boat, actually."

"No wonder I haven't heard a peep from Cole," I chuckled.

"Yeah, he's been sweating a little bit," Jack said as he backed into a tight space. "I enjoy watching him freak out, though. It's entertaining."

"That's mean." I laughed and stuck my tongue out at him. *Boys.*

"Oh, I'm just playing. The day you catch any of us guys *not* giving each other some form of hell is the day you need to worry."

"That's fair," I said. "Jack, I can't open my door." He'd parked so close to the next car over that I wouldn't be able to get out.

"Well, it was the last speck of land on the property." He pulled the key from the ignition and adjusted in his seat. "Just slide on over here," he said as he reached for me.

"Jack!" I squealed as he grabbed my hips and pulled me over the center console and into his lap. "You're crazy."

"I'm sorry! You're just sitting there all gorgeous, looking so damn kissable." I sat straddled across his lap with my hands on his shoulders as he reached up and pulled my face to his for one last kiss before we stepped back into the real world. Our time together had become something I didn't recognize—when it was just the two of us, we were goofy and flirty, joked around, and had our hands all over each other. We spoke up and out about what was on our minds, and we did it all so easily that it seemed like we'd been that way forever.

It still baffled me how quickly things had fallen together with Jack. We hadn't put a label on our relationship, and I hadn't even brought it up to my friends. We had more talking to do ourselves, but the way he kissed me told me everything I needed to know. In any other situation, I would have cautioned someone who moved in with a guy she'd just met and let herself fall in love after a few short weeks. But I knew how I felt, and I knew Jack Dixon. Whatever was going on between us was real, and it was safe, and it was right. Whatever it was, I just hoped it would last. I'd said too many goodbyes already.

"Come on," I said as I pulled away from his kiss. "Your family is either watching us or waiting on us. Either way, we better get out of the car."

"Do we have to?" His hands gripped my thighs, inching closer and closer to the shredded hem of my blue jean shorts. I grabbed his hands and kissed his cheek.

"Save some for later." I opened the driver's side door and leaned to get out.

"You're killing me," he groaned as he stepped out behind me and adjusted his shorts. He cleared his throat and shifted his tee shirt over his shoulders, gathering himself before we walked down to the dock. No sense in giving everyone a show.

"Remember the first time I found you here?"

"Very well," I said. "Although I'm not as worried about you seeing me naked these days."

"Me either," he said as he slapped my backside.

"Jack!" He raised his hands.

"Okay, okay. I'll be good." He stepped up beside me and walked us down to his parents' boat.

"Uncle Shak!" Tate—dressed in brown leather loafers, a pinstripe swimsuit, a life vest, and a white bucket hat—jumped up from the boat and onto the dock.

"What's up, Gilligan?" Jack ruffled a hand on Tate's head.

"Who's Gilligan?"

"Nevermind," Jack laughed. "Did you bring your fishing pole?"

"Sure did. Pop even stopped on the way so we could get a bucket of live shrimp. Look!" Just as quickly, he jumped back into the boat and ran toward a cooler in the back.

"Hi, Mr. Dixon," I said as I took Jack's hand and stepped into the boat.

"Oh, Val. It's Daniel. And I'm sure you remember my wife, Grey." I reached to shake her hand but was met with a hug instead.

"We're so glad you could join us, sweetheart." She walked back to the cooler just as Tate pulled a bucket from inside. "Can I get you a drink? I've got sweet tea, lemonade, and coke."

"Don't forget the grown-up juice," Tate said confidently, standing next to her. "Look, Val. This is our shrimp." He opened the lid and shoved the bucket toward me as shrimp jumped up and down in the water.

"Wow, they really are alive!"

"Better for catching the good fish," Daniel said.

"Grown-up juice?" Jack asked as he took Tate and the bucket up toward the front.

"It's our new description of alcohol. Apparently, he told one of my co-workers last week that mommy likes tequila." Everyone erupted in laughter, and Jack high-fived Tate, who looked mighty proud of himself. "So we've decided to call it grown-up juice. I'd like to keep the adult explanations to my four-year-old at a minimum."

"That's fair," I laughed. "I'll have a sweet tea, Grey. Thank you." She poured from a fresh pitcher over a glass of ice and slipped it into a cover that looked custom-made for her glassware. That was something my Golly would have done. In fact, I was surprised I'd never seen such a thing.

"Everyone, take a seat, and we'll head out." Daniel shifted the boat into gear and took us out of the marina toward the open water ahead of us. Once he was cleared of the docks, he picked up speed, and I settled a bit more into the bench seat next to Jack. Etta, Tate, and Grey sat in the back. As we moved faster, the wind got louder and muffled out the giggling coming from Tate, who was still holding onto his shrimp bucket, excited to catch a fish.

Jack reached his arm up and around me to hold onto the railing. I didn't know if he actually wanted to hold on or if he was just getting closer, but I leaned in, happy to have an excuse for my being so near to him. Although I got the impression from Etta's close attention that we weren't doing a great job at hiding whatever was going on between us. Not that I thought it was necessary.

As we drove, my emotions were bittersweet, but this time they didn't overwhelm me to the point of tears. I wondered if that was a sign that I was healing. I'd never had a boat full of family, or even that many people at the dinner table for that matter. Sharing a simple meal with my parents, a sister, and a nephew was something I would have loved growing up. The experience may have been trivial to some, but it was new to me. If a boat ride like this was typical for them, I was already desperately hoping to be invited again.

After about ten minutes, we slowed to a halt at the edge of the marsh. "Is this where we're eating dinner?"

"We can eat dinner anywhere," Jack said as he stood and pulled his sweatshirt over his head. "This is where we fish!"

"Yeah!" Tate jumped in the air with a fist held high in excitement. Jack lifted the bench seat across from me and pulled out Tate's child-sized fishing rod, a larger one of his own, and a tackle box.

Etta sat next to me, and we watched as Jack helped Tate put a shrimp on his hook and cast it into the water. Watching Tate carefully, he put another shrimp on his own hook and set the pole into some kind of grip on the edge of the boat.

"Want to give it a try?" He said, turning to face me with the smile I'd come to crave. I could feel Etta nudge my elbow, but she never said a word.

"Oh, I...I'm fine. You boys look like you have it under control."

"Nonsense!" Daniel said. "First trip out calls for a line in the water—and if history serves as a good reference, you'll catch one, too. This boat is said to be a good luck charm, you know."

Jack stood with his hands out, like he didn't have a say. He joined everyone in egging me on.

"Okay, but you'll have to show me. I have no idea what I'm doing."

"Come," Jack said, "and let the master show you how it's done." He sounded like Dumbledore, about to unleash a tough lesson on Harry.

I stepped up to the edge of the boat, and Jack situated himself behind me. He stood behind me with an arm on either side, putting the fishing pole in my hand and wrapping his left hand around mine. Then he reached his right hand around to the reel."

"You see how all that water out there is flat," he pointed ahead of us, "except for that choppy circle right there?"

"I see," I nodded.

"That's where the fish are." The excitement came out of my mouth as a giggle. Who knew fishing would have me so on edge? In all fairness, it was probably the fisherman who made me feel that way and not the fish. "So you're going to face where you want it to go," he said as he laid a hand on my hip and shifted me around a bit. "Put your thumb right here under this button—that's what controls the reel." His soft but steady grip felt perfect around my hands. He moved my thumb to press the button, and the shrimp dropped a few inches.

"Oh!"

"It's okay; it's just letting go of the line. He won't go anywhere." Jack laughed, seeming entertained with our lesson.

He reached around to the rod with his other hand, surrounding my face with his strong arms and holding me into his chest. "We lift it up and back behind us…"

I turned to make sure there wasn't anyone behind us.

"Remind me to tell you about the time Etty hooked my ear on a cast out," he said.

"No way," I said, shocked.

"Then, you just toss it and release it." He made the motion and cast the line out into the water ahead of us, directly into the center of the choppy part he'd aimed for. "Then you just reel him in nice and slow until you feel a tug."

He made all the motions and explained everything he did without taking his hands from mine. Suddenly, a tug on the line filled me with anticipation.

"Was that it? Is that a fish?" I was so excited to see what we'd caught that my hands shook.

"Let's see," he said, starting to reel the line back in. I held the fishing pole with both hands, and he held mine and reeled at the same time. The muscles in his forearms flexed as he moved the rod where he wanted it, pulling our catch in a little at a time.

"What is it?" I shrieked as Etta, their parents, and Tate crowded around us.

"Well, hot damn!" Daniel cheered. "The legend lives on!"

"That's a big fish," Jack said, still reeling.

"We did it? We caught a big one?"

"You did. Look!" He gave me the rod, knelt down on the bench, and reached into the water with a net to scoop up our fish.

"That's a keeper, for sure," Daniel said.

"How do you know?" I asked.

"Come here," Jack said, carrying the net to the back of the boat. At the cooler, he laid the fish down on the lid—which I noticed had a ruler etched into it. "Twenty-five inches," he said. "Definitely a keeper."

"Yay, Val!" Tate jumped and clapped his hands. "Cook him up!"

"Let's get a picture with your first catch," Daniel said.

"Want to hold him?" Jack asked, raising the fish toward me.

"Oh, no. No way. Nope. You uh…you look like you've got it just fine right there." It was cool, that fish. But I didn't need to touch it.

"Here, turn around and smile." Etta stepped in front of us and raised her phone. "Hold the fish up, Jack."

He stood behind me and held the fish up in front of us, surrounding me with his strong arms again. I reached to help him hold the fish, but couldn't bring myself to wrap my hands around the slimy ball of scales. Instead, my hands settled on the forearms that had just helped me reel in my first fish. I heard the shutter sound click on Etta's phone, and smiled uncontrollably. He really was a good catch. The fish was too.

CHAPTER EIGHTEEN
JACK

My dad pulled out a knife and lit the grill faster than I'd seen in a while. "Want to learn to skin a fish?" He'd taught me, Etty, and even Tate how to catch and cook our own fish when we were each four years old, and he looked as if he was about to impart his wisdom on Val.

"Oh, I absolutely could not," she said, stepping backward as if she had somewhere safe to go. Mom and Etty laughed, and when Val looked to them for an explanation, Etty gave it.

"It wasn't as much of a question as it was an indoctrination," Etta said.

"What's a doctor nation, mama?"

"*Indoctrination*, Tater." I rested my hand on his head. "It's a way to welcome a new friend."

"Is Val your friend or Mama's friend?" The most innocent child had a way of stirring up trouble, and Etty seemed to enjoy it.

"She was Mama's friend from college, baby," Etty said. "And now that she moved here, she's Uncle Jack's friend, too."

"And Aunt Bay?"

"Yes, baby. She's Aunt Bay's friend too."

"Hey, Val? Are you going to be my friend, too?" He stood in front of her with eyes that could have earned him damn near anything.

"I would love to be your friend, Tate." She crouched down to him, and they bumped knuckles like old pals.

"Well, all of my friends know how to cut up a fish," he said after his tiny little fist bump. A collective *ooooh* came from the rest of us on the boat, and Val stood, squared her shoulders, and joined my father at the cutting board.

"How do you ever say no to him?" She joked quietly.

"It's hard," my dad said.

I sat back with a beer and watched as the greatest man I knew taught Val how to cut her fish. He explained his every move as he slipped the knife underneath the skin, down the backbone, above the fin, and all the way to the tail. He came back, separating the meat from the bones and up through the rib cage. Val cringed with every slice but never backed away. Dad continued, separating the skin from the meat, flipped the fish over, and handed the knife to Val.

"Oh, my God," she mumbled quietly, biting her bottom lip.

"Your turn." She reached to grab the fish. "That's it, grab him right there by the head. And be careful now—that knife is sharp." She looked up at me for just a second but went back to her fish and took a deep breath. And I have to tell you —I really didn't think she'd do it. But for the next ten minutes, I watched as my Dad walked her through the other side of the fish, helping when she needed it but letting her do the work. A few times, I thought she might throw up over the side of the boat, but she'd just shake her head, clear her throat, and get back to it. If she was trying to impress me, it worked.

"There she is!" Dad held what was left of the fish in the air. "Want to toss the scraps back in?"

"That's so gross…" She laughed.

"That's good eating," Dad said, handing her the carcass. She reached to grab it by the head just as my dad had, and swung it into the water before turning back to us with her hands out in front of her.

"Now what?"

"Now we eat!" Dad gave her a high five and walked past her with the fresh filet to the grill, but Val stood stiff with wide and uneasy eyes. I burst out laughing when I realized what she was thinking.

"You can wash your hands off right here," I said, walking to the rinsing station dad had installed on the side of the boat.

"That was disgusting. I feel so…ruined. And so proud of myself at the same time." She reached for the towel I held out to her, and I held onto her hand when she took it.

"You did a really good job, though. Maybe you can come with me to Big Rock next month. I'm my dad's first mate. You can be mine."

"Count me in, Captain." She winked and tossed the towel at my chest.

Back at the cooler, I poured us some drinks while dad grilled her catch, and mom unwrapped the side dishes she'd brought. Mom always packed a bag full of peanut butter and jelly sandwiches too—just in case we didn't catch anything. Dad always argued that he'd starve before he admitted to not catching a single fish. I usually ate the sandwiches anyway.

By the time we finished eating, Tate had fallen asleep in my mom's lap. Etty and Val cleaned up our dinner while Dad and I went to the front of the boat to clean up the mess. We worked in a routine that had been well established, talking while we moved around each other to a steady rhythm.

"I like her," he said quietly as he hosed off the cutting boards.

"That's good, Dad."

"I mean, you know. If you were wondering what I thought about your new, uh…roommate."

"I wasn't. It's really not a big deal, Dad." I hung my head and kept on working, although every bit of me knew that the way I felt about Val was in fact a huge deal. And my dad's approval, though it didn't surprise me, meant a lot.

"Maybe not yet, son, but you're going to marry that girl. I know it. Your mom knows it. Inviting her to dinner was Etty's idea, you know."

"She's nosy."

"She's your sister. That shouldn't shock you." He laughed and wiped off the seats and the surface around us before stepping back toward the helm.

"Hey, Dad?" He turned to face me. "Thanks." He nodded with the same content smile he'd given me when I scored a goal, reeled in a good catch, got into law school, and a variety of other things.

Dad took it slow on the ride back to the dock, trying not to wake Tate. There was nothing like a nap on the boat. I remembered doing the same thing as a kid and still enjoyed it as an adult. Etty sat to my left and Val to my right while Dad brought us all home. Another family dinner on the boat had come and gone, and this time it felt as if my family was a little more complete.

We said a short and quiet goodnight as Etty buckled Tate into his car seat, and they all climbed in to head home. Val and I walked back to my truck which had since been given just a bit more space in the parking lot.

"At least I don't have to climb over you this time," she said. "I smell like..." She pulled her hands up for a sniff. "...Fish scales, and...guts...and...gross."

"I can't believe you did that," I laughed. "I really thought you were gonna tell my dad where to put that fish."

"Well, you see." She stepped toward me slowly with her hands clasped together. "I met this guy recently, and I've been looking for ways to impress him." She stopped right in front of me.

"He was already impressed, Val." I smiled and nearly leaned in to kiss her when my parents drove by, waving at the windows. Val turned around quickly and waved back, and we both got into the truck without saying another word about it.

On the way out of the marina, a familiar chain of piano notes came through the speakers. I'd heard *Sunday Drive* many times before, and I loved the song. But now, with Val in the seat next to me and the future looking a little different, I think I felt the words of the song deep in my bones. It was as if I wasn't ready for a Sunday Drive of my own until I had the right person to share it with.

Driving home that night, I watched the world through newly opened windows. The trees lined up on the side of Irvin

Garrish Highway were more than familiar but played a different pattern now. I'd taken this path home a million times before, but I'd never felt so eager to get home as I did having her with me. Home meant something new these days. Home was worth getting back to. It seemed like the world I'd known had changed; nothing would ever be the same again now that I knew Val Foster—now that I was in love with her.

I'd come to realize that no matter how much time you get, it's never enough. Life was always too short, and all we really had was the moment we were in and the ones we were in it with. I reached over into her lap to grab hold of her hand, and I smiled as she wrapped her fingers in mine, tangling herself in me. I'd have driven forever to keep her hand in mine like that.

No sooner than the song was finished, we pulled into the driveway. Going home felt different with her. I'd gone home alone for so long that I barely knew how to do anything else. I hadn't even considered the idea that one day I wouldn't be alone when I went home at the end of the night.

At the door, Val turned around. "Jack, is that what your childhood was like?"

"What do you mean?" I waited in front of her, trying to figure out the emotion that filled her face. It wasn't sadness, or question, or concern. It almost looked like she wanted to reminisce but couldn't.

"Boat rides. Your dad teaching you...outdoorsy things. Your mom rocking a little one to sleep. Peanut butter and jelly sandwiches tucked in the cooler just in case."

"You noticed those," I smiled.

"It's a way she shows she loves him—making sure he has a meal, even when he plans to fix his own."

"Yeah, my childhood was exactly like that." I smiled as I briefly reminisced on the life I'd been given and the way I was raised. "That and...treehouses, a couple of broken bones, and a few stitches. A burnt Turkey every year when my Dad tried to deep fry it, and a good turkey in the oven in the kitchen—"

"Just in case," she laughed.

"Just in case," I nodded and continued. "Hot apple pie that my mom made every Christmas morning. Big Rock with my dad every summer."

"A whole family," she added. All I'd said, and that's what she'd heard: I'd always had a family.

"The luckiest." I leaned down to kiss her cheek, knowing exactly what her emotion was now. I couldn't fix the past. I couldn't bring back the one family member Val hung on to so desperately. But I saw a different future for her, and I think she was starting to see it, too.

ANNALEE THOMASSON

CHAPTER NINETEEN
VAL

I washed my hands six times, nearly scrubbing the skin right off. I could still feel the fish scales and guts on my fingertips, and I barely wanted to walk through the house, let alone wash my hair until it was all thoroughly removed. I'd done a lot of new things recently, and as gross as it was, I was proud of myself for learning how to catch and filet a fish.

I pulled my brown leather journal from the nightstand and opened it to the last page I'd written. It was the day Golly died. Since then, my journal had remained closed. I hadn't had all that much to say or all that much I wanted to look back on and remember. Until today, that is. I turned the page, grabbed my pen, settled against my pillows, and took a deep breath.

Well, hey.

Today I did something I never want to forget. I would have laughed with Golly at the dinner table over this. She would have made me show her the pictures the next day to prove it. Today I caught a fish, and then I held him by the head and cut him up just right so that Daniel could throw my catch on the grill.

I wasn't going to do it, but Jack stood there looking so handsome and so proud of me that I just couldn't say no. I wanted him to see that I was willing to do anything...anything reasonable, of course. That, and I had some underlying intentions to impress the rest of his family. I think I already had Etta on my side, but Jack and his parents could still be influenced. The way I see it, learning how to cut up that fish earned me some solid bonus points with everyone.

Jack said I never *needed* those bonus points. It's not like I'm running on a deficit. I like to think I'm a hell of a catch—no pun intended. I'm smart. I'm interesting. I'm not afraid of a challenge. And today, I proved to myself and to them that I could do new things. Sure, the whole *buy a house that's falling apart and fix it* thing was new and challenging. But I haven't finished that one yet...we can't call that one a success just yet.

But the fish? Success. Jack watched me like he knew I could do it the entire time. His father never took his eyes off my hands and the knife. His mother sat on the bench, enjoying the show. And for a second, I felt it. That feeling of...being surrounded. Having a family. I always had Golly and even Pop for a long while. But it was always just the three of us, and in recent years it was just the two of us. There's something different about being surrounded by such a crowd.

Everyone offers something different. Jack radiated confidence. His father; pride. His mother; a place of rest. Etta; an entertained sibling. And me? I was feeling so many things all at once.

I like it here. My life—until now—has been a puzzle cut into just a few large pieces. But the longer I stay here in Ocracoke, the more I realize that puzzles with a thousand pieces are cool too. I still fit— differently, of course—but I fit. I belonged with Golly in Raleigh. But my story didn't end there.

I can belong here too. At least...I think I might.

I tucked my journal back into the nightstand and got into the shower, satisfied with the day. Some might have called it just a typical day, but to me it felt like so much more.

When I finished and dressed, I returned to the living room to find Jack relaxed on the couch with his feet propped on the coffee table. He had a drink in one hand, the remote in the other, and a movie on the screen.

"Hey," he said as he adjusted in the corner of the couch. "Want to join me?" He lifted the edge of the blanket over his lap, and I climbed in close. When I got settled against him, he tossed the blanket back over us and stretched his arm around my shoulders, pulling me in.

"Jack, what kind of tree was your treehouse in?"

"Oh, man. I think it was…" He ran his fingers through my hair while he thought. "Yeah, it's the live oak trees on the back of the property. Why do you ask?"

"I never had a treehouse. I was thinking, when the house is finished, maybe we could build one for Tate."

"That sounds awesome. He would love that."

"The kid deserves a treehouse."

"We're going to need to work on a landscape plan first. That backyard is a jungle."

"I was thinking maybe you could help me with that. I know there are a few big trees back there, but I don't know what they are. Do you think we could take a look at the yard tomorrow?" I was sad but excited. Fulfilled but dreaming. Settled but curious. It was all overwhelming. These days, rather than feeling embarrassed when I was overwhelmed with emotion, I felt safe. I could feel everything with Jack, and he would sit there with me while I processed through it all.

"I'd love to." He kissed my head and continued to play with my hair. "Did you get all the fish scales off of you?"

"Yes," I giggled. "I hope you enjoyed the show. I can't say I'm eager to do that again."

"How about this—you catch the fish, I'll cut them."

"Deal. And I'll cook, you do the dishes." I turned to look at him.

"I'll kill the bugs, and you handle the decorating."

"Pffft. I'll take care of everything inside if you promise to take care of everything outside...and every creature that belongs outside."

"Deal," he laughed. "Val..."

"Hm?" I laid my head on his shoulder and reached for his glass to take a sip. "Delicious."

"Val, I..." He sat up and adjusted in his seat. "I wanted to talk to you about something."

"What's up?" Our conversation had been so lighthearted that I didn't know how to feel about the seriousness that had just fallen across his face.

"I've just been wanting to...well, I just want you to know this." He smiled, which helped to ease my feelings that something was wrong. "When I invited you to stay here, it was a temporary thing. You know...until your house was...livable."

"I know," I said, worried that I'd been misreading what was happening between us. "I...I mean, the kitchen is going in, so I suppose I could move over there this week if—"

"No, no. Val, that's not what I meant."

"Okay," I sat up and turned to face him. "What's wrong?"

"No...nothing is wrong. The thing is, Val. I know you are excited to have Bailey and Etta move in with you, and I think it's a great idea. I know they're excited, too. And I think it's a really good use of that house."

"But?"

"I, uh, just wanted you to know that...I'm excited for you, and I can't wait to see what you do with the place. But I'm really going to miss having you here. I can't say I'm too excited for you to...you know...to leave."

Leaving had been the plan all along, but it hadn't exactly been at the top of my mind recently. When I first moved in here, I felt an urgency to move out and get out of Jack's way. But now that I'd been here a while and had gotten settled in his house and with *him*, I wasn't exactly eager to leave him either.

"You know, I hadn't really thought about that," I said. "I don't really...want to—I mean, I don't really want to leave you."

"I just wanted you to know how I felt. I wanted you to know that...I love having you here. That my house is your house. Because I..." He stopped to clear his throat. "I just... I've fallen in love with you." He held back a smile and a laugh caught in his throat as if he was embarrassed. "And I...well...I just wanted you to know that."

"I've fallen in love with you too," I said, smiling.

He leaned his forehead into mine and rested his hand in my hair, rubbing his thumb across my cheek. He kissed me as he leaned me backward, falling on top of me on the couch and pulling me into his side as we settled in. As I snuggled in closer against his chest, he wrapped his arms tight around me and tangled his legs around mine.

"So, what do we do?" He asked.

227

"I don't know," I said. "Just...don't go anywhere."

"Deal," he said, kissing the top of my head again. "I picked your favorite movie." I looked at the screen and realized that the freeze frame was paused at the very beginning of *How To Lose A Guy In 10 Days*.

"Oh, my favorite!"

"I have my sources," he said. "Etta had me watch it recently...she said it was your favorite."

"And you're willing to suffer through it again for me?" I was impressed.

"I'd do anything for you, Val...also I might have watched it the other day after Etta told me it was your favorite."

"Ahhh. That's how you knew about Bullshit in Bayonne."

"Guilty."

We stayed there together and watched the movie from start to finish; he never even complained. I'd never felt as comfortable as I did on that couch, in his arms. I never wanted it to end.

I didn't need to ask him where we stood; it was clear. What I did need to figure out was what the future looked like for us. I wasn't going to leave this island, but we'd quickly established a home of our own while I worked to renovate the cottage on Lighthouse Road. I came to Ocracoke as an orphan and had since managed to find myself belonging in two places at once.

"Jack, do you think two people can really fall in love in ten days?" The ending credits scrolled along the television screen as my head rose and fell with the deep breaths in his chest.

"I fell in love with you faster than that," he said.

"You did?"

He kissed the top of my head and twirled his fingers through my hair. "You drove me absolutely insane for a few hours."

"Thanks?" I laughed, unsure of how to take that.

"But then I learned that Bailey loved you. And my sister loved you. After that, I was a lost cause. And now, I wouldn't make it without you. I want you to drive me crazy every day, Val."

"Challenge accepted," I said, giggling as he kissed my neck and shifted around me. We fell asleep there on the couch listening to the soundtrack that played at the end of the movie.

I woke up the next morning wrapped up in exactly the same position: secure in his arms. Except now we were in his bed, and the sunrise was starting to peek through his window and land on us. His curtains swayed in the breeze from the crack at the windowsill, and my heart and mind flooded with an overwhelming sense of calm. I was right where I was meant to be—with him. I'd need to figure out where I was physically going to live, but I'd never question again where my home was. My home was with Jack Dixon.

ANNALEE THOMASSON

CHAPTER TWENTY
JACK

We stayed in bed a lot longer than we should have that morning, but not for a single minute of extra sleep. After a few rounds of each other, a shower, and breakfast, we left my house for the day.

"Well, I'm getting into the office a bit later than usual this morning, but I think I can still swing a trip to the house later this afternoon if you want to take a look at the backyard."

"I'd love that, Jack. Thank you." She lifted herself onto the tips of her toes to plant a kiss on my cheek. I never wanted to leave for work any other way.

She took off for Lighthouse Road, and I drove the other way toward my office, trying to think of an excuse to tell my dad and Aunt Cora about my late arrival.

"There he is," Aunt Cora said as I walked inside. My dad reached into his back pocket to pull out his wallet, removing a twenty-dollar bill and slapping it down on the desk in front of my aunt. "Thank you very much," she said.

"You bet money on me?" I asked as I set my briefcase down on the couch. "I'm appalled."

"Oh, please. I knew full well you'd be late at best." Dad chuckled.

231

"Actually, he bet you wouldn't show up at all today. I told him I had confidence in you. My bet was that you'd be here before lunch."

"Thank you, Aunt Cora."

"I take it you had a good night," Dad asked, wedging his way into my love life one aggressive step at a time.

"Yes, dad. Dinner on the boat with y'all was fun. We should do it again soon."

"Mhm, that's absolutely *not* the part of the night I was asking about."

"I know." I laughed and stepped into my office to get to work.

Later that afternoon, I closed everything up on my computer and left for Val's house. She hadn't answered my text message from earlier in the day, which was unlike her, but I knew they were busy installing the kitchen appliances. We had plans to talk about the backyard landscaping, one of the final pieces she had in mind for the renovation.

I couldn't believe my eyes when I pulled into the driveway. The once crumbling stack of a home was now somewhat resembling a grand estate. The exterior had been painted a fresh bright white, and the shutters a deep hunter green. Empty flower boxes sat at the ledge of each window, and unfinished wood surfaced the stairs and the front porch. Val emerged from the front door, looking like she'd just stepped out of heaven.

"You're here!" She clapped her hands as she ran toward me in the front yard. I caught her in my arms, smelling the orange and vanilla notes of the shampoo I loved so much. "I missed you," she said just before she kissed me. I loved the way she kissed me—unrestrained as if we'd been together all along and the whole world knew about us. At this rate, the whole world would know soon enough. If she kept kissing me like *that* when Lord knows who was around us, the island wireless would take care of the news for us.

"I can't believe this, Val. I can't believe how much has been finished."

"I told you, Link Nicholson is a miracle worker. That or he dabbles in wizardry of some sort. I haven't decided yet. Actually, I'm still a little worried that it's cocaine." My hands settled on her shoulders as she stood in front of me, leaning back into my chest. We stood there lost in admiration of the home she'd created. "It's not finished, of course, but I'd love to show you around."

"Oh, you have to," I said. "Show me everything." She took my hand and pulled me forward, leading me into the project that had brought her so much happiness in recent months. I knew before we even walked inside that one day, this place would be our home.

She stopped on the front porch and clasped her hands together. "So, this morning, I put these flower boxes up on the windows. I don't know what I want to put in here yet; I just thought it needed a little something. I was thinking about maybe a swing on that side and some wood rocking chairs on this side. I'll probably want to plant another tree in the front here, too. It needs some shade."

"Sounds amazing," I said as I looked around to imagine what she'd suggested. She went to the front door and pushed it open.

"Are you ready to see the inside?" I followed her over the threshold and about fell back outside when I took it all in. The place had been refinished top to bottom. The restored wood floors, the opened-up main level, and the grand staircase in the center of the home. It was all brand new, and it was way more than I could have imagined.

"So, the family room is much brighter now." She spun around in the center of the floor. "I want to add some built-ins along this far wall over here and a giant sectional around here with two chairs over there." She pointed as she described where each piece of furniture would go. "On the other side of the staircase, there is what used to be the formal dining room. I think I'm going to turn it into a bit of a playroom for Tate for now though, because of the kitchen."

"What do you mean?"

"Come on," she said with wide eyes, tugging my hand to follow her. "Look."

We walked around the staircase past the powder room and through the new butler's pantry into the largest kitchen I'd ever seen.

"Holy hell," I said, mouth dropped wide in awe. "This is…Val. I can't believe this."

"I hope you like it," she said quietly as she rested her hands on the center island, watching me take it all in. "The reason I'm not going to use the dining room quite yet is that we built this kitchen with an open space large enough for a huge table of its own." She pointed to the area between the kitchen and the porch. "Watch this." She walked over to the edge of the kitchen to flip what I assumed was a light switch, except the lights didn't change. Instead, the large window that was nearly an entire glass wall began to move and fold as it opened across the back of the house. The kitchen, dining area, and back porch became one large room as the wall settled neatly behind the refrigerator. "What do you think?"

"Oh my God, Val. It's…" I had no words. The place was almost unbelievable. It was absolutely stunning and made for entertaining. "What are you going to do with a place like this?" I laughed.

"Well, I love those dinners at Glenn's place. I was hoping that with a kitchen like this…a whole house like this, I mean…I could do a lot of entertaining." She rested her chin in her hand on the countertop. "I've always dreamed of having enough friends and family to fill a home. And these days, I'm starting to feel like it might actually be possible. One day."

"You have that right now, Val. You have all of us," I said, grabbing her waist and lifting her up to sit on the counter in front of me. I rested my hands on her thighs and took another look around.

"I know it hasn't been long, and we're…you know… new."

"Eh, it's been more than ten days," I joked.

"Yes," she laughed. "That's true." She looked around and wiped a tear from her cheek. "Bailey and Etta are going to move in here with me, but we each have our own space. And, I mean, I need to show you the upstairs still, but the master suite is…well. Just remember, this place was huge. I've tried to make really good use of the space."

"Oh, I definitely want to see the master suite." I slipped my hands underneath the edge of her shorts.

"Easy, slugger." She lifted her hands up and laid them on my shoulders. "But the master suite…I think that you would love it." She took a breath before continuing quickly as if to get it all out before I could argue. "And I know you probably never dreamed of living with a bunch of girls, least of all living with your own sister. But the place is huge, and I really think we could still have privacy of our own. So,"

"Yes."

"Yes?"

"Hell yes." I lightly touched my lips to hers, rubbing my hands along her legs. "I told you I wasn't ready to let you go, and I'm still not. I never will be. If you want to live in my house, good. If you want me to move into this house with you, good. Whatever it is, as long as we're doing it together, then my answer is *yes*. Hell yes."

"Oh my god," her eyes widened. "Oh my God!"

"You excited?"

"I'm so excited!" She wiggled around in my arms. "But one more thing…"

"Anything."

"Let's go see where we can build a treehouse."

CHAPTER TWENTY-ONE
VAL

Rather than rush into my new house as soon as it was livable, Jack and I decided to stay at his place for a while. Not shockingly, Link had finished the work at an extraordinary pace, taking it from shambles to show-stopper in three months flat. I'd decided his blood type was chaos; I'm pretty sure the man never slept. Although funny enough, I did walk in on him getting to know a woman quite well on my kitchen floor. Turns out Jack's concerns about the contractor were valid. The poor woman was shocked to see me; apparently, he'd told her that it was *his* place at the bar the night before. It was a less than pleasant wake-up call, I suppose. She grabbed her clothes and ran out the door before Link could come up with an excuse. When I looked to him for a good one, he didn't even try. I told him he was responsible for bleaching my brand new tile floor, and he did.

I'd had the keys to the place for a month now. The walls had been painted, the utilities were up and running, the landscaping was finished—complete with a freshly cleaned-out backyard lined with small but growing magnolia trees—and we were just three weeks shy of calling the place home. We were waiting to move in until Etta had everything packed up in her place. She didn't want to stress Tate out any more than a move already would, so we were hoping to pull the switch off nearly overnight at the very end of her lease.

Jack and I explained our plans to live together, which was received exceptionally well by everyone. Etta and Bailey finally admitted that they knew about me and Jack all along, but in an effort to be the supportive sisters they were, they kept their distance and let us do our thing.

After work every day, Jack came home to help me pick out furniture and final touches, all of which were set to be delivered in the following weeks. I'd closed up shop in Raleigh and brought all of my equipment back to Jack's place, fulfilling orders on our kitchen counter every Wednesday evening. It wasn't a permanent solution, but it was good enough for the time being. I'd tabled my ideas for moving forward with my ideas at work until everything with the house was settled.

I'd taken on so many new things all at once, but the more time went by, the more I realized that most of my ideas were just a response to grief. I needed something to do, things that would distract me from missing Golly. Eventually, Jack helped me decide that I was plenty satisfied with the house and moving and that I could let the business wait patiently on the back burner until I could give it the attention it deserved. That, and the bungalow I'd looked at had sold relatively quickly. I took it as a sign that I shouldn't rush into another big purchase quite so soon. Tucket Teas was doing just fine, and it would continue to do so until I was ready to make a change.

"What on earth did you order?" Jack walked into the house after work, laughing at me as I sat on the couch, trying to figure out what he might have been referring to.

"Depends," I said. "How many boxes?

"I stopped counting at twenty-six. Large rectangular boxes from Ikea."

"Oops," I smiled. "It's possible that my tea ingredients have been delivered to the new house then." It was an easy mistake these days, with as much as we had going on at so many different locations.

"Good Lord," he laughed, collapsing into the couch. "I'll rally the troops. We'll get it all switched. We'll probably owe the boys some beer, though."

"That's easy," I agreed. Jack made his phone call to the guys and came back inside, crashing into the couch with me.

"So I've been thinking. Once the house is done, you were talking about moving on to restructuring Tucket Teas. What if you and I...and maybe Link, if you don't hate him yet...find a space and go ahead and build that kitchen." I sat up and listened, surprised at what I was hearing. "We don't have to tell Bailey about it. We can just build whatever you need as far as getting a kitchen approved for your business. Then, down the road, if she wants to move forward with the cafe, the space will be ready for her."

"Jack, that's such a good idea." I stopped to kiss him again. "I don't know where we're going to find a space, though. This island seems to get a little smaller every day."

"Give it time. My dad tends to be a miracle worker."

"You're incredible, you know that?" I turned to slide up and over his lap.

"I try," he said as he grabbed my waist and pulled me in. "I could kiss you forever, you know that?"

"Show me." I giggled, and he wrapped his arms underneath my hips to hold me close as he stood from the couch. I squealed and laughed again as he kissed my neck and walked us upstairs to his bedroom. So many things had changed since we'd first met. I couldn't get away from him fast enough back then, and these days I couldn't stand even the clothes between us.

I was in love with Jack Dixon. We'd made great use of the months we'd already spent together, and the future was only looking brighter.

CHAPTER TWENTY-TWO
JACK

Val thought I was kidding when I'd suggested she join me at Big Rock as my first mate. The tournament had been popular for generations, and my dad and I had participated each year since I was in elementary school. It started as a trip that my dad and his cousin Rhett used to take with their fathers. They'd bring me along, but for the most part, the two of them did all the heavy lifting. As I grew up—and got stronger—I became more useful and helped them out.

Each year the crowd grew, and eventually, the boat did too. This year the team consisted of Val and me, my mom and dad, Hank, Glenn, Etta, and Bailey. I never asked how, but my dad managed to get us onto a seventy-four-foot sport-fishing yacht for the tournament. You can be damned sure that Hank and Glenn signed up for that trip real fast. They would have bit the heads off live shrimp with their own damn teeth to get on that boat.

I was excited about the trip for many reasons, but on the top of my list was the fact that Val and I were renting a place of our own to sleep in each night. Hell, the boat was big enough that surely I'd find a way to sneak away with her there, too. Then again, she'd proven how good she was at pulling in a fish. My dad probably had plans to put her to use.

We arrived in Big Rock the morning before the tournament. The week in Morehead City was typically hot and humid with a side of sweat, but since this year's tournament had been delayed due to storm damage, you could almost feel a touch of crisp fall air. Everyone wanted the day to get settled in their rentals, but I wanted the extra time with my girl. My dad was staying on the boat with Captain Denny, a friend of his from college. The rest of us had arranged for cottages near the marina.

"Where are we going?" She asked as she climbed into the passenger seat. We'd only just dropped off our luggage in the place I'd made sure to reserve for just the two of us. As much as I wanted to toss her in that bed, I knew that if we got that settled in, we'd never make it out.

"First, we have to get you the appropriate gear." She looked confused. "Gear? You said I didn't need to bring my own pole! I told you we should have stopped for bait. Your dad's going to think I'm useless." I felt bad for laughing at her, but her concern was just too cute.

"Val, babe. There's not a fishing pole large enough that you could possibly find in a store. You won't believe the fishing poles on this boat."

"Oh! Well, what are we getting then?"

"Your Big Rock gear, of course."

We spent an hour in the shop loading up on hats, sun shirts, stickers, and everything else we didn't need for the tournament but wanted to take home to remember being there. Mom always said the shopping was the best part. She'd tell you she loved fishing, but truthfully, I think she just enjoyed the time with my dad and the view.

I didn't know all that much about the tournament, and I was pretty sure that I was in the way more than I was helpful, but it was tradition. At the very least, I helped to keep my dad, Hank, and Glenn well fed and well hydrated.

We all met back at the marina for the Captain's party that night and followed my mom and dad around as they caught up with all of his fishing buddies and their wives. As if I'd forgotten that our whole world was watching, I walked hand in hand with Val like we had always been that way. I pointed out different people I remembered and told her stories of the tournament years before.

"What are you thinking?" I asked as we neared the bar.

"Being here feels like...like the treehouse," she answered with a nostalgic smile.

"What do you mean?"

"I kind of feel like I'm living vicariously through you. The things you got to do as a kid, all the things your family does together. The way you share those things with me, for a minute it feels like I'm remembering too."

"Well, from here on out, they *will* be your memories. Welcome to Big Rock, Val Foster."

"Thank you for bringing me here," she said as she squeezed my hand. "I love seeing the things that are important to you."

"It's not as much about the fishing for me as it is getting to spend a fun weekend with my family." She looked up at me, and I winked. "And now, you."

"It's the best."

"Five million, kiddo." My dad walked up to us, wrapped an arm around my neck, and noogied my head. "We only need one good catch, Val. You feeling lucky?"

"I don't know," she laughed. "You might have been better off with someone else."

"Nonsense. It's all about having a good time."

"Well, sign me up." My dad tossed his arm around Val and walked her off toward what I assumed was a mile-long introduction of his friends, leaving me with my mom and Etty.

"Your dad and I really like her, Jack." Mom tucked her tiny frame underneath my arm, wrapping around my ribs and squeezing for a hug.

"I really like her too, Mom."

"It's a shame you didn't meet each other years ago when she'd come home from school with Etty."

"I've been thinking about that, actually. She would have met some playboy college kid who was either studying or drinking himself into oblivion. I don't think we would have gotten anywhere if we met back then."

"My boy's done some growing up, that's for sure."

"Thanks, Mom."

"In case I don't tell you enough, I want you to know that we're very proud of you."

"Oh, Mom—" I shrugged. Why did mothers always have to turn an easy conversation into something so emotional?

"No, you listen. I know your dad really relies on you at the office these days. You've proven time and time again that you can handle things when he's ready to retire." She rubbed her hand across my back. "But, as your momma, I wanted to remind you that if taking over the company isn't for you, we don't want you to do it. Don't accept the business from your father and Aunt Cora just because you're next in some… generational lineup. If it's not what you want, it's not expected of you."

"I don't know what I want, Mom. Except maybe that girl." I nodded ahead of us where my dad toted her around like she was his own. In a way, I think he was showing me that she already was.

"You want a life, Jack. You want Val, and you want a life with her. You'll need a job, of course. All I'm saying is, don't let us pressure you into keeping up with real estate for the rest of your life. Whether or not it's with Val."

"I think it might really be…"

"Well, isn't that something?" She smiled and wiped a tear from her eye.

"Oh, Momma. Don't do that." She cried at the drop of a dime—the same as she'd done my entire life. The littlest moments always were that important to her.

"I just love seeing you happy, Jacky. I'm glad you found someone who does that for you."

"Me too, Momma." I kissed the top of her head and smiled. I had it good. My family was something else.

My dad and Val returned with arms full of swag bags. If we weren't well stocked before, we were now. Val's new house would have glasses, mugs, and cozies to last a lifetime. My parents had a whole basket in the kitchen dedicated to the can cozies from other boats.

"How about it, kids? Yellowfin's for dinner?"

"I made the reservations four months ago," Mom said with a confused look on her face as if we'd even consider anything else.

"Atta girl," Dad said before kissing her cheek. "Let's go!"

All was as it should be. Fishing in Big Rock was one of my greatest memories growing up, and now it included the girl I loved. I didn't know how it could ever get better.

It sure as hell did, though. Beginner's luck was a real thing—ask any fisherman—and my dad swears that having Val on the boat sealed the deal. That and, he made her throw the bananas overboard before we pulled out of the docks. She'd been so excited that she packed so many snacks for everyone. At the end of the third day, on her turn in the rotation, my girl reeled in the fish we thought could have won it all.

I stood behind her as everyone coached her on reeling it in. She looked back at me a few times, and I could tell she wanted to tell me she was done—she probably would have tapped out if I'd let her, but I knew she could do it.

"You got it, girl." I tried my best to encourage her the first few times, and then when she looked back at me, I just winked, smiled, and nodded her on. She needed to know that she could do it—to know that she had every heart and hand around her that she'd ever need to do hard things.

She was overwhelmed, unsure of herself, and completely out of her comfort zone. It would have been easy to let someone who knew what they were doing reel the fish in instead. But I knew that later on that night, the next day, and the next year, she'd be the most proud of herself if she kept her ass in that seat and caught that fish.

When it was finally close enough and the mates took a net to the water, Val sad wide-eyed in shock at how everyone worked with her to pull it in. I never did see them fall, but tears pooled in her eyes as she looked up at me from her seat. Her face was beet-red and her chest nearly exploded as she caught her breath.

"That's a good-looking fish you caught," I said, coming around her to kiss her cheek. "Didn't think you could do it, did you?"

"No, I didn't. But then I realized that I wasn't doing it alone."

I knelt down in front of her and laid my hands on her knees. "Remember, Val. You aren't alone anymore. You never will be." She nodded in understanding, agreeing with me, and acknowledging that her world had changed. I was damn glad that I got to be a part of it. Right there in front of God and everyone else, I wrapped my hands around her head and pulled her in for a kiss; not the kind that told her I was horny for a lady angler, but the gentle and thorough kind that told her that I loved her. While the mates and our friends were cheering around us about the fish, I was feeling the same happiness about the girl in front of me; the girl who would be my co-captain for the rest of time.

I took Val up to the flybridge for the ride home. I joined her at the railing, watching over her shoulder as the sun set over the inland side of the Crystal Coast. I pulled my hat off and placed it backward on her head, holding down the long waves that blew back and over us in the wind.

"Stay with me?" I whispered into her ear as I held her between my chest and the rail. I'd beg her if I had to, but something told me that begging wouldn't be necessary. She didn't answer with so many words, but reached up to lay her hand on my cheek and then turned her head toward me, pressing her temple to my cheek. I held onto the railing in front of us with one hand while I held on to her with the other, sneaking my fingers up underneath the hem of her tank top to rest on her hip. I didn't ever want to let go of her again. She was cemented into my life now; the good days, the bad days, and each moment in between. Driving back to the docks on that yacht was the moment I decided with certainty: Val Foster was my future, and all of it. She'd be my wife one day, and I couldn't wait for the lifetime we'd share full of days like this.

We rode and listened to the silent roar of the ocean until Captain Denny docked us at Big Rock Landing, backing into the scales that would tell us how well she did. No matter what that fish weighed, Val had an amazing day. We'd be celebrating regardless.

We met the staff at the weigh station and waited to the side as they pulled the fish up onto the scale. Official records would say that Angler Valerie Foster pulled in a three hundred and forty-two-pound blue marlin. On the last hour of the last day of the tournament and with no boats left to return, it was official: she'd caught the fifth largest marlin in the tournament, securing winnings of twenty-six thousand dollars.

She beamed with a joy that I'd die trying to recreate. Nothing would ever compare to the pride and excitement that poured out of her on that dock.

The mates pulled her from my arms to hoist her up on their shoulders next to Captain Denny. The picture I snapped on my phone would be framed in our house one day: my girl up on the shoulders of some of the greatest fishermen in the Carolinas, surrounded by the cheering hands of everyone we knew and loved. My whole world was together, and for the first time in a long time, everything felt balanced—just as it should have been.

Everyone went back to their rentals long enough to run through the shower and throw on some clean clothes. Back at the Landing for the awards banquet, I stood between Hank and Glenn as Val joined Captain Denny to receive their check. She'd argued with me at first, suggesting that my dad do it instead. But we insisted that she wrap up her experience and tie it with a bow. She'd done it all, and I didn't want her to miss a single bit of it.

As we watched the winners' ceremony, my friends finally spoke up.

"You're gonna marry that girl, aren't you?" Hank asked quietly.

"Hell yes I am," I said.

"Who'd have thought?" Glenn asked, watching her claim her prize. "Crazy girl turned out to be a good friend and a half-decent angler."

"I thought we agreed to—" My eyes nearly rolled out onto the floor.

"I'm sorry, I'm sorry. Who'd have thought, when *Val Foster* walked into our bar, that you'd end up falling in love with her?"

"I guess sometimes life surprises you."

At the table later for dinner, I leaned over to Val. "The guys are pretty impressed," I said as the chatter continued around us. "Glenn might tell stories about you for years to come."

"Oh stop it," she said, waving at me. "You're just saying that."

"No, I'm serious. You continue to surprise me, Val."

"I love you, Jack," she whispered as she laid her hand on my knee. "When do we get to go home?"

"Home?" I didn't understand why she was eager to get back to town.

"Er...not *home*. To the cottage, I mean. Just the two of us." Now I understood. And boy did I ever.

"Dessert will be coming around in a few minutes. Then I'll tell them we're going to turn in for the night."

"I don't think I'm settled enough to go to bed yet," she said.

"Oh, Val. That wasn't my plan."

CHAPTER TWENTY-THREE
JACK

Big Rock was a big deal, and bringing home a winning catch earned one hell of a celebration.

"It's about time to go," I said. "Party is at six." My dad had organized a party at Howard's to celebrate after Big Rock.

"I just talked to my parents. Everyone's starting to get there, and they're asking where the champion angler is," Bailey shot her eyes to Val, who settled into me.

"Let's go," Val shrugged, still irritated that we were making the party all about her. Well, her and Captain Denny.

We left our cars at the house and jumped into the back of Hank's old pickup. At Howard's, we all jumped out and walked inside, where we were met with a round of applause and cheers and beers.

"I've got four pizzas, two calzones, a salad, and drinks on the way," Bailey said as she set her phone down on the table. Anglers and captains from the other boats had joined us, too. The few weeks after the tournament almost became a round-robin of celebrations; the whole group went town to town to celebrate with each winner. We all gathered around on the porch and settled in for the party of the season.

A horn sounded in the parking lot just after the girls walked inside to get our food. The rest of us looked out to find

Cole Stewart pulling into the parking lot. We weren't expecting him; he'd been working non-stop for days to finish up a major dock repair at the marina. I stood up to greet him, skidding to a halt when my stomach flipped. I watched the second man step out of the passenger side of the truck.

"Holy shit," Glenn said quietly behind me.

"Go get the girls," I said as a knot formed in my throat. "Tell them inside. Make sure you give them a minute."

My dad stood on the porch and walked toward me slowly. I waved him off, hoping like hell that he'd take a breath and let this go as smoothly as possible.

Cole stood by the driver's door as Robert Brooks circled the front of the truck with his hands tucked into his pockets. He glanced over at Cole in a way that looked like he was asking permission. Cole looked back up to me and shrugged his shoulders like he didn't know what to say. I didn't either, so I walked down to meet them at the truck.

"It's really good to see you, man." I reached my hand out toward him, and he looked back at me for a breath before he shook it.

"Hey," he said quietly and cleared his throat. "Hey, man."

"I got an interesting phone call this morning," Cole said, leaning against the hood of his truck. "Seems Robert's attorney had a chat with the judge. Someone decided he'd done enough time, and..." Rather than finish that sentence, he just waved a hand out toward Robert. "I guess I was his emergency contact. His lawyer thought he might want to see a friendly face when he got the news."

Robert listened while Cole explained, looking at the ground behind me like he was staring right through me. "I didn't know y'all were here, I swear. I just wanted to come to see Bailey."

"He's right. We thought Bailey would be here setting up before the party."

"Nah, we all decided to head over early. No sense in having beers at home when we could be having beers here." The guys laughed softly behind me, but any attempt at a joke didn't crack Robert's hard shell.

"Dude, it's okay." I grabbed his shoulder and jostled him a bit. When he looked up, I stepped into him and wrapped my arms around the friend I'd missed for years. It took him a few seconds, but he slowly raised his arms behind me and hugged me back. "It's really, really good to see you." The idea that life had come so full circle in one day, and in this place, was just beyond anything I could have imagined.

I thought about Val, still inside with my sister and Bailey. The three of them were completely unaware of what was happening, and I wondered how it would all go. My thoughts were tossed around in my head at warp speed.

A lifetime had already been had on our island. The restoration of Val's home was about more than the frame of a house. Lives were being restored, and it was all going to happen here too. Ocracoke was everyone's home already, and the thought that I'd tried to talk Val out of coming here hit me like a punch to the gut.

I was thankful that she'd been adamant enough not to listen to me. I was so very glad that she saw something in the house on Lighthouse Road that I couldn't. She saw second chances. A girl who only knew loneliness was able to see some really crowded tables. And in the same fashion, Robert had managed to come home to find an entire crowd waiting for him.

I stepped back and held my friend by the shoulders.

"There's uh, a lot to tell you." Through a flood of his own emotions, he managed to crack a smile.

"I can't wait," he said.

"Uh, guys," Cole nodded behind me, and I turned to see the girls on the porch between Hank and Glenn.

"I'm sorry, I should have called," Robert said quietly with his hands in front of him. He took a step back as if the distance might help. Bailey blinked and finally seemed to unfreeze when she heard his voice, lunging from the porch toward her brother. When she crashed into him, a sob blew out of her lungs that sounded as if it had been held there since the day he went to prison—which, come to think of it, might actually have. Bailey was one of the first ones to hear Robert's angry demand for no visitors. She'd held the most pain over it all these years.

There in front of Howard's Pub, a place we'd all shared so much of life, she cried in his arms for a solid minute before anyone moved or said a word. Every girl deserved a big brother that loved her as much as Robert loved Bailey; as much as I'd tried to love her while he was gone. I couldn't imagine that kind of time away from my sister. I'd die before I let Etta do life alone. In his own way, I knew that Robert had to feel a bit of relief too.

I turned around again to find Etta still standing back between Hank and Glenn and Val off to the side. My friends stood on either side of her like they were on guard and ready; for hell, for high water, or for the next world war should she decide she wasn't ready for this moment, or for whatever Robert might have to say.

"I should probably go," Robert said to Cole.

"No," Etta choked out from the porch. She stepped forward between Hank and Glenn, looking to Cole and then me before stepping down the front steps cautiously. She approached us slowly—as if the ground might fall from beneath her—and quietly, rolling one hand in the other like she couldn't find the place for them. Bailey stepped out from between them and stood next to her brother, unsure of exactly what to do. I understood the feeling—I had no idea what to do either, other than to let Robert and Etta lead the way. My heart raced in a heavy beat that I could feel in my fingertips as I watched it all unfold. Every attempt to move or speak was met with a hesitant pause.

I tried to calm myself as I watched my sister stare into the eyes of the man who'd been legally responsible for Jake's death. I struggled to breathe as it all played out. As much as I tried, I never could imagine how she would react, seeing him standing there in person. Regardless, I knew that I wasn't going to interfere. This was something I thought we'd have time to plan for. It was a conversation I planned to have with her…one day. It never occurred to me that we'd need to be prepared for an early homecoming like this.

We all waited patiently as Etty and Robert seemed to have an entire conversation in complete silence.

Suddenly, as if they'd rehearsed it, they each took a step toward each other into an embrace that could have moved mountains. Robert sobbed over her shoulder, and Etty cried into his neck—indiscernible words from both of them. In that moment, friends had been reunited and trespasses had been forgiven. An endless amount of healing still sat ahead of everyone involved, but that one step made the rest possible.

Life—the way I knew it could be—was in reach again and possible in a way I never thought we'd know. Years ago, chaos had interrupted everything we knew. Since then, the unfinished healing had lingered above us all. Now, it was all happening. The future was back in our hands.

Robert Brooks was home.

CHAPTER TWENTY-FOUR
VAL

I waited at a distance while everyone took turns reuniting with Robert. In my view, it was easy to see that every single one of them loved that man with an unconditional reach. A terrible thing had happened, and he'd gone to prison for it, but each one of them had a balanced happiness to have him back. It was like their love for him had never even stopped— but had just been nearly impossible to express for so long.

On the other hand, Daniel and Grey sat with me at the table in painful silence. Jack had explained that his father was never able to forgive Robert the way Etta had, or even close to how everyone else seemed to *want* to forgive him. I pretended not to hear the conversation between them while I watched Jack's whole world shift in the parking lot.

"I think we should go," Grey whispered.

"Just…give me a minute," Daniel answered, grabbing her hand tightly. He'd watched every second of the reunion unfold and hadn't moved an inch. I didn't know how to help or if I even could.

As they all neared the porch, I couldn't stand it any longer. The group that had welcomed me so warmly had finally found their missing piece. As far as I was concerned, he was always there.

"Great timing," I said. "We were just about to eat." I reached a hand out to their old friend—my new one. "I'm Val. I've heard so much about you." He shook my hand with cautious ease. "I hope you like pizza."

"I love pizza," he laughed through tears. His relief seemed to unlock the last straps around them all, and they all erupted in laughter with him. Jack took my hand, and the two of us followed the group back onto the porch, where I noticed that Daniel and Grey had disappeared. The boys settled at the table, and I went inside with the girls for a refill.

"You okay, Etta?" We'd situated ourselves at the bar. "I swear I had no idea..." Bailey raised her hands in unnecessary defense.

Etta cut her off quickly. "I wish I'd known sooner. I have a welcome home present for him somewhere in one of the boxes back at the house," Etta laughed. A sigh of relief poured out of Bailey's lungs before she moved to wrap her arms around her friend.

"I love you so much," she said. "I just always want you to remember how much I love you and how much I love Tate." Bailey held onto Etta for dear life. The two had obviously worked through the situation years before, but Robert's surprise return had brought on a wide variety of fair emotions in everyone.

"We know you do, Bay. And we love you, too." She stopped to dry her eyes. "I'm glad he's home. I really am. It's long past time we all moved on with our lives. Having him back on this island where he belongs... it will be good for us—all of us."

"Hey, girls!" Jack's voice floated into the bar, and we returned to the living room with drinks in hand. "Girls. What do you say to an old-fashioned night out? Let's stay a while. All of us," he looked at his sister and argued before she could decline. "Tate's taken care of. Robert's home. We all have some celebrating to do. Tonight can be just like the old days."

"I appreciate the invite, you guys. But I should probably head home." The weight of Robert's words seemed to hit everyone at the same time. Visiting his sister might have been the first stop he made outside of prison gates, but he had an entire world to reenter. It would take time.

"Well, I'm in," I said.

"Me too," Bailey added as we all looked at Etta.

"Come on, Etty. Loosen up." Jack had the best chance at getting her to go out with us for the night. She finally had a weekend off from mom-mode and deserved to enjoy it. I just hoped she'd allow herself the freedom.

"Come on, Etty," Hank added in plea.

"Please?" I batted my eyes for extra flair.

"Okay, okay!" Etta laughed. "Let's go out."

The boys stood and cheered like they were front row on the fifty-yard line at a Carolina football game, and the girls and I just stood back and laughed. I'd gotten myself into one hell of a wild new family, and I loved every minute of it.

"God, this town is small. We need another bar about as much as we need another cafe," Bailey said. The girl finally took a night off, and we took her right back to work.

"Now there's an idea," Etta said. "You open up that cafe, and we can do coffee all day and drinks all night."

"We'll see," Bailey shrugged off the idea. I nearly burst at the mention of it and wondered if Bailey would actually consider the suggestion. We talked through the possibilities until the boys returned with another round.

"Half price margs, girls." Hank set the pitcher down in front of us and handed us each a glass. "Etta," he gave her the first glass as if she was a princess and he was her royal servant. I could have laughed, but I was too caught up in trying to figure out the interaction I was seeing. That and Hank's large and bulky hands were covered in tattoos and made the glass look like a child's toy.

"Thanks, Hank." Etta Dixon had a sparkle in her eye that I wasn't going to ignore. When he joined the rest of the boys at the other end of the table, I pried for more.

"Excuse me," I said as I took a sip. "God, that's good."

"What?" Etta asked, taking a sip of her own. "Jesus. A little mixer with tequila?"

"Oh, Kate's working tonight. She's a bit heavy-handed." Bailey turned toward the bar with her hands around her mouth. "Kate! Babe! Let's not kill anyone tonight, kay?" She made a good drink, but she was right. This Kate girl had a heavy pour.

"Dare I suggest that your eyes just twinkled a bit toward our favorite tattooed nurse?" I asked Etta. I wasn't going to let her off the hook that easily.

"No," she rolled her eyes. "Don't be silly."

"What's so silly about it?" I asked.

"It's Hank. He's like...one of our friends. One of the guys."

"So?" Even Bailey was getting in on the game.

"So? He works constantly. And when he isn't working, he's bringing home his latest hooker from the bar. Not exactly my type."

"Okay, first of all, he works endlessly, but he's like… saving people's lives," Bailey clarified, leaning in to whisper. "Plus, he's totally hot, and you know it."

"Oh, let it go. Hank doesn't want anything with a girl like me."

"A girl like you?" I asked.

"He's…fun. Outgoing. Loud. A bit…wild."

"And you are?" Bailey asked.

"I'm…well, I don't know his type, exactly. But I highly doubt he's after a single mom, elementary school teacher who lives the most quiet and predictable life imaginable."

"Maybe the lion could be tamed," Bailey suggested with widened eyes, making the three of us laugh. "Or maybe the lamb could be—"

"Stop it!" Etta blushed.

"What's so funny?" Jack asked, finally leaning in from my other side.

"Nothing," I said.

"So, you'll tell me later?" He asked confidently.

"No, she won't. Girl code." Bailey said.

"That's fair," Jack said, looking back to the guys.

Even when Golly was alive, I didn't have this: a night out with so many friends. Lives so intricately intertwined that multiple conversations happened at the same time. I'd never sat around a table so crowded, and I loved it. I hadn't felt this rooted since college, and I'd let it all go entirely too easily. Here on Ocracoke, I had the life I'd dreamed of. I'd found—and even contributed to—the life I always wanted. What more could a girl ask for?

For hours that felt like brief minutes—we drank and talked and even took control of the sound system to play a few songs we all loved. The tourists were starting to roll into town, so we even found ourselves mixed in among strangers—an odd but fun addition to the party.

Over-served and celebrated to our heart's content, we each began making plans to head home for the night. Bailey, Glenn, and Scott climbed into an Uber, leaving me and Jack with Hank and Etta. Though, Etta was nowhere to be found.

"Where's Etty?" Jack said as he wobbled into me, planting a kiss on my cheek.

"I don't know. She went in for the bathroom a few minutes ago.

"I'll go get her," Hank offered. "You two sit down. Maybe drink some water."

"No fun," I said, sipping from my fifth—or maybe sixth —margarita of the night.

"I want to take you home, Val Foster," Jack whispered into my ear as his hand drifted down my back and over my hip. "I want to take you home, have my way with you, and never let you go." He gripped the curve underneath my back pocket and pulled me snugly against him, dropping small kisses from my ear, down my neck, and over my shoulder.

"Take me home then," I mumbled. I mean, where else was I going to go? I already lived with the man.

"I'm gonna marry you, Val Foster."

"You are?" I backed my face away enough to lock my surprised eyes with his. Don't get me wrong; I loved him. I absolutely *would* marry him. I just didn't think he was the type to consider it after just a few months.

"Yes, I am. One day. I'm going to put a ring on your finger and make an honest woman out of you." As drunk as he was, I was impressed by his clear words and intentions. "Until then, I want to take you home and practice living in sin."

"Yes, please." I smiled just before he kissed me again, entirely too handsy for a public place, but most of me didn't care. I would have kissed him there on the porch of that bar if the whole world was watching. This was what I wanted my Saturday nights to look like for the rest of time: going home with Jack Dixon.

"Why don't we go inside? You can settle up the tab, and I'll go find Hank and Etta."

"Deal," he said, slapping my backside again as I walked ahead of him. It didn't take long to find Hank in the bar. He was a head taller than the average guy and was easily identifiable by his many dark tattoos. I walked up to him, ready to tap him on the shoulder and ask if he'd found Etta, when I saw that he most definitely *had*.

Sandwiched between Hank and the bar was Etta Dixon, perched on a stool and on the receiving end of one hell of a kiss. His palms rested on the top of the bar behind her, surrounding her with his strong arms on either side. His shoulders bulged against the hems of his shirt as he pressed into her. When she moved to stand, he lifted a hand from the bar, wrapped it around her waist, pulled her into his chest, and leaned in for what he thought was a whisper. Alcohol made it hard to whisper, though.

I stood off to the side—just distanced enough to be out of sight yet close enough to listen in. I wondered when she'd gone from "not his type" to making out with him in public.

"I don't like seeing other guys hit on you," he said.

"So don't let them," she answered, more flirty and forward than I'd ever seen her before. "Are you kissing me to keep that guy away, or are you kissing me because you want to?"

"Because I want to," he answered. "I've always wanted to."

"Why haven't you?"

"You never come out with us." An expression I could only identify as a near-pout crossed the otherwise stoic man's face.

"And here I am." Her grin was easily identifiable: as trouble.

"And here you are." They shared a devilish smile.

As Hank leaned into Etta again, presumably to continue making out with her right there at the bar, I made a beeline for Jack, hoping to distract him long enough to get outside. A girl didn't need her brother interrupting a kiss like that.

"All settled?" I asked, turning him to face the other direction.

"All settled. Where's Etty?"

"She and Hank found some friends…they're going to get a ride later." I had to think fast. "But I want to go home…"

"Well then, let's get you home." He took my hand and led me out of the bar, leaving Hank and Etta to themselves.

I pulled my phone out as we climbed into our ride outside.

Val: Your brother and I are on the way home...so have fun.

I added a winking emoji to the end of my text and hit send. It was about time Etta had some fun. She never did answer, but I wasn't worried. Hank's hands seemed...more than capable. *Dreadfully capable.*

The next morning, I rolled over to peek at my phone and check the time. A response from Etta topped the screen.

Etta: He took me home. Like he actually just brought me home. As in, he walked me to the door and said goodnight.

Val: What? Didn't you invite him in?

Etta: Of course I did. He said I'd had too much to drink.

Val: Damn, gentleman. So rude.

Etta: I know. - laugh emoji- Keep last night between us? Please?

Val: Deal.

It really was a good move on Hank's part. From what I'd heard, he was less than a gentleman on most occasions and brought home a wide variety of female friends over the years. But with Etta, he did the right thing. He took her home, ensured she was safe, and walked away. In my mind, that was different. I'd suspected that there was something different about Hank. There was more to him than some horny man who couldn't get out of the party life from his college years. There was a soul hidden deep inside that man that I suspected he kept to himself intentionally. Someone hurt him: someone or something. I didn't feel the need to press the issue. I figured he'd reveal himself in his own time, little by little, the way he was right now.

The way I saw it, the fact that he *didn't* take her home and jump in her bed said a whole lot more about him than if he had. A man had to actually care about a woman to take her home and not sleep with her. Maybe this thing between Etta and Hank was more than just a spark. Maybe they were on the edge of the real deal.

"Who are you talking to so early," Jack mumbled.

"Just checking on the girls…" I set the phone down and rolled to face him.

"Last night was fun." He took a deep breath in and exhaled slowly, thinking. "It's like everything is the way it should be again."

"Having Robert home?" I asked.

"And having you here," he said as he turned to face me. "I think I've been waiting for you."

"Well, you got me."

266

He wrapped an arm around me and pulled me into him, tucking the covers around us. We fell asleep again right there in my favorite place: in the corner of his shoulder, lined up along his muscular chest and his hips, and wrapped up in his legs. I could have laid there forever.

We woke up later on to the doorbell, and Jack left me in the bed to answer it. It wasn't but a few seconds before I heard the loud crowd of voices and knew that the living room was full of the guys. Jack came back into the bedroom a minute later.

"What's the party for?" I asked, still comfortably tucked into our bed. He climbed in on all fours and rested above me.

"It's Saturday morning. The boys want to go surfing. They came here because I wasn't answering my phone." I laughed, and Jack hung his head. "Would you mind if I went with them for a while?"

"Of course not!" I laughed. "Go! Have fun." He kissed my cheek.

"You're the best." He touched his nose to mine, kissed me again, and jumped off the bed to throw board shorts over his boxers. The man looked terrific in a bathing suit, that's for sure. The view I'd had in his bedroom recently was back on full display as he got ready to head to the beach, making me feel a bit sad that I wasn't going at least to watch.

"Hey," he stopped at the doorway. "I love you."

"I love you, too," I said, sitting up and smiling at him. He dropped his towel and lunged into the bed one more time, smothering me in one last kiss before he left. When he walked back into the living room, I heard the same excitement as before until it traveled in a muffled crowd and the door closed behind them.

ANNALEE THOMASSON

CHAPTER TWENTY-FIVE
JACK

A few weeks later, after Link had finished every nook and cranny of the house and triple-checked every outlet, faucet, and deadbolt, it was finally time to move the girls into their home. Val decided to stay with me until Etta and Bailey were settled in with Tate. I was happy with the decision since it allowed me to keep her right where she belonged—with me, in my house, and our bed.

Gravy and Pop took Tater down to Charleston for a long weekend, and the rest of us got to work. Hank, Glenn, and I started with Bailey's things at her parents' house, which took all of two hours. She didn't keep a whole lot when she moved back into their place and hadn't accumulated much since then, either. While we did the heavy lifting, Val and Bailey helped Etty to pack up her apartment. They loaded the small things and lighter boxes into their cars, and later that afternoon, we met them with the pickup trucks to move the furniture.

Val had prepared to furnish the house entirely, but everyone agreed that Etty should keep everything she already had. We wanted Tate to settle in easily and figured if things all looked similar, it might help him to feel at home. I had ideas for my place, too—ideas that would help it feel less like mine and more like ours.

269

Etty had suggested that she and Tater share a room at the new house for a while; she still hadn't gotten over the idea that Val was just giving them a place to live. Val agreed, but just in case, she asked me to help her with another secret project. The room next to Etty's was initially planned to be an office, but with more than enough room to spare, she decided to give Tate an extraordinary bedroom of his own—for when he and Etta were ready, of course.

We'd managed to keep the plan between the two of us, and the morning of move-in, Val got an alert that his bedding had been delivered to the new house.

"Who's that?" I asked when her phone alerted her to a new message.

"Well, we're all here…" she laughed, picking up her phone to check the notification. "Oh, just a delivery!" She flipped the phone around to me and winked.

"What are you two doing over there?" Bailey asked from the front door with arms full of throw pillows. "You look like you're scheming…"

"Us? Never," I scoffed, handing the phone back to Val.

"Right," Etta said with a grin. "You two are the definition of secrets."

"That's fair," Val laughed. "Come on; we're almost done loading up."

When our caravan of six vehicles and two hitch trailers pulled up to the house, I realized how thankful I was that Val had chosen to extend the driveway. When everyone stepped out of their cars and onto the front sidewalk, a quiet appreciation filled us all.

"A lot of things sure have changed this summer," Glenn said.

"All for the better," I agreed with a fist bump.

"Hank, I'm suddenly finding the need to find myself homeless." Glenn laughed and pouted a terribly dramatic sad face at Val.

"You have to cross that one with the girls," she said, waving a finger back at Glenn. "So far, this house is burp, fart, and foolery-free."

"I'm kidding," Glenn laughed, knowing full well that his foolery would never be allowed.

"I'm not," Hank argued. "Val, you've really outdone yourself. This place is amazing."

"Thanks, guys. I just hope everyone is happy here."

"Not everyone," I shot back. "You've got your own home, ma'am."

"I know," she said, looking over her shoulder at me as she walked toward the front door. I reached to grab her ass, but she squealed and ran off. I chased her inside, knowing damn well that it was only a matter of time before we called this place our home, too.

"Y'all are cute," Hank yelled. "Don't worry; we'll do the hard work. Y'all just go make out in the kitchen." I heard their burst of laughter as I crossed the threshold.

"Where'd you go?" I yelled into the empty home.

"Come see," she said, sounding close.

I walked into the kitchen. It's where I usually found her. "What's in that head of yours, Val Foster?"

"I was just thinking about how full this place will be." A glisten of tears filled her eyes, but I knew they were the happy ones. She wasn't even going to be moving into this house, and she was so excited that her emotions seeped out of her. The overwhelming joy in her eyes reminded me of my mom. "I didn't know...you know?"

"What didn't you know?" I circled the kitchen to meet her by the back door, settling my hands on her shoulders as we looked out to the backyard.

"I came here to...to get away from everything. I just needed a night or two in a safe place, and I ran here. Turns out...I was running home." She looked up and around at the enormous country-coastal style kitchen she'd designed herself. "I didn't know I could feel this kind of joy again."

"You're missing her, huh." I lifted her up onto the countertop and stood between her knees. I reached up to wipe the tears from her cheeks, and her head fell into my hands.

"Golly would have loved this place. She would have loved all of you so much." Her smile was always incredible but paired with those happy tears; it was almost more than I could handle. I never wanted to see her cry, but I loved it when she offered her soul to me, completely unguarded and honest. "She would have loved *you*," she added.

"I bet I would have loved her too," I said, wiping underneath her eye once more. "I wish I had the chance to get to know her."

"I have a feeling...if you stick around here long enough, you'll find bits and pieces of her everywhere." She looked around again and shook her head, sniffing the tears back the best she could. "She would have loved the view." Val nodded to the large sliding glass wall that separated the kitchen from the back porch.

I looked out through the porch to the backyard and the dock at the edge of the property. Tate was going to love playing in that yard. My mind quickly got ahead of me, and I had no thoughts of stopping it. I imagined my own kids playing in that same yard—Val's children, *our* children.

"Time is a funny thing," I said. "Tate will be grown up and out of here before we know it."

"Don't worry," She said, laying a hand on my chest. "I think there will be plenty of others running around here one day. This house will never be empty again."

I closed my eyes and smiled, understanding that our minds were on the same wavelength. We'd be more than content in my apartment for the time being. But there was one hell of a future waiting for us in this place, and I was more than ready for it to start.

"It's just an armoire," Glenn groaned sarcastically from the front room. "I can carry it myself. No worries, dude."

"I'm going to go help them," I said through a laugh before I kissed her cheek. I walked into the front room and watched as Val stopped in the foyer. She'd framed Betty Ann's letter and hung it by the front door. She laced her fingers across the frame and smiled before heading back outside. I picked up the other side of the armoire with the guys.

"About damn time," Hank said. "Been busy in there loving on your girl?"

I wasn't even going to try to hide it. Ever since Big Rock, I'd had no intentions of masking my feelings for her. I was hers, and she was mine, and every single person on Ocracoke would know about it as soon as I had the chance. "Yeah," I smiled proudly.

Three hours later, the trailers and pickups had been unloaded, and all of the furniture was in place in the house. The girls had brought in all the boxes they'd packed that morning and set them in the appropriate rooms. All that was left was to unpack and put things away, but it was dinner time. The girls wanted to get to the little things slowly, a piece at a time.

CHAPTER TWENTY-SIX
JACK

When my dad retired in the fall, we decided to bring on another real estate agent full-time so that I could step away and just manage things from a distance. After endless talking about whether or not to take over my dad's business, I finally figured out that building wealth by owning real estate excited me more than managing other people's homes and purchases. I would never have figured that out if it wasn't for Val. When she moved here and demanded to rehab a home that I thought was beyond repair, she changed how I saw my island's bones. Betty Ann's house wasn't the only place with a story, and Val and I were on the brink of something big.

Val and I moved forward with the idea of buying and rehabbing homes on the island one at a time. We figured we could buy, flip, and sell or keep them and rent them out to tourists. She seemed to agree, and though I still thought she was too eager to dive in way too deep, I knew that Link Nicholson would always be around to help us with whatever poor renovation decisions we made.

When my lease ended, we bought a small cottage on Pamlico Boulevard. We moved in immediately and started our overhaul of the place one room at a time. Every now and then, when we got too deep into a project, we'd stay a few nights on one of Cole's boats just to get out of the mess. We'd gotten to know a lot more of each other since the first time I found her on that boat.

The cottage was small enough that we knew it wouldn't be our permanent home. It would never have been big enough for the circus full of kids we talked about having. Instead, the Pamlico house would likely become our first rental property.

Shortly after Big Rock, I took a quick trip with Cole and bought her a ring. I came home and tucked the box away in one of Etta's dresser drawers, just waiting long enough to find the perfect time to ask her.

On a Friday in the middle of October, my plans finally began.

When I got home from work that afternoon, I faked an urgency to go back to the office for paperwork I'd *forgotten*. Of course, Bailey and Etta were in on the whole thing and arrived at our place just in time to keep her occupied and prevent her from tagging along.

"I'll be as fast as I can," I said as I walked out the door. The girls all lifted their glasses in my direction and I knew that they'd be plenty distracted, at least for a little while. Val loved talking about design plans with the girls. They'd google for hours over cabinet knobs, window valences, front porches, and paint colors.

I drove over to the house on Lighthouse Road where Hank, Glenn, Cole, and my dad met me in the backyard.

I looked up at Tate's treehouse in the distance and realized that it had all come back around in the best of ways. My life was everything I thought it could be and more. I only needed one more thing.

A feast was arranged on the tables that sat in a long line in the backyard. Glenn tended to the grill while Hank and Glenn strung lights from the oak trees along the edge of the water.

My mom pulled in a few minutes later and Tate jumped from the backseat to join us.

"Uncle Jack! Did you marry her yet?" He leaped into my arms.

"No, buddy. We're not getting married tonight...you know that right? I have to ask her first."

"Oh. So she won't look like a princess?"

"She always looks like a princess, buddy. But one day, if she agrees to marry me, she'll be dressed like the most beautiful princess in the whole world."

"Can I dress up like a prince? With a crown?"

"Yes, Tater. You can." I laughed as he spotted my dad behind us, and took off running. "Pop! Was Gravy a princess when you got married?" Kids had such a wild understanding of how things worked—or I suppose, a wild *lack* of understanding.

"You ready?" Cole said, walking up to me with the bouquets of flowers he'd stopped to pick up on the way.

"More than ready," I said.

"Well, here are your flowers. And don't worry. I also brought tequila in case she says no." He lifted a brown paper bag up between us.

"Asshole," I laughed. "Some of us still believe in happy endings."

"Eh. To each their own." He whacked me on the shoulder as he set the bouquets down by the tree I planned to use as the perfect spot. Robert stood a few feet away, setting up his phone and tripod to record it all and hopefully catch a few good pictures.

A little while later, Bailey and Etta walked down the stairs of the back porch and joined everyone at the bottom of the hill.

"She'll be right out. She's just putting away the groceries." My sister hugged me and kissed my cheek before standing next to my parents underneath the tree.

"Hey, Jack!" The sliding glass door opened quickly as Val stepped out with a plate full of fresh fruit. "Can you help-" She stopped and stared into the yard, jaw-dropped in shock and what I hoped was a happy understanding of what she'd found in front of her.

She set the plate down on the table and started to walk down the grass toward me. My future wife, the mother of my future children, the woman who came here to my island and turned me upside down: she was finally on her way to me.

I bit my lip as she got close, trying like hell not to run to her. I'd planned everything out down to the smallest detail, and I was going to ask her right here under our favorite tree. She lifted her sunglasses to the top of her head and moved toward me with her hands at her mouth, barely hiding the smile I'd come to need every minute of every day.

"Hey, baby," she squealed quietly. "What are you doing?" She asked in a whisper as if no one else could hear her, laughing and crying as she took her last steps up to me. "Bailey? What?" The girls giggled and the guys stood silent like the emotionless pigs they are. But not me. I was filled with joy, knowing what came next.

"Hey, girl." I reached for her hands and watched as she looked at everyone around us. After a few seconds, I cleared my throat and tried not to choke on my words. "Val, when you first got here, I thought you were crazy."

"Understatement," came from the crowd—Hank or Glenn, no doubt. I just laughed and shook my head. A loud *thwack* told me that Cole took care of the culprit for me.

"I know that your life has been nothing but chaos this year. After Golly died, you moved here, and we've been chasing life together ever since. I know we haven't really had a chance to settle down or catch our breath, but I think that's kind of the point."

She wiped the back of her hand across her cheeks before reaching back to my hands between us.

"I know things will quiet down eventually, and when they do, I want to be quiet with you. And when things get loud and crazy again, I want to do that with you too."

"I don't mind loud and crazy," she said through laughter and tears.

"The thing is, no matter what life looks like, I want you to remember that you aren't alone." She looked around us at all the people who loved her, even though some of us had only just met her within the past six months. "I know you moved here because you thought it was a safe place to be alone. But Val, I don't think you're ever going to find yourself feeling that way again." She shook her head and smiled.

"I don't think so either," she whispered.

"So, first of all, I want you to know that I already spoke with Alex and Louise. I drove up to Raleigh a while back, and they gave me a blanket approval to marry you whenever I wanted." She shook her head in happy disbelief. "They said if you kept me around long enough for me to start thinking about marriage, you were probably completely in love with me; and that was enough for them." My parents laughed at the sentiment they must have understood. "They seem to have confidence in your ability to kick a man to the curb if necessary." She laughed again and squeezed my hand. "And so…I know this might seem fast. But you know better than anyone that you don't know what you have til it's gone. And I don't ever want to lose you, Val."

I stopped and reached into my back pocket before I knelt down in front of her. I opened up the black velvet box that I'd been hiding and lifted it toward her.

"I don't ever want you to be alone again, Val. And I don't ever want to be without you. Even if you're crazy." Laughter came from all around us again. "So let's jump, Val. Will you marry me?"

"Do you still think I'm crazy?"

"Yes, Val. I do."

"Then let's jump." I thought I knew what she meant, but I still needed her to say it. "Yes, Jack. Yes, I'll marry you."

My whole world erupted in hoots and hollers around us as I slid that ring onto her finger. She barely even looked at the diamond before she lunged into my arms, clinging to me tighter than she ever had before.

"I love you, Jack," she said quietly as she buried her face into my neck.

Bailey and Etta collided with us and the onslaught of girl-shrieks began as Val held her hand out in between them.

"Oh my God, Jack!"

"It's beautiful!"

"Mrs. Dixon!"

"You're going to be my sister!"

The rest closed in around us, hugging and clapping, and raising their glasses.

"I think this calls for dinner to celebrate." Glenn rubbed his hands together like he was ready to grill.

"Dude, it's Sunday." It's not like we were going to do anything else.

"Well, isn't that convenient?" Glenn clapped his hands. "I've been preparing our catch all afternoon." He turned to go back to his place at the grill and I walked back to Val who stood at the edge of the water with her hand in front of her face. I stepped up behind her and wrapped my hands around her hips, pulling her up against my chest.

"What do you say, future Mrs. Dixon?"

"I say…life with you is very crowded, Jack. And I love it."

I kissed her cheek and toyed with the ring on her finger while the waves washed over our feet. Everyone partied behind us as we soaked in the moment: the one where we went from now to forever.

"We're just getting started, you know. There's always room for more."

ANNALEE THOMASSON

EPILOGUE
JACK

"Morning, Dad!" I walked into my parents' house for breakfast with my dad and closed the door tight behind me. The winter chill had set in, forcing me to wear a sweatshirt these days. Val would usually *accidentally* spill coffee or a bit of her breakfast on me if I put on one of my Duke hoodies before I left. She drove me nuts—in the very best way. My Dad met me in the foyer with a manilla envelope in his hands. He handed me the stack of paper that still felt warm from the printer.

"What are you working on?" I flipped through and began to read over the first page. I'd finished everything at the office for the month and wasn't expecting anything else to do until Link had finished with the permits for our new renovation. For as much as my dad claimed to be retired, he had developed a knack for showing up with more work for me.

"Albert's place..." My dad began. "I'm buying it."

"You what?" I was always excited to see my dad making strategic business moves, but I was frustrated that he hadn't waited to talk to me more about this one. Val mentioned buying the place a while back, and she'd be crushed to find out that someone had swooped in and made a deal. If it was on the market again, I wanted her to get it. For her, and for Bailey. "Dad, you can't buy this one."

"I already did, son. I'm buying it outright. I already talked to Albert about their plans to close the diner. It's going to need a bit of an upgrade, but I get the sense that you and Val can handle all of that." He had me excited but confused. "I'm buying it, but if you take a closer look at the paperwork, you'll see that it's not my name on the deed."

"What do you mean?" I flipped through the familiar pages. We didn't usually handle commercial purchases, but the terminology was similar enough that I understood what I was reading. Behind the deed of purchase was another form I hadn't seen before.

"North Carolina Quitclaim Deed," I started. "Made effective this date between Daniel Dixon, the Grantor, Bailey Brooks and Robert Brooks, the Grantee of Joint Tenancy…that the Grantor, for and in consideration of the sum of one united states dollar, to it in hand paid by Grantee, the receipt whereof is hereby acknowledged, does hereby quitclaim, convey and release unto Grantee, all interest the Grantor has in the real property located at 201 Irvin Garrish Highway of Hyde County, North Carolina…"

I stopped to read through the words again. It sounded like scrambled eggs, but I understood. My dad bought the bungalow and was transferring the ownership to Bailey *and Robert.*

"I've been thinking…nothing should stand between Bailey and her dreams."

"You're right, Dad. This is…"

"And Robert…" Dad cleared his throat and choked back tears while he caught his breath. "Robert deserves a second chance. He deserves an opportunity to make something of the life he's been given." He paused again, and I noticed a quiver in his lip that I'd rarely seen before. "I've always prided myself on the way we love you kids. You know we've always extended that to your friends. It would be...hypocritical of me...to continue to blame Robert for what's happened. If it were you..." Tears fell from his eyes, and I stepped forward to hug him.

"It's okay, dad." I pat his back. "It's all right."

"No, son. If it were you," He grabbed onto my shoulders and separated us before he continued. "If it were you, I would have fought the world for forgiveness on your behalf. I would have given my life to make sure that you had a second chance. I never offered that grace to Robert, and I should have. That boy..." The walls my father had built up after the accident were starting to crumble. "You are my boy. And Jake, he...he was my son, you know? I mean, I know he and Etta hadn't gotten married yet. But he loved her." He cried. "He loved your sister, and he would have been a good father."

"Yeah," I agreed, wiping tears from my own cheeks on my sleeve. "He would have been the best."

"But...so would Robert." My dad finally admitted what the rest of us had believed all along. Robert was a good friend and a good man. He was a good brother and a good son. And though he'd been at the unfortunate end of a terrible night, we knew that the heart of the man was good. I think deep inside, my dad always knew it, too.

"I know you've always tried to get me to...to work through my anger toward him. But son, I think...when I saw him at Howard's, and I saw his eyes—my God, the sadness in his eyes. And then I saw how Etty was with him. She's so gracious. She was so sweet. I just...I want to be that way too. So I just...I think it's time I tried."

I set the folder down on the desk as my dad stood in front of me. "Thank you, Dad." I wrapped my arms around him again, grateful beyond all understanding for the forgiveness my father had chosen at that moment and the way he chose to move forward with it all.

Bailey was going to have her shot at the cafe she and Robert had dreamed of opening. Robert was going to have another chance at making something of his life. And Val...Val wasn't going to believe it.

"If you'll go ahead and do your thing...file those papers appropriately...it will be as good as done. I figure I'll have a chat with Bailey sometime soon. Maybe, as soon as you see that it's all finalized."

"Of course, Dad. Wow." A part of me always knew that my dad would come around, but the burden of the heartbreak he carried all this time was palpable. I'd always worried about the effects that it would have on him over the years. Now, to have gotten the weight off his shoulders in such a redeeming and honorable way, I couldn't believe the relief I felt.

"Let's keep this to ourselves for a while, son. I think we should let the purchase settle before we go shaking things up anymore. That and, I think I'd like to talk to Bailey...and Robert...myself, if you don't mind."

"Got it, Dad. No problem." I tucked the folder into my briefcase and reached to shake his hand. He nodded and turned to walk into the kitchen as if nothing had happened. That was just like him: one quiet and quick movement, undetected and off the radar.

"Breakfast is ready whenever you are," he hollered.

I walked into the kitchen and tried to catch my breath. Redemption was always the piece of the story I'd questioned. I had no idea over the years how any bit of the ordeal could have been redeemed. And yet, here it was—finally happening right before my eyes.

A few weeks later after a morning fishing trip with Hank and Glenn, I came home to find my fiancé sopping wet on our front porch, stripping out of her wetsuit.

"How was your morning?" I leaned on the porch railing and watched as she towel-dried her long sexy legs.

"It was incredible. That storm really kicked up some surf." She'd quickly developed a talent for surfing, and I might have asked her to slow down. The trouble was, she was really good at it. I didn't have the heart to stop her.

"I thought Glenn told you girls to stay out of the water this week?" I was a little frustrated at her lack of respect for the water. Glenn kept close tabs on the currents and was quick to let us know when it wasn't safe to go out. I shouldn't have been surprised that Val didn't bother to listen to him. If I had to guess, Bailey and Etta were right there with her. Bailey is the one who got her into surfing in the first place. After a few lessons, I could barely keep up with either of them.

"Oh relax, Jack. We're all fine." I followed her inside and joined her on the couch.

"One of these days, your fearlessness is going to bite you in the ass." She leaned over to kiss me and batted her eyelashes—that always got her on my good side. "So, I have something I wanted to talk to you about." I pulled the envelope from my bag and handed it to her. "This has been in the works in the background for a while, but today I got all the final paperwork and the keys."

"What keys?" She sat up, looking thoroughly confused.

"Don't freak out, okay?"

"Contrary to popular belief, that's not actually a great way to start a conversation." She glared at me as I handed her the envelope. I watched as she pulled the paperwork from it and began to read, but most of it was way over her head. "Why don't you give me the simple version," she said, flipping through the pages.

"So, you know how my Dad feels about Robert and the accident."

"Yes…" she said slowly.

"Well, it seems that time, and maybe grace, have worked in him a bit. Remember that bungalow you looked at a while back?"

"The commercial property…of course I do."

"So, when you first mentioned it, I talked to my dad about it. He liked the idea and wants you and Bailey to go and…you know, do your thing there."

"Okay…I'm still not following. The building already sold."

"That's right. My dad bought it."

"Try again. I'm so confused. What does your dad want with the bungalow?"

"That's the crazy part." I took the paperwork from her and flipped to the important page in the middle of the stack. "Read this."

To her, the paperwork probably looked to have been written in German. Real estate wasn't known to use simple language. It was all way more legal-sounding than it needed to be.

"North Carolina Quitclaim Deed...Daniel Dixon, the Grantor, Bailey Brooks, and Robert Brooks, the Grantee of Joint Tenancy...that the Grantor, for and in consideration of the sum of one United States dollar...the real property located at 201 Irvin Garrish Highway of Hyde County, North Carolina." She looked even more confused than before.

"Do you know what that is?" I asked.

"I think...so your dad bought the bungalow?"

"Yes."

"But he's selling it to Bailey and Robert Brooks?"

"That's right."

"For a dollar?"

"That's right."

"Jack!" The pieces started to fall together, and she nearly burst when it all clicked. "Her cafe!"

"That's right," I said. Her smile grew exceptionally wide before she reached to grab my face and kiss me. "She's going to have her cafe!"

"And Robert will co-own the building," I added.

"Your dad is giving this to Robert?" She couldn't believe it, and in all fairness, neither could I. The Daniel Dixon she'd come to know had no room for Robert Brooks and wouldn't even hear of his name spoken out loud. Now he was generously setting Robert up for one hell of a future.

"I kind of can't believe it myself. But I think Etty finally got to him. I think his heart finally broke down, and…he just wants the kids to be all right, you know?"

"Does Bailey know?"

"That's actually what I *really* wanted to talk to you about."

"You are full of surprises, Jack Dixon."

"I wasn't even supposed to tell you about this place, but when my dad saw how well you and Link did with the renovations at the house, he wanted you in on this one too."

"He wants me to renovate it?" She looked so excited that I started feeling the need to buy ever old and run-down property in the state of North Carolina. If renovations had her this happy, I'd see to it that she had renovation projects for the rest of time.

"I thought we could sit down with Link and come up with a plan. Maybe, work on it as a surprise for now—a secret project."

"Let's build a cafe," she said. The future Mrs. Dixon was going to make me one very happy man.

ABOUT THE AUTHOR

Annalee Thomasson is an author of sweet, small-town, island-based romance. She loves a character who gains self-confidence, adds seats to their tables, and finds themselves learning something new. She lives in Wilmington, North Carolina with her husband, three children, two dogs, and four ducks.

KEEP IN TOUCH

Instagram: @annaleethomasson
Facebook: facebook.com/AuthorAnnaleeThomasson
www.annaleethomasson.com

Made in USA - Kendallville, IN
73623_9781737790457
08.19.2022 1348